SILENT NIGHT,
UNHOLY NIGHT

At first the chapel seemed to be totally dark except for the red light of the sanctuary lamp, hanging in front of the altar. Then I realised that a group of candles were burning unevenly in front of a statue on my left. I picked up one off its little spike and held it in front of me. I was quite sure I was not alone in the chapel, that the mysterious visitor could not have left by any other door, and must still be lurking in front of me in the shadows.

The strangeness of her silence grew. Why did she not speak? Or at least make some signal. As fear, for the first time, began to catch up with me, there was a rush of cold air behind me and my candle went out. At the same time I put my hand down against the first wooden pew to steady myself, and found my hand touching warm flesh. . . .

Bantam Crime Line Books offer the finest in classic and modern British murder mysteries
Ask your bookseller for the books you have missed

QUIET AS A NUN

A NUN

Antonia Fraser

BANTAM BOOKS

NEW YORK · TORONTO · LONDON · SYDNEY · AUCKLAND

*This edition contains the complete text
of the original hardcover edition.*
NOT ONE WORD HAS BEEN OMITTED.

QUIET AS A NUN

*A Bantam Book / published by arrangement with
W. W. Norton & Company, Inc.*

PRINTING HISTORY
Norton edition published 1982
Bantam edition / February 1991

CRIME LINE and the portrayal of a boxed "cl" are trademarks of Bantam
Books, a division of Bantam Doubleday Dell Publishing Group, Inc.

ISBN 0-553-28311-1

Published simultaneously in the United States and Canada

---

*Bantam Books are published by Bantam Books, a division of Bantam
Doubleday Dell Publishing Group, Inc. Its trademark, consisting of the
words "Bantam Books" and the portrayal of a rooster, is Registered in U.S.
Patent and Trademark Office and in other countries. Marca Registrada.
Bantam Books, 666 Fifth Avenue, New York, New York 10103.*

PRINTED IN THE UNITED STATES OF AMERICA

OPM   0 9 8 7 6 5 4 3 2 1

For Rebecca
Who read it first

Contents

QUIET AS A NUN

1

Out of the past

Sometimes when I feel low, I study the *Evening Standard* as though for an examination. It was in that way I found the small item on the Home News page: NUN FOUND DEAD. It was not a very promising headline. Nevertheless I conscientiously read the few lines of print below. It staved off the moment when I would look round the empty flat resolving to cook myself a proper meal for once, and knowing that I would not do so.

'Sister Rosabelle Mary Powerstock,' the story continued, 'of Blessed Eleanor's Convent, Churne, Sussex, was found dead today in a locked building on the outskirts of the convent grounds. It is believed that the forty-one-year-old nun, known as Sister Miriam at the convent where she had lived for eighteen years, had been taken ill and was unable to raise the alarm. Reverend Mother Ancilla Curtis said today that Sister Miriam would be a great loss to the community of the Order of the Tower of Ivory, and would be sadly missed by her many pupils, past and present.

'Sister Miriam was the daughter of a former Lord Mayor of London.'

Before I had finished reading the short item, I had been transported back a whole generation. I knew that ruined building. It was in fact a tower. Blessed Eleanor's Retreat, as the nuns called it, in memory of the foundress of the Order of the Tower of Ivory. Sometimes irreverently referred to by the girls as Nelly's Nest.

For that matter I knew Sister Miriam. Or I had known Rosabelle Powerstock? Rosa. Had I known Sister Miriam? On consideration, no. But for a short while, long ago, I had known Rosabelle Powerstock very well indeed. For a few moments the cold elegant surroundings of affluent London in the seventies dissolved. It was wartime. A little Protestant day-girl sent by the vagaries of her father's career to a smart Catholic boarding convent conveniently next door. Bewildered and rather excited by the mysterious world in which she found herself. The resolute kindness of the nuns – was there any kindness like it for the undaunted firmness of its warmth whatever the reaction of its recipient? Reaching its final expression in Reverend Mother Ancilla.

I learnt that the nuns in their religious life adopted a name, Latin or otherwise, for some virtue or religious attitude they particularly admired; failing that, the name of some especially inspiring saint. Ancilla meant Handmaid of the Lord – echoing the great submissive answer of the Virgin Mary to the angel's unexpected announcement of her coming motherhood, 'Behold the handmaid of the Lord.' No doubt the Lord had been happy with his handmaid, Ancilla Curtis: but it was difficult even now to envisage any relationship in which Mother Ancilla was not the dominant partner.

And Rosa – the late Sister Miriam. So she had taken that name in religion. She had always declared her intention of doing so – if she became a nun. It had been a fashionable topic of conversation at Blessed Eleanor's.

'If I become a nun, and of course I wouldn't dream of doing such a thing, I'm going to marry and have six children, then I'll be Sister Hugh. After little St Hugh of Lincoln.'

'I'll be Sister Elizabeth. After St Elizabeth of Hungary who gave bread to the poor and it turned to roses when her husband tried to stop her.'

'Did the poor eat the roses?' I enquired. I was not trying

to mock. I was fascinated by the whole concept. To cover up, I said quickly: 'If I become a nun, that is to say if I become a Catholic first, and then become a nun, I'll be Sister Francis.'

How lovely. The birds. The dear little animals. That met with general approval.

'No, not St Francis of Assisi.' Honesty – or cussedness – compelled me to add, 'St Francis Xavier.' I had just been reading about the origins of the Society of Jesus, and the heroic struggles of that St Francis to convert the Japanese, dying in the attempt. Like many non-Catholics I was morbidly intrigued by the Jesuits. Secretly, the one I would really like to have chosen was St Ignatius.

'Jemima should be Sister Thomas,' said Rosa sweetly. 'Doubting Thomas.'

'Isn't Miriam rather an Old Testament sort of name?' I countered. I meant rather Jewish.

'It's one of the titles of Our Lady. Our Lady Star of the Sea.' Rosa loved to snub and enlighten me at the same time about the intricacies of her religion. Humbly, I loved to listen to her. I thought of the other titles in that great litany. Star of the Sea, pray for us. Mystical Rose, pray for us. Tower of Ivory, pray for us.

Like most Protestants, I knew the Bible much better than my Catholic friends. Besides, my terrifying nonconformist grandfather had been fond of reading it aloud. He was particularly fond of the Song of Solomon. 'Thy neck is as a tower of ivory,' sang Solomon – and thus my grandfather in his booming voice, 'Thine eyes like the fishpools in Heshbon by the gate of Bath-rabbim ...' Fish pools. Not very pretty to modern ears. But thinking about fish pools, dark, with swirling depths, the phrase was not inapt to Rosa's eyes in certain moods.

Mysterious Rosa, once my Star of the Sea, was now dead – in her ruined Tower of Ivory.

I shook myself, to remove the touch of memories long buried. Wartime had brought strange schooling to many, and quick changes. After the war my parents had decided to go back to their original Lincolnshire and make their home there.

'Goodbye, Jemima,' Reverend Mother Ancilla in our final interview. She combined the roles of Reverend Mother of the convent and headmistress of the school, an awesome conglomerate of power. This time it was very much the headmistress who was to the fore.

'What a clever girl you have been. Top of your form. The nuns all say they will really miss teaching you. A very nice impression to leave behind. Don't forget us.'

'Oh Mother, I couldn't,' I gushed. That was one thing the convent taught you – how to return a soft answer. Mother Ancilla paused. I knew quite enough about nuns by this time to know that they never left you with the last word.

'This cleverness, Jemima. A wonderful gift from Our Lord. You must develop it of course. Go to university perhaps?'

A mutter. 'I hope to, Mother.'

'But there is the spirit too as well as the intelligence. The spirit which bows itself and in doing so finds its true happiness. Self-abnegation, Jemima.' She paused again. At no point had the nuns ever tried to convert me from the thin Protestantism spread upon me by my parents. It would have been quite outside their philosophy to attempt by words what example could not do. I felt her pause was a delicate acknowledgement of that restraint.

'St John of the Cross, one of our great mystics, once wrote that unless I find the way of total self-abnegation, I shall not find myself.'

'Yes, Mother.' I bobbed a curtsey.

At the time her parting words had seemed singularly inappropriate. And later even more so to a successful career, carved, sometimes clawed out, by methods which always contained a great remembrance of self. Ironically enough, it now occurred to me that in my relationship with Tom I had probably realised self-abnegation at last.

The thought of Tom brought me back sharply to the

empty flat, as it always did. He had said that he might telephone about ten.

'If I can get to my study and she has a bath so that she doesn't hear the click of the telephone as I pick it up.'

It was a proviso which had been made before.

I once said: 'Tom, why don't you get a telephone which doesn't click?' He said nothing, but kissed me gently. So it was the way of total self-abnegation. It was now eight o'clock. There were two hours to wait. I turned on the television and turned it off irritably, deciding that the critic who said in this week's *Listener* that my own programme was really the only thing worth watching these days had after all a great deal to be said for him. I picked up the autobiography of the children's doctor from Nigeria I would interview on Friday. I forgot Mother Ancilla. I had long forgotten Rosa. Sister Miriam I did not know. I even forgot Tom for an hour and a half, and the last half-hour passed not too slowly, considering it was actually an hour, and nearly half-past ten before he managed to ring.

The letter from Mother Ancilla arrived about a fortnight later. The small convent writing paper, covered clearly and carefully in a still familiar handwriting, unlocked its own memories. Nuns did not waste writing paper: waste was not only extravagant, but also displeasing to God. I was curiously unsurprised by the arrival of the letter. It was as though I had been expecting it. The previous memories had warned me: we are after you, out of the past.

Mother Ancilla's letter was complimentary on its first page, sad on its second page and astonishing on its third. The compliments referred to my own career, 'which although we did not play, I fear, the whole part in your education, we have nevertheless followed with interest. And of course like all our old girls, you have always had the prayers of the community. Our girls nowadays regularly watch your programme on television—yes, we have colour television in St Joseph's Sitting Room, the gift of an old girl. Your programme is one of the few we can safely trust to be both

5

entertaining and instructive. Sister Hippolytus often tells the girls about your earlier triumphs in the debating society, and how she predicted a public career for you.'

It was a surprise to me that Sister Hippolytus had predicted anything so favourable in my future as a public career. Famous for her sharp tongue, Sister Hippo was one of the few—no, the only nun who had made me conscious of my alien status. Then I remembered that 'a public career' on the lips of certain Catholics was not necessarily the golden prospect it would seem to the rest of the world. Motherhood, sanctity, those were the true ideals. Neither of them had I satisfied.

The sadness referred to the death of Rosa. 'You will perhaps have read in the papers of the death of Sister Miriam, whom you knew as Rosabelle Powerstock. Perhaps like us, you felt that the coroner's remarks were a little unfortunate.' In fact I had not actually seen a report of the inquest. My newspaper-combing phase had passed. I had been busy, and besides, Tom's wife had gone to stay with her mother. Later in the month, there was the prospect of a really long trip to Yugoslavia for the two of us.

'But even in these enlightened days,' Mother Ancilla's measured letter continued, 'I suppose we must remember that the Catholic faith was once persecuted in this country. There is still a great deal of prejudice about. Poor Sister Miriam, she did not have a very happy life latterly, she had been ill, and although the manner of her death was tragic— Sister Edward blames herself dreadfully and of course unnecessarily—one cannot altogether regret the passing of her life on this earth. R.I.P.'

The third page astonished me by containing a remarkably pressing invitation to visit the convent as soon as possible. It was couched in language which, even disguised by Mother Ancilla's precise calligraphy, sounded remarkably like a plea.

'In fact, in general, these have not been very happy times for the community as a whole. I want to ask your help, dear Jemima, in a certain very delicate matter, which I cannot explain in a letter. Will you make time in a busy life to come down and see us? After all these years. As soon as possible . . .'

'*My* help,' I thought lightly. 'Mother Ancilla must be desperate to want *my* help.' But as it turned out, that was quite a sensible reaction to her letter.

2

'I want to find myself'

I arranged to drive down to the convent the following Saturday. My work would be over for the week – my programme was recorded – and by Friday I was generally filled by a post-programme adrenalin in which all things were possible, whether the programme had gone well or badly. In this case it had gone well, and on Friday night I was going to have dinner with Tom. He also said that he would be able to spend the whole night with me, in my flat.

'What if – she – telephones you at home?' I did not particularly like saying Carrie's name, or introducing her into the conversation. But the question had to be asked. In the past we had both endured some unsuccessful stolen nights, when Tom lay sleepless in my bed, wretchedly imagining the unanswered telephone and Carrie's subsequent anguish.

'She won't,' said Tom cheerfully. 'Mother-in-law's telephone has broken. She chatted the wire through. Thank God. Long may it stay that way.'

I thanked God too. The Almighty suddenly seemed to be taking a more friendly interest in my affairs. Perhaps it was the influence of Mother Ancilla and the prayers of the community? That reminded me to tell Tom that I had to be off early the next morning. For a moment I was almost tempted to postpone – no. It would do Tom no harm to find that I too had some personal commitments beyond the vicarious ones imposed on me at second hand by Carrie. Though Tom might frown.

Later, Tom did frown. After all he loved me. We were in love. He pushed back his hair off his forehead. It was a gesture almost as familiar to me as his kiss. Tom's hair, straight, floppy, unmanageable, was another of the persistent problems in his life. Still frowning, he said:

'Blessed Eleanor's Convent. Wasn't that the awful place where the nun starved herself to death? Quite mediaeval, the whole business. Nobody knows what goes on beyond convent bars, you know. It was pure chance this case got out in the open because the nun actually died. I think the coroner was quite right.'

'Oh Tom,' I burst out. 'Don't be so ridiculous. 'There aren't bars. It's a school. I was there in the war and afterwards. I must have told you. As for the coroner, I thought it was disgraceful what he said. Now Popery rides again.' (I had since looked up the clippings.) 'It was accidental death, no-one denied that, and he had no business blaming that poor young nun who gave evidence. Nuns have feelings just like anybody else.'

'Well they don't look like anybody else,' said Tom.

'Really—' Mother Ancilla's letter had made me feel curiously protective, even in the face of Tom.

'Or rather they all look just like each other. I saw a couple on the tube today. Couldn't possibly have told one from the other, even if one had been my sister. Two identical black crows.'

'What extraordinary prejudice from Tom Amyas, M.P., that well-known hero of liberal causes.'

Tom grinned. 'Sorry. Some rooted anti-Papist prejudice in me somewhere. Relic of my childhood I think. The Inquisition and all that. I remember reading *Westward Ho!* — connections with my name — and being full of British indignation about it all. It still horrifies me: the idea of the imposition of *belief* upon others ... you should know that.'

9

'I hardly think that an obscure convent in Sussex full of harmless middle-aged women can be blamed for the horrors of the Spanish Inquisition four centuries ago,' I said coldly. I was oddly narked by Tom's remarks. I tried to tell myself that at the first hint of Catholic persecution returning to this country – perish the unlikely thought – Tom would be the first to throw himself into the cause of quelling it. Save The Nuns: I could see him marching now with his banner. It was one of the things for which I loved him. But we had never discussed Catholicism before – why should we – and I hated to find even this corner of prejudice in my kind and gallant Tom, the champion of all those in trouble.

I thought of telling him that Mother Ancilla too was in trouble, or thought she was. I decided not to. We dropped the subject.

But I remembered Tom's remarks the next day as I drove up the long gravel drive to the convent. It was autumn. In the sunshine the convent grounds were immaculate. It was the season in which I had first arrived at Blessed Eleanor's as a day-girl. I walked with my mother from my parents' leaf-strewn autumnal garden, which had a kind of rich self-made compost under-foot throughout at this season, through to gardens where evidently no leaf was permitted to rest for very long before being tidied away.

'The nuns must catch the leaves before they fall,' said my mother jokingly, to leaven the slightly tense atmosphere of a new school. She paused and gulped.

'My God, look at that.' We both stopped and observed a nun – young? old? who could tell? – carefully catching a leaf long before it fluttered to the ground. She put it carefully away in a pocket, or anyway somewhere in the recesses of her black habit.

'Catching leaves is lucky.' My mother was quick to seize on an occasion for optimism. 'We'll find out who the lucky nun is, and you can make friends with her.' I assented rather dubiously. But we never did find out who the lucky nun was.

As Tom observed thirty years later, from a distance they really did all look exactly the same.

At that moment two nuns pulled a crocodile of small girls into the side of the drive as I passed. Identical. Two black crows. The children's uniform, a blur of maroon blazers and pink shirts, seemed singularly unchanged from my own day. I smiled. The children smiled amiably back. Both nuns smiled. The autumnal sun continued to shine, mellowing the rather fierce red brick of the convent façade. That too seemed much as I remembered it. Peaceful. Tidy. Even the creeper on the walls did not romp but climbed up in an orderly fashion. It was difficult to imagine what possible troubles could lie behind that calm exterior – troubles, that is to say, that could not be solved without recourse to the prying outside world. That was after all the world that I represented: Jemima Shore, Investigator, was how I was billed on television. It was a deliberate parody of the idea of the American detective, a piece of levity considering the serious nature of my programme. I was nevertheless an alien to the convent world. But Mother Ancilla had deliberately sent for Jemima Shore.

I stopped feeling an alien when a nun answered the door. She was very small. Ageless, as all nuns tended to be, with their foreheads and throats covered, so that the tell-tale signs of age were hidden. The short black cape covering the upper part of her body, whatever it was called, part of the nuns' uniform, also partially hid her waist. It had the effect of making her figure into a sort of bundle. She looked a bit like Mrs Tiggy-Winkle – hadn't there been one nun we named Tiggy? Perhaps all small nuns looked like Mrs Tiggy-Winkle. I gave my Christian name just in case.

'It's Jemima Shore to see Reverend Mother Ancilla.'

'Ah Miss Shore,' she beamed. So I didn't know her. 'We've been expecting you.' Into the reception room, a large room just by the front door, known for some reason as the Nuns' Parlour – although it was very much not part of the nuns' accommodation, being used exclusively for confrontations between secular and religious worlds. Here parents bringing quivering offspring to the convent for the first time were welcomed, smoothed down by Mother Ancilla, and made to feel – so my mother had told me – that they themselves were about to enter a disciplined but friendly institution.

The Nuns' Parlour really was exactly the same. The reproduction holy pictures in their dark frames, with their dully gold backgrounds. Fra Angelico seemed the prime favourite. On the table lay the familiar pile of wedding photographs, still surely dating from the forties. At any rate they were still mainly by Lenare and not by Lichfield. Perhaps the old girls of Blessed Eleanor's had abandoned their propensity for lavish white weddings, like the rest of the world? These wedding photographs, when I was at school, had exercised the same secret fascination over me as the Jesuits. I used to gaze at them covertly when my father was discussing my need for better science instruction with Mother Ancilla.

'But Mother Curtis,' he would say at the beginning of every term, finding the name Ancilla evidently too much to stomach: 'Science instruction by *post* is really not enough to equip your girls for the modern world.'

'Oh Captain Shore,' Mother Ancilla would regularly reply with a tinkling laugh. 'I keep asking Our Blessed Lord to send a vocation to a good young science mistress to help us out, but so far, He, in His infinite wisdom, has not seen fit to do so.'

'I seem to remember a saying about God helping those who help themselves,' began my father. No doubt he intended to refer to such unsupernatural expedients as advertisements and educational agencies. But no-one bandied words with Mother Ancilla and stood much chance of emerging the victor. Especially about Almighty God, someone whose intentions, mysterious as they were to the whole world, were somehow less mysterious to Mother Ancilla than to the rest of us. In the language of today, one would have referred to Mother Ancilla as having a hot line to God: or perhaps an open line was the correct term.

'Exactly, Captain Shore. Helping ourselves. That's exactly

what we're doing with our postal science lessons. Just as Our dear Lord wants us to do.'

My father gave up: till the beginning of the next term. I stopped gazing at the brides. Even then I suspected that I should never make that honorific folder. God might help those who helped themselves, but he did have a habit of not marrying them off. At least not in white.

As I turned over one photograph – the face was vaguely familiar – I heard a single sonorous bell ring somewhere in the convent. I recognised the signal. All the nuns had their own calling signal, like a kind of cacophonous morse code. One ring, then another for the Infirmary Sister, two then one for the Refectory Sister and so forth. One bell on its own called for the Reverend Mother.

Silence.

A pattering of feet on the heavily polished floor. The swish of robes outside the door, the slight jangle of a rosary that always presaged the arrival of a nun, and then –

'Jemima, my dear child.' Reverend Mother Ancilla kissed me warmly on both cheeks. I reflected ruefully that probably to no-one else in the world these days was I, at nearly forty, still a child. My parents were both dead. Tom? I could not remember him using the term even in our most intimate moments. Besides Tom, as a crusader, liked to see in me a fellow crusader. He had his own rather demanding child in Carrie and, for Tom, to be childlike or childish was not necessarily a term of endearment.

I studied Mother Ancilla's face as we talked, and I answered her preliminary polite enquiries. Nuns' faces might not show age but they did show strain. On close inspection, I was faintly horrified by the signs of tension in her mouth. Her eyes beneath the white wimple were no longer the eyes of a fierce but benevolent hawk as they had been in my youth. They reminded me of some softer and more palpitating bird, the look of a bird caught in the hand, frightened, wondering.

'You never married, my child?' Mother Ancilla was asking.

13

I hesitated how to reply. There was still something compelling about Mother Ancilla. 'Too much involved perhaps in your work,' she said tactfully, after a minute's silence between us.

I nodded, relieved and disappointed at the same time. That would do. Besides, it was true. Until I met Tom I had been too much involved in my work – for marriage, if not for love.

'We here, of course,' continued Mother Ancilla smoothly, 'understand a life of devotion, for which the ideal of home and family is sacrificed. We too have made that sacrifice, in honour of Our Blessed Lord.' She fell into silence again. 'It can be very hard. Even at times too hard, unless the grace of God comes to our aid. Sister Miriam –'

'Yes, Mother?' I said as helpfully as possible.

'Perhaps the sacrifice was a little too much for her? Who can tell? Perhaps Sister Miriam should never have become a nun in the first place. I wondered so much about her vocation.'

This was surprising. I had anticipated some more religious bromides, as I described them to myself, about the value of the sacrifice.

Mother Ancilla took my hand and said suddenly and urgently:

'Jemima, we must talk.' This time she did not call me her child. 'We don't have much time.'

'I'm not all that busy,' I began. I realised with a faint chill that she was talking about herself.

'I'll begin with Sister Miriam; Rosabelle as you knew her.' It was a pathetic story, not uncommon perhaps in a single woman these days, a spinster. But I was conventional enough to be shocked by its happening to a nun. A decline in health. A form of nervous breakdown, culminating in a hysterical outburst in the middle of teaching. Sister Miriam was whisked away to a sister house of the convent in Dorset by the sea, a convalescent home. There she found the greatest difficulty in eating, although with the help of tranquillizers

14

her composure returned. After six months Sister Miriam was adjudged ready to return to Blessed Eleanor's. But she was given light duties, French conversation with the Junior school –

I gave an involuntary smile. 'That wouldn't have been a light duty in my day,' I explained hastily.

'We have a language laboratory nowadays. The gift of an old girl.'

A laboratory. That reminded me of the old days of my father's arguments. I wondered if God had ever sent Mother Ancilla that experienced science mistress. And was it too much to hope that God would also have inspired an old girl to endow a science laboratory?

'And the most beautiful science laboratory, by the way. How pleased Captain Shore would have been to hear that, wouldn't he, Jemima?' So she had not forgotten. Mother Ancilla never forgot an adversary.

'Did you get the science mistress too?' I couldn't resist asking.

Mother Ancilla opened her eyes wide.

'Why, of course. They both came together. Sallie Lund, an American girl. When she joined the Order in 1960 she was already a trained scientist, so naturally she could teach science here. And as her father pointed out, she could hardly teach science without a laboratory. A very dear man, and most practical about money, as Americans generally are. So he gave us it.'

I was only surprised that it had taken Mother Ancilla till 1960 to iron this matter out.

We had been distracted. Mother Ancilla returned to a sadder topic than her scientific victories.

'As I was saying, Sister Miriam appeared to return to normal, although she still found great difficulty in eating. Difficulty that persisted for all her valiant efforts to overcome it. She told me once that strange visions seized her, that God wanted her to die, to go to Him, so that it was His will that she should not feed the flesh ...'

For a moment, I felt a strong distaste for the whole convent and all its works expressed in such language.

'I told her that it was God's will that she should make a good nun and eat up her supper. Such as it was,' said Mother Ancilla sharply. I remembered that uncanny attribute she had of seeming to read one's thoughts.

'A form of anorexia nervosa, I suppose.'

But the story got worse. Rosabelle began to talk of her visions, eat less, hide her food, got thinner, a doctor was called, more doctors. She got fatter again. She seemed more cheerful. She took more interest in life around her. One day when attention was no longer focused on her and her affairs she disappeared. A typed note was found: 'I can no longer hide from the community that I have lost my vocation. I have gone to London to stay with my relations. Please don't try to find me. I want to find myself.'

'I want to find myself!' I echoed. It was the phrase Rosa had used to me years ago in our teenage discussions about our future, lasting half the night.

'But of course she never went,' I said.

'No, poor unhappy Sister Miriam. She went to Blessed Eleanor's Tower and locked herself in and – well, you probably know the rest. You probably read the newspapers.' I nodded.

'What's her name? The nun who knew all the time where she was and never told.'

'Sister Edward.'

Sister Edward. She was the one I felt sorry for. But how she could have been such an idiot – 'She is young, young in religion, she has only just stopped her postulancy. I think she really believed Sister Miriam when she spoke of her vision and the need to undergo a period of trial and purgation. And then when she realised that all along Sister Miriam had lain there, that the old key had snapped off, that she had tried to escape and been too weak, the door locked, growing gradually weaker, she nearly broke down herself.'

'It might have been better not to go into the court with that story all the same.'

Mother Ancilla opened her eyes wide. 'That would have been against the law, Jemima.' I was reminded of the formidable rectitude of the convent.

'All the same, to give the coroner the opportunity to refer to the centuries-long tradition of perverse practices and cruelty of the Church of Rome, and the suggestion that Sister Edward *gloried* in Sister Miriam's death.'

'Our reputation is very low around here now I fear. They are simple people. It's quite deep country you know. Churne village has people in it who have never been to London, for all the short distance. The nuns hate to go shopping alone at the moment. Some very hurting remarks are made.'

At last I perceived why Mother Ancilla had sent for me. It was, I assumed, to rectify the convent's 'image' in the national, or at any rate, the local mind. With the touching faith of ordinary people in television, Mother Ancilla obviously thought her former pupil could do it for her.

'Jemima,' said Mother Ancilla sharply, interrupting this train of thought. 'You've got to tell us. Why did she die?'

3

Jemima knows

I realised that the object which Mother Ancilla was twisting between her fingers was not, as I had imagined, a black wooden rosary such as all the nuns wore at their side. It was a scrap – no more than that – of white paper. Mother Ancilla pushed the paper towards me.

I began to read. I recognised the handwriting immediately: it was Rosa's. I thought how little it had changed over the years. That's because she's a nun. Was a nun. Frozen. Mine must have changed beyond all recognition. Not that I really use it much these days except for the odd secret note to Tom, perhaps after a speech at the House of Commons – 'Darling. You were terrific. All my love, J.' I always imagined that he destroyed such notes instantly, for fear of Carrie finding them in his pockets. Yet, perversely, I could not resist writing them in a form too compromising to be preserved. I had a secretary for everything else and then of course there was the telephone.

Rosa on the other hand would have honed and fashioned her handwriting A.M.D.G. – *ad majorem Dei gloriam* – To the greater glory of God. It was odd how quickly that phrase came back to me. The nuns wrote it on everything. We wrote it piously at the head of Scripture papers, and on other papers too where we thought it would help.

I looked down again at the piece of paper. No, Rosa had not written this message for the greater glory of God. At least if she had, she had not thought fit to embellish it with the customary initials.

'Jemima will understand what is going on here. Jemima knows why I have to do this,' I read carefully aloud. 'Jemima knows.'

I paused. Mother Ancilla's bright dark eyes, the focus of her face, were regarding me intently.

'I don't understand,' I said after a moment's silence. My voice sounded rather flat. 'This is written in her own hand. And you said her farewell note was typed.'

'It was in her missal. Her old Latin missal she used as a child. Not her breviary. It was dated the day of her death. We only found it later. That's why the police never saw it at the time. They took the other note away of course.' Mother Ancilla pursed her lips.

'She must have been in two minds at the time. I mean, about it all . . .' I thought: she must have been in more minds than that. And all her minds distracted.

'Poor Sister Miriam,' said Mother Ancilla sharply, 'was certainly a very disturbed person.' Disturbed: and disturbing. Disturbing to the peace of Blessed Eleanor's Convent. Potentially highly disturbing to my own peace.

On the back of the little white slip was a picture of the Virgin Mary in her blue robe, surrounded by a halo of stars.

I breathed a fairly devout prayer of thankfulness – I was almost tempted to cross myself – it was odd how these practices so slightly learnt at the time were returning to me – to whatever tutelary power had kept Rosa's message hidden. Imagine the newspaper headlines. Yes, I could imagine them only too well. Jemima Shore in Dead Nun Drama. Mystery of Last Message. So much more appetising than the simple 'Nun Found Dead' which had originally attracted my attention. Suddenly a feeling of the craziness of it all overcame me. I had not seen Rosa for – how long? It had to be fifteen years, no, more. After school there had been some unsatisfactory meetings in London. I remembered particularly one girls' lunch in a store – D.H. Evans was it, somewhere in Oxford Street. It was definitely not Fortnum and Mason, as Rosa had suggested. I knew that was too expensive for me and had said so.

'I generally go there with my friends, but I don't like it particularly,' was Rosa's comment. She sounded rather blank on the telephone.

In any case, I could not even pay the price of the set lunch at D.H. Evans, so it was just as well we had eschewed Fortnum's.

'Don't be silly,' said Rosa easily, paying both bills. She took a wallet from her leather handbag. Fascinated I saw that it contained another thin white fluttery note – as five-pound notes were in those days. I suppose that note was the single positive object which told me that Rosa was rich. Our school uniform, strictly imposed, made us all equal just as the nuns' black imposed uniformity on them. Rosa the nun – Sister Miriam – would have seemed no richer or poorer than say that little nun who had let me in at the door. Because I did not want to think back into the past for too long, I allowed a more modern thought to strike me. Rosa had been rich. Even, perhaps, very rich. What happened to her money when she entered the convent? What happened to it now that she was dead?

'She was a great heiress of course.' Mother Ancilla's voice broke into my thoughts in a way I was beginning to take once more for granted. The words came to me on a sigh. 'All the Powerstock money from generations back came to her. She had no close relations left.'

I thought back.

'Land in Dorset somewhere?'

Mother Ancilla smiled sadly.

'Alas, no. Not just that. That would have been simple. But there were all the great London properties as well. Her family estates in London. The Powers Estate.'

I began to put two and two together.

'You mean Powers Square, Powers House, and all that. Good God – sorry Mother.' I had done a programme on it all some time back, a particularly successful one as it had turned out. Combining as it did questions of the environment (Powers Square was said to be Cubitt's finest achievement) and social policy (the poor families on the nearby Powers Estate were being ejected from decrepit but still elegant houses so that a monster high-rise development could take place). I had also managed to discover that a good many of my colleagues at Megalith Television were living in the aforesaid decrepit houses and had done them up very nicely, thank you. They too objected to being removed yet essentially were being asked to make way for working-class housing ... It was all very confusing. So confusing that I could not immediately remember who Jemima Shore, Investigator, had finally decided was in the right. Tom of course had been full of special scorn for my television colleagues in their refurbished homes ('A series of I'm-all-right Jills and Jacks masquerading as liberals'). I think I decided as usual that justice lay in the middle – that is to say nowhere.

Then there were the Powers Project fanatics. I'd temporarily forgotten about them. They too had been represented on my admirably impartial programme in the shape of an interview with their leader Alexander Skarbek.

Before the programme went out, several of the directors of MGV had taken fright and suggested that Skarbek should be cut.

'We're not here to promote the social ideas of mad extremists,' was the general line taken. Cy Fredericks, Megalith's colourful boss, groaned to me in private:

'Jem, what are you doing to me? Lord Loggin-Smith is an insomniac and rings me up throughout the night. Dame Victoria believes in making a brisk start to the day and calls me any time from six-thirty onwards.' But in public he merely murmured a few platitudes about television being open to all sides of the question. Actually I had rather enjoyed interviewing Skarbek, who was quite young and was certainly a more sympathetic type to me, fanaticism and all, than most of the directors of MGV.

The Powers Project aimed quite simply to set up a type of workers' commune all over the Powers Estate. The Projectors, as they became known, dismissed with equal contumely the existing concept of Cubitt's Powers Square and Powers House, and the council's future high-rise blocks. I was never quite clear what kind of rudimentary housing would replace the present Victorian façades, but there would be acres of it, that was certain. I think they were going to grow vegetables there too, like the Diggers, and keep pigs and hens.

Tom poured scorn on them too.

'Darling, when we're trying so hard to institute a proper housing policy in that part of London, to have some dangerous loony advocating a return to the standards of the seventeenth century – yes, Skarbek is dangerous. Power mad. You watch out.'

'Everyone on this particular programme is power mad,' I countered. 'Or rather Powers Mad. In the sense that everyone wants something different from everyone else for the Powers Estate. And wants it like crazy, with no ability to compromise. To coin a phrase, this programme is turning out to be an allegory of our society.'

'Your programmes always turn out to be an allegory of our society,' said Tom crossly, 'and if you don't say it beforehand, the critics say it for you afterwards.'

But he had at least provided me with a title for this programme. Powers Mad it became. And Powers Mad it went out, Alexander Skarbek and all.

'And of course she owned the convent land itself,' continued Mother Ancilla delicately with a little cough.

This time she had really astonished me.

'Blessed Eleanor's. You mean Rosa *owned* Blessed Eleanor's?'

'No nun owns anything, dear Jemima,' said Mother Ancilla calmly. 'In the sense that you in the world own things. A nun has given everything to God. It is just a case of the formalities of the arrangement.' I had a vision of God's lawyers – hatchet-faced men, as Tom would have them – behind whom the warm and benevolent God was able to shelter. 'Of course it was all handled by the lawyers and made part of a trust. Set up by Sir Gilbert Powerstock long ago. You probably remember him at Parents' Day: an enormous man. I remember thinking what an imposing sight he must have made in his Lord Mayor's robes, quite different from Rosabelle – Sister Miriam. She took after her mother. Poor Marie Thérèse was a Campion of course and all the Campions were small and dark ever since the marriage of the 1st Earl Campion to one of dear Queen Mary's Spanish ladies-in-waiting.' I suddenly realised she was not referring to the late Queen Mary of betoqued fame, but to Mary Tudor. In my convent days I had to learn not to refer to her as Bloody Mary.

'You won't remember Lady Powerstock. She died very young – the Campion chest, you know. We were going through a period of grave financial difficulty at the time. And then dear Sir Gilbert stepped in and bought most of the land on which the convent stands and endowed it in perpetual memory of his wife. But for some technical reason to do with the trust, although the convent buildings became a charity, the land itself was different. I am afraid, as his heiress, Sister Miriam still owned it outright.'

'You're *afraid* she owned it outright?'

It was an odd choice of words, even for a nun.

'Oh Jemima, I am so worried that the whole wretched business of the land drove her to what she did.' It was Mother Ancilla at her most human and appealing. She stretched out and held my hand in hers. I remembered what ones the nuns were for physical contact, hugs, embraces, kisses, hands warmly held. The contacts whose natural corollaries were denied to them ... No, that was Tom's kind of talk. They were just a bunch of affectionate and sweet, slightly girlish women, frozen perhaps in the girlishness of the age at which they had joined the convent.

'It worried her so, the responsibility of it, on top of her illness. Our Lord certainly knew what He was talking about when He told the centurion to sell all that he had. How poor Sister Miriam longed to lose all her great wealth into the arms of God. But the lawyers, you know. Even for a nun. They wouldn't let her alone. They kept saying: we must regularise the situation. And then she began to get such odd ideas about it all into her poor sick head. Not at all what Sir Gilbert intended, I can assure you. Ah well, Our Lord saw fit to put an end to all that. He knew that she would have never got such an idea in her right mind.'

'Mother, you must tell me. What was it that Rosabelle wanted to do with the land?'

This time Mother Ancilla looked quite genuinely surprised.

'But, Jemima, don't you know? You must know. I thought she must have written to you, when I found the note. It was after your programme. She wanted to take it away from us and—'

'Yes?'

'Give it to the poor.'

'Give it to the poor,' I repeated. Then the funny side of it all struck me. There had been such absolute horror in Mother Ancilla's voice. I could not resist adding: 'Just like the centurion in fact.'

'Not at all like the centurion,' replied Mother Ancilla icily. 'The centurion, you will remember, was a responsible man in a high position. Sister Miriam was a very sick woman. Her own lawyer begged her not to perform such a destructive and—one cannot avoid the word—crazy action. It would have ruined the convent of course. No grounds, no land. Right up to our very gates. No, beyond our gates. To our front door. It seems that the chapel itself would have gone. Our own chapel! Oh, we could no longer have existed. All our work gone for nothing. So very very far from the intentions of her father and the memory of her dear mother.'

She sighed again. There seemed to be more irritation than charity about the exhalation. I felt encouraged to continue.

'The poor – that's an awful lot of people. How did she choose?' Mother Ancilla gave me a smile of great sweetness.

'The poor. As Our Blessed Lord said, they are always with us. I remember it was the title of one of your programmes, wasn't it? "They are always with us." I wondered at the time how you selected *them*.'

'I doubt if Sister Miriam used the methods of Megalith Television.' Once again I regretted the decision to strike back. Another clasp of the hand. Another desperate look. A nagging feeling that something – or someone – was frightening Mother Ancilla, returned.

'Look, Mother Ancilla,' I said in my gentlest Jemima Shore manner, 'I want to help you. Please believe that. But you must explain to me what's going on here. Or what has been going on. I'm really quite at sea. Let me state a few simple facts –' Oh that phrase! Why couldn't I resist it? Even now when I was desperately trying to be honest. A phrase parodied by satirical programmes, which generally had me following it with a load of absolutely incomprehensible gibberish. 'No, Sister Miriam, Rosabelle, never wrote to me about the programme. In my enquiries I certainly never came across the fact that a nun of the O.T.I. had any connection with the properties – why, that would have made a terrific addition to the programme, come to think of it –'

I reined myself in. This was scarcely the time for such enthusiasm.

'"Jemima knows," she wrote. . .But Jemima doesn't know. You must tell me. Otherwise I cannot begin to help you.'

There was a silence. It was interrupted by a knock at the door.

'Yes, come in,' said Mother Ancilla sharply. 'Yes, Sister, what is it now?'

'Oh, I'm sorry, Reverend Mother, I didn't realise you had a visitor –' A slightly breathless voice behind me. But I did not quite like to turn round and stare. I waited for Mother

Ancilla to introduce me. But Mother Ancilla continued to gaze over my head at her visitor with barely concealed annoyance.

'As you can see, Sister, I'm really rather busy at the moment,' was all she said. The unseen visitor – a nun, evidently, but I knew no more than that – departed.

Mother Ancilla frowned. I noticed that she suspended speaking until there could be no question of the recent intruder overhearing us.

Then at last she explained. How Rosabelle Powerstock, in her new life as Sister Miriam of the Order of the Tower of Ivory, had never shown any particular interest in her previous wealth. She took her vow of poverty extremely seriously. Naturally she brought a dowry with her to the convent as all the nuns did.

'A substantial dowry,' said Mother Ancilla, nodding. The language laboratory? The swimming pool? I did not like to interrupt her by asking. 'Our Blessed Lord saw to it that at last we were able to mend the chapel roof, which has needed the most expensive repairs since the day of Reverend Mother Felix.' Ah. I felt reproved for the secular nature of my speculations. But beyond that she had renounced the vast trusts once administered in her name, the beneficiaries being a series of Catholic charities and educational projects.

Of course, Sister Miriam had made the usual will required by a member of the O.T.I., leaving the residue of her dowry to that community. But that in itself was not expected to be a great fortune. And what with chapel roofs and other religious luxuries . . . In the years which had passed since dear Sir Gilbert's death – his dear death, I almost thought Mother Ancilla would say – no-one had had the faintest idea that Rosabelle Powerstock still retained outright ownership of every single inch of the so-called convent grounds of the Blessed Eleanor's. It was, it seemed, an oversight on the lawyers' part that the trust deed which covered the buildings did not in fact cover the lands. A technicality.

'One can't help wondering why, if they were to make the

mistake in the first place, Our Blessed Lord ever guided them to discover it so many years later,' observed Mother Ancilla with something approaching waspishness. But discover it, they had. And in their interminable way had begun the long, long process to rectify it. To establish the deed by which Rosabelle Powerstock would hand over the grounds to the convent, as once her father had officially handed over the buildings.

'She agreed to do so?' I interrupted.

'At first. Without hesitation. I told you that Sister Miriam cared nothing for the things of this world. In her right mind.'

'But lately, there was a change. She wanted to give these same lands away?'

'Oh, those lawyers, they took so long. And wrote so many letters. And came to see her, and insisted on explaining to her what she was doing. As if Sister Miriam was *doing* anything. She was simply being a good nun. And putting her signature to a piece of paper which should have been over and done with years ago. And then she became ill.'

'And everything changed.'

'She changed. Nothing round her changed in the slightest.' Mother Ancilla began to speak more rapidly. 'It was after she saw your programme on television. She was convalescing at the time. She wanted to give it to the poor. Not just any poor, Jemima, but those poor people in the demolished houses of Powers Square. The Powers Projectors they call themselves. She talked of the rich man and the needle's eye. But she was, alas, mad. We know that now – too late. I thought she wrote to you. I thought she must have written to you. But somehow she got in touch with that man, the leader of the demonstrators or the residents' association or whatever they were called. She wrote to him. She offered him our lands. She said they were hers to give. Alexander Skarbek his name was.'

Alexander Skarbek. The man I had secretly found more sympathetic than the directors of MGV. Secretly and not only because of my job but because he was Tom's *bête noire*. Tom once said Alexander Skarbek existed to give good causes a bad name. A man without scruple, at least in Tom's opinion: it depended of course upon what your own scruples were. A man who certainly possessed qualities of decision and leadership. A man, a fanatic, sufficiently convinced of the rightness of his cause, who would not have hesitated to accept such an offer, even made by a half-crazy nun. A man who would also have understood exactly how to beat the Power-stock family lawyers at their own game. Had he not defeated the combined efforts of the Ministry and local Council in his efforts over the Greatpark Housing Estate?

Jemima knows: but I had known nothing of this, even if my programme had been responsible for touching it all off.

'She talked of Christ's poverty. How she would settle at our gates like Lazarus and teach us the true meaning of the Christian message.'

I could see that Mother Ancilla in her capacity as Dives, would scarcely welcome such a Lazarus as Alexander Skarbek at her gates.

'But in the event, Mother Ancilla, it didn't happen,' I heard myself say in my best unemotional manner. 'For I gather she never changed her will. Blessed Eleanor's inherited every-thing she still possessed.' The old nun shook her head. 'So the community has – forgive me for putting it so bluntly – by the untimely death of Sister Miriam Powerstock acquired the lands for itself.' I almost said: 'Timely death.'

Mother Ancilla did not seem to notice. She merely nodded. Behind her head there was a reproduction picture of the Virgin and Child in a bevelled burnished gilt frame. By Lippo Lippi. That had not changed since my day. But then Lippo Lippi could hardly be said to date. The Virgin looked infinitely sorrowful. But detached. As though she knew that all the concern she felt for the pitiful human scene taking place beneath her calm sad gaze could not alter the course of the stream of human passion by one iota. Her high round brow, the tendrils of her perfectly delineated golden hair, gave her an implacable beauty.

Mother Ancilla's brow on the other hand was not visible beneath the white band of her wimple, and no tendrils escaped from this prison. Any hair that did show would be grey and wispy, if not white. Nuns' hair had been a preoccupation when we were at school. The delicious thrill of shock when Sister Thomas, a young nun, had appeared in class with a distinct curl of brown hair showing. She must have dressed in a hurry, poor child. As nuns were not allowed to look in mirrors, she was probably unaware of her solecism. Another delicious thrill at the idea of Mother Ancilla's tart regret when the offending wisp was glimpsed. It all added up to the fact that nuns were not bald and did not shave their heads; they simply cut their hair conveniently short.

Gazing at Mother Ancilla now beneath the tumble-locked Virgin, I found that I had not altogether lost my preoccupation with nuns' hair. Or their appearance generally.

'You know, my child, I have not been very well recently,' said Mother Ancilla. I realised that there had been quite a silence between us, although to me her little room – even the headmistress's study was not allowed to waste space – had seemed filled by a voice from the past.

'Supposing a nun just refused to have her hair cut –' Rosa, young and audacious. But one day Rosa's own hair had been chopped off. That unruly brown curling hair I loved, hair which I used sometimes to brush furiously. Cut into the shape of Sister Miriam. Buried forever, first beneath the severe black headdress, now in the perpetual blackness of the grave.

Back to Mother Ancilla, another blackness and the shadow of her health.

'I'm sorry to hear that, Mother.' The conventional gush.

'Don't be sorry. Our Lord has been very good to me. He has allowed me to spend many years at the head of this convent, trying to serve Him. I cannot complain if now He feels that my work here is over. In many ways,' she paused, 'I shall be glad to lay down the burden.'

'Oh surely things aren't quite so serious.' Another easy riposte. Then with more conviction: 'I can't imagine this

29

convent without you. You've made it what it is. You *are* the Blessed Eleanor's to most of us.'

'Nonsense' – briskly. 'We are none of us indispensable. I should be gravely wanting in humility if I believed what you have just said to be true.' But under the air of reproof she did look slightly pleased. I was reminded of a recently retired Trades Union leader, appearing on my programme. I had made the same sort of observation along the lines of 'You are the Union'. He too could eliminate ambition but not pleasure in the success of his work. Another admirable martinet, I suppose. At any rate the camera had caught the fleeting expression of self-satisfaction. There was no camera to catch Mother Ancilla's momentary pleasure, and now she was frowning.

'Like Simeon, I would wish to make haste to be gone. If only I could leave the community as it should be ... Not divided, frightened.'

She began to speak much faster again.

'Jemima, something is going on here. It is not simply the death of Sister Miriam, nor the reports in the Press. Although obviously those shook the community gravely. I feel it. I have been, you know, nearly fifty years in religion. I should have my Golden Jubilee next summer if ...' A pause in the rush of words, and then she dashed on, 'I will be frank with you. If I live that long. I have been warned by our doctor that I may not. That I *will* not, unless I take things easier. That means of course retirement: maybe to our little house at Oxford. Maybe to our convalescent home in Dorset, built incidentally on part of the Powerstock Estate. Mindful of my vow of obedience I would go any time. I should go willingly. But how can I leave the community now? When they are–' A long pause. A single sonorous word: 'Troubled.'

'Jemima, I want you to help us. I told you there isn't much time.' It was a return to the old voice of authority. 'I want you to find out what is going on here amongst us. No, please don't say no, not immediately. I have prayed long and earnestly about this. Think about it.'

One bell tolled in the distance. One bell for Reverend Mother.

'My bell.' Mother Ancilla arose and with surprising alacrity for a sick woman approaching seventy, moved to the door, automatically putting one finger in the tiny holy water stoup and crossing herself. 'I have arranged for you to have lunch in the refectory with the children, dear Jemima. They are thrilled at the prospect, naturally. They are all great fans of yours. Sister Clare will give you coffee later in the Nuns' Parlour. A visit to the chapel, perhaps?'

I smiled noncommittally. Things were going altogether too fast. I wanted to retain what control I still had of the situation. The chapel represented a form of capitulation I was definitely not prepared to make.

My last sight of Mother Ancilla was of a figure like a little black bird skimming down the corridor. The corridor itself was plain except for a series of alcoves containing incongruously garish statues of assorted saints.

'Miss Shore,' said a gentle voice more or less at my elbow. I realised that a little nun, hardly more than a novice from her face, had been waiting for some minutes to speak to me. With her twitching mouth and neat nose, she looked rather like an unhappy rabbit.

'I'm Sister Edward. I must talk to you.' Sister Edward: the name rang a bell. Yes, the nun who had so unfortunately not revealed Sister Miriam's crazy plan of self-purgation. And only sounded the alarm about the locked tower when it was too late. I also realised from her voice that Sister Edward had been that intruder in the headmistress's study whose appearance had been so unwelcome.

'Talk away,' I replied with false cheerfulness, my voice unnecessarily loud.

'Not here.'

At that moment the bell sounded again, three strokes then four. Sister Edward literally blanched.

'My bell. I must go.' All the same she continued to stand

twisting her hands. 'They're after me. They don't want me to talk to you –'

'Sister Edward, I really think –'

By way of reply, Sister Edward dragged me into the narrow alcove beside me.

'She killed her,' she said, panting, and poking her little face into mine. 'She wanted her dead. So she killed her.'

'*Who?*' I might have said 'What' with equal force. I had no idea what Sister Edward was saying.

'Why Mother Ancilla of course.' The rabbit's face was turned up in innocent surprise. 'Mother Ancilla killed poor Sister Miriam.' The next moment Sister Edward was in her turn skimming down the corridor towards the nuns' part of the building. Another black bird. I knew that it was Sister Edward. But of course from the back it might just as well have been Mother Ancilla or any other nun. They really did look exactly alike.

I was left alone except for a statue of St Antony holding the Infant Jesus in his arms.

A balanced
programme

Lunch in the refectory did not last long. Actually the refectory had been turned into a cafeteria since my day, complete with counter and plastic cases for food. All the nuns behind the counter had beaming rather flushed faces. We used to divide nuns into Snow Whites and Rose Reds, as the religious life (or the wimple) seemed to have the effect of sending their complexions to one or other extreme. These were all Rose Reds.

The food was delicious. I said as much to the girls sitting with me at table. They all affected considerable surprise.

'Would you like a second helping, Miss Shore?' enquired a girl at the end of the table politely. It was the first remark she had made throughout the meal. She had a long, interesting face, with a straight nose, like a crusader modelled on a tomb. As she brought back the plate, she bent over my chair and said quite low: 'This was Sister Miriam's favourite pudding as well, you know.'

Afterwards I asked Mother Ancilla who she was.

'Why, that's Margaret Plantagenet!' cried Mother Ancilla. She sounded delighted at my cleverness in picking out such an eligible candidate for my attention. 'Lady Margaret

Plantagenet,' she added in passing – no-one could throw away a title like Mother Ancilla. 'The Bosworths' daughter.'

'It's not a very Catholic name,' I muttered. In my irritation at having given Mother Ancilla such an opening, I quite forgot to ask how a mere schoolgirl could have known of my friendship with Rosa.

'It's true that her mother was –' and Mother Ancilla mentioned some incredibly grand-sounding Italian name which I had genuinely never heard before, although I should have tried to look blank in any case. 'Lord Bosworth is a convert. But Margaret herself looks pure Plantagenet, don't you think?'

It was clear that Mother Ancilla regarded the presence of Margaret Plantagenet at the Convent of Blessed Eleanor as a latter-day triumph for the Counter-Reformation.

I did not go to the chapel.

I did receive coffee from Sister Clare in the Nuns' Parlour. Sister Clare was extremely plump, and the sight of her swelling front beneath her black habit tempted me to wonder anew whether nuns wore bras (another perennial topic of discussion, and one which as far as I was concerned had never reached a satisfactory conclusion). If we had been on television I would have asked her, 'Sister, there is one question I know our female viewers are dying to ask ...' Everyone would have expected something about sexual frustration; instead of which I would have continued: 'In an age when many women are boasting of burning their bras ...' and so forth. We were not on television. I put temptation from me. It was unlikely that Vatican II had left the topic untouched in any case, whatever the mode when I was at school.

To distract myself, I reapplied my attention to the pasteboard brides in and out of their portfolio. At least I could picture Lady Margaret Plantagenet featuring here in a few years' time, stern in white, on the arm of some suitably aristocratic bridegroom. And the convent would send them a wedding present of table napkins embroidered by the nuns in which the Plantagenet arms mingled with those of the

Blessed Eleanor . . . This agreeable fantasy lasted until I had finished my coffee.

Shortly after that I made it clear to Mother Ancilla, kindly but firmly, that Jemima Shore, Investigator, was a character who existed more or less for the benefit of television. I could not undertake a special secret mission to iron out the problems of Blessed Eleanor's. My encounter with Sister Edward had nevertheless given me an inkling as to the nature of these problems. Clearly a host of celibate women cooped up together could ferment from time to time like yeast. In the Middle Ages Sister Edward would have seen visions. Nowadays she merely accused her superior of murder. She probably watched too many thrillers on television. The gift of an old girl. In St Joseph's Sitting Room.

As I drove back to London, I felt that the long fingers of the past had stretched out to grasp me. And I had eluded them. I was sorry for Mother Ancilla. But I could not help her.

Besides, I was shortly off to Yugoslavia with Tom.

Two days later, he took me for dinner in our favourite restaurant, a trattoria behind Victoria station, discreet, convenient for the House of Commons. I wore my treasured Hanae Mori dress. A motif of scattered hearts. The heart: my lucky symbol. I tended to scribble a heart on my notes to Tom. Not so lucky tonight, it seemed. For I was not in fact off to Yugoslavia. Or at any rate, not with him. The Welfare Now Group, on which Tom had lavished so much of his prodigious idealism, was calling for urgent meetings with the Minister before the autumn session of Parliament. In the expectation that these meetings would be unsatisfactory – and they always were – there was to be a rally in Trafalgar Square. Tom of course would be one of the principal speakers. His tall thin figure, bowing slightly in the gale of his own words, was an inseparable part of the W.N.G. platform.

'It's not that I can't get out of it,' Tom said unhappily. 'It's just that I don't want to. We've got to make them see that our demands are reasonable. You understand what I mean, darling.'

As a matter of fact I did not understand. It occurred to me that the Archangel Gabriel with the resources of Mycenas would not be able to satisfy the demands of the W.N.G. But this was not a time for saying so.

'Tell me we shall go to Yugoslavia one day.' My voice had a mournful spaniel's note which I disliked.

'I promise.' Tom was a totally truthful person, even sometimes when I wished he wouldn't be. I believed him. Perhaps it was Tom's honesty that now compelled him to let drop the news that Carrie's mother was also unexpectedly altering her plans and coming over from the States. To me at a suffering distance, Carrie's mother had the power and caprices of a Byzantine Empress. Much of Carrie's innate disturbance of personality was laid by Tom at her door. Carrie's fear of having children for example:

'Can you wonder with the sort of mother that she had, that she doesn't want to take on the role herself?'

'Why don't you adopt a Vietnamese orphan *pour encourager?*

Tom looked reproachful. Vietnamese orphans were not subjects for humour. I was well aware of that. My own programme on the subject had been deadly serious. He also looked reproachful now when I murmured how convenient it must be for Carrie to have Tom with her after all to help stave off her mother's onslaughts. But I did not pursue the point.

That night was perhaps the tenderest we had ever known. It was also a whole night. I do not know what story, if any, Tom told Carrie. She was quite forgotten by us both, along with everything else.

The next morning at breakfast I told Tom all about Mother Ancilla and the Order's inheritance and Rosabelle's will and her intention to leave the land away from the Order. I did not, of course, mention poor crazy Sister Edward's accusation. Then, out of nowhere, or so it seemed at the time, we quarrelled violently about Rosa's right to give away the convent lands. I felt buffeted by a series of prejudices, my own and his. On the one hand, Tom had clearly not overcome his innate revulsion for convents, nuns and their like. The words 'black crows', although not spoken again, were implicit in several of his remarks. On the other hand, he criticised anew a social system which allowed an individual – Rosa – to own so much land.

I pointed out several times that Rosa's ownership was an anomaly, which it was intended that time would set right. Community ownership after all was exactly what Sir Gilbert Powerstock had in mind when he handed over the buildings to the Order. I also pointed out that the nuns had worked the lands honourably for many years – generations of them – long before Sir Gilbert bought it in fact and, like the working-class residents of the Powers Estate, were now in danger of seeing the fruit of their labours handed over to another body. All this because of an arbitrary accident of birth which gave Rosabelle Powerstock the legal – if not moral – right to do so.

'Well, she's dead now. Your old friend. So you can't argue with her,' replied Tom heatedly. 'Mind you, I still think there's something fishy about her death. A little too convenient if you ask me –'

It was those last words that did it. That, and the cruel awareness of three blank weeks in my life. A week later, I was once again driving down to Churne. It was precisely the date on which I should have been boarding a plane to Dubrovnik with Tom, I reflected, as I pressed into the deep countryside. Various skeletal trees reminded me that winter was coming. How quickly autumn passed! Like every pleasure, it seemed momentary.

It was dark when I arrived at the convent. The same small hedgehog of a nun let me in at the gates. On the telephone I had been brief and reserved to Mother Ancilla. I merely told her that after all I had decided to accept her offer of a few weeks' relaxation at Blessed Eleanor's. To the curious, it might be hinted that I was contemplating a programme on women in religious orders in the modern world, i.e. post Vatican II.

'I am not sure that we are the best example of such changes,' said Mother Ancilla drily down the telephone. 'A great deal of prayer and thought has persuaded us that to move with the times is not necessarily to move according to the will of God. Or indeed the intentions of Our Blessed Foundress.'

'Precisely. A balanced programme. In other words, it takes all sorts.'

I did not see Mother Ancilla that evening. The girls had already eaten. The small nun – Sister Damian – brought me supper on a tray in the Nuns' Parlour. The food was delicious. Each dish not only tasted good but was also exquisitely presented, reminding me of food in Japan. Later Sister Damian took me to the guest corridor. Botticelli (a Virgin), Titian (a Madonna with Child) and Fra Angelico (an Annunciation) were represented on the walls. By the bed I observed two books. One, bound in black leather, turned out to be the Treasury of the Blessed Eleanor, a work whose name if not its contents, was familiar to me. The other, still in its dust jacket, was the recent autobiography of a prominent Roman Catholic. I knew him from a rather unsuccessful programme of mine about birth control.

Under the circumstances, I picked up the Treasury of Blessed Eleanor.

I read: 'As a Tower points towards heaven, so should a man build his whole life in the direction of God. Yet even the highest Tower can never touch the sky; nevertheless man by the grace of God and his own Faith may expect to reach heaven one day. This is the supreme mercy of God, to set man higher than his highest buildings, to make of him a living Tower who will one day touch the sky.'

Towers clearly obsessed Blessed Eleanor. She had been born a French princess and briefly married in youth to an ageing English king. Childless widowhood had clearly suited her; she had made no effort to marry again, but had retired thankfully to Churne Palace which formed part of her marriage jointure. To the palace she had affixed the buildings of a large convent, and founded the Order of the Tower of Ivory.

It wasn't quite clear if that name actually dated from the lifetime of the Blessed Eleanor. There was some suggestion that she had already thought of commemorating her own name. Would the nuns have been called Queen Eleanor's Own, I wondered, as a modern regiment is named for royalty? Be that as it might, the O.T.I., as it had become, was certainly a very old foundation in Mother Ancilla's words. Even the vicissitudes of the Reformation period, the years of persecution, had been overcome without extinguishing the Order altogether. The Order itself transferred to Belgium, the buildings, less mobile, transferred to the ownership of a friendly Catholic-sympathising family. Then in the happier times of the nineteenth century and Catholic Emancipation, the O.T.I. was ready to flourish on English soil all over again.

As Reverend Mother, Blessed Eleanor continued to inhabit Churne Palace, leaving her nuns to the somewhat lesser state of their convent. Even her retreats had not exactly been taken in the bosom of the community. That was where the tower – Blessed Eleanor's Retreat – came in. Now all that was left standing of the ancient foundation, it had originally been constructed slightly apart from the convent for a sinister reason. Outside its extra thick walls, Rosa had ghoulishly assured me, the screams of the Blessed Eleanor, as she scourged herself remorselessly in penance for her sins, could not be heard.

'She did not want to be rescued from herself,' Rosa went on, large eyes opened wide. She loved to impress me with the more horrific details of her Faith. I shivered. It reminded me too vividly of the details of poor Rosa's own death: and I was not ready to think about those tonight. I should have to think about them and many other things tomorrow.

Let the Blessed Eleanor, dead for so many years, rest. And

Rosa too. *Requiescant in pace.* But I could not wrench my thoughts so easily away from the pair of them. It came back to me, unbidden, that the Blessed Eleanor too had died in her tower. In her case there had been an Arthurian deathbed, with the dying woman carried to the tower by six black nuns, and laid on the stone flags.

I could not resist checking the story in the brief biography of the saint at the back of her Treasury. Yes, I was right. And there was something else too which I had forgotten. 'And then our blessed foundress called for her royal robes, the robes of a Queen of England and a Princess of France, and they brought them to her, whereon the lions and the lilies were splendidly entwined. "Now good sisters attire me," she commanded them. And they wondered that she who had given up the riches of the world so willingly should call for them in the hour of her death. But she reproved them for their lack of understanding, saying, "Is it not thus in my finest raiment that I should go to meet my bridegroom, the King of Heaven?..."' And so on, till the Blessed Eleanor with a great many last words and admonitions and pious ejaculations, finally expired. Leaving her body to perform those necessary miraculous feats of healing which ensured her beatification in the nineteenth century.

I felt rather more warmly towards the Blessed Eleanor after learning that she had insisted on dying dressed up in full royal gear. Personally, I was not deceived by the excuse she gave the nuns. Once a queen, always a queen. She wanted to sport those lions and lilies once more. Otherwise why preserve them all those years?

My attention was caught by something outside the narrow world of my own thoughts. Far away there was a small distinct sound. The sound of a door opening and shutting. No, the sound of swing doors being gently helped to close. There were two swing doors to the left and right of the guest corridor. One led to the children's dormitories and the other to the vast nuns' wing. That was quite an unknown area to me. Nevertheless I assumed it included a stairway directly to the chapel. Then why was someone attempting to leave the nuns' wing as silently as possible, in order to descend to the chapel by the visitors' staircase? For I could now hear distinct soft steps on the flight outside my door.

It made no sense. It was not particularly late by my metropolitan standards. But it was extremely late by the standards of the convent. The whole place was plunged in darkness, except for the occasional light reflecting from a corridor window where the children slept. Moreover the night owl, whoever she was, was not moving in that busy rapid fashion of all the nuns, intent on not wasting time in the service of God. She was taking step by step very carefully, stopping occasionally as though to listen for any extraneous sounds.

I waited until I reckoned she must have reached the side door of the chapel. On an impulse, and without in any way thinking of what I was doing, I opened the door of my room and slipped out as silently as I could. I too ventured quietly, slowly, down the winding stairs. I touched the oak door to the chapel. It was not latched and pushed open in my hand. It made no sound at all as it swung forward.

At first the chapel seemed to be totally dark except for the red light of the sanctuary lamp, hanging in front of the altar. Then I realised that a group of candles were burning unevenly in front of a statue on my left. Some patronal feast day or other. I picked up one of the candles off its little spike and held it in front of me. I steadied it, and waited for my eyes to grow accustomed to the gloom. I was quite sure I was not alone in the chapel, that the mysterious visitor could not have left by any other door, and must still be lurking in front of me in the shadows.

The strangeness of her silence grew. Why did she not speak? Or at least make some signal. As fear, for the first time, began to catch up with me, there was a rush of cold air behind me and my candle went out. At the same time I put my hand down against the first wooden pew to steady myself. I found my hand touching warm flesh.

I screamed.

5

Unnatural lives

Shortly after my scream, two things happened. Someone or something rushed past me into the chapel from the outside, by the route I had used, out by the nuns' door and away.

The flesh turned out to be a face turned up towards mine in a rather dazed way. There was a nun kneeling at the end of the pew I had touched.

'Miss Shore,' said the nun in a low voice, 'I'm sorry if I startled you.'

'Who was that?'

A rustle. The nun rose to her feet. I could not see her face and did not recognise her voice.

'I'm Sister Agnes.'

'No, who was that? The other person who rushed past us.' I was still trembling and could not let go of the pew. 'Who blew out the candle?'

'There was no-one else here, Miss Shore; see, the chapel is empty.' Deftly Sister Agnes took the candle from my shaky hand and relit it at the shrine. I saw that the statue was of the adult Jesus pointing to a large red heart prominent on his breast. Sacred Heart of Jesus, *Sacré Cœur!* I felt like exclaiming it aloud as a relief to my feelings.

'I've been on duty in St Aloysius's dormitory, the big

dormitory. I came here on my way down to say my night prayers. I'm sorry to have disturbed you.'

'Down the visitors' staircase?' I enquired sharply. If Sister Agnes was surprised at my inquisitorial tone, she did not show it. But she did take a moment to reply. Then she said easily:

'It is quicker that way than going back into the nuns' wing and all the way round by our own stairs. I'm making a novena to the Sacred Heart of Jesus,' she added.

'Then I'm sorry that I disturbed *you*, Sister Agnes,' I answered politely. I was recovering my poise. 'I will leave you to your prayers and peace.'

With as much dignity as I could muster I turned to go back up the winding staircase to my little room, which now seemed like a haven compared to the rustling chapel.

'Let me put on the stair light for you,' said Sister Agnes. 'No wonder you were frightened. We nuns get used to the darkness here in the chapel.'

Sister Agnes stepped swiftly ahead and flipped a switch outside the door. Light flooded the stairs. Enough light to show me an alcove at the bottom of the stairs. It was sufficiently large to conceal a person who might shrink back into it. A person who knew they were being followed and did not want to be seen.

For of course Sister Agnes could not be telling the truth. There was no question of that. There was no way in which she could have slipped out of the children's wing, down the visitors' stairs and reached the pew to be kneeling there calmly and silently ahead of me. Her story was implausible from many angles. For one thing there had not been enough time. For another, the mysterious prowler had definitely come from the nuns' not the children's wing. In any case, if Sister Agnes had arrived from the big dormitory why did she not use the ordinary front staircase to the main chapel entrance, past the refectory?

Last of all, there had been another human being there with us, someone as yet without a face, behind me in the alcove, who blew out my candle before beating a fast retreat to the nuns' part of the building. Ergo: she was a nun. Ergo: Sister Agnes must have seen her over my shoulder, her eyes accustomed to the darkness, my candle held high. Ergo: Sister Agnes was lying.

All of this occupied my mind as I passed back up the staircase to my room.

My last sight of Sister Agnes was of an upturned face wearing an expression of gentle concern. She reminded me of someone. Then I realised that she resembled a Murillo I had once admired of St Agnes with her lamb, the saint as a charming young creature with dark eyes and loosely playing locks. Perhaps it was that resemblance which inspired my new friend to choose the name of Agnes in religion. I had no idea what the inspiring virtues of St Agnes might be beyond a weakness for lambs like Mary in the nursery rhyme. Or was that merely a play on her Latin name? In any case it was tempting to think that Sister Agnes had secretly been prompted by human vanity. I was still thinking of the story of the Blessed Eleanor and her royal robes. It struck me that Sister Agnes must have been a pretty woman once.

Later, when the door of my room was safely shut, it occurred to me further that Sister Agnes probably still was a pretty woman – under that confining coif and veil. It was a commonplace at Blessed Eleanor's that one could never tell the real age of nuns. The tell-tale throats and foreheads were securely hidden. From my brief glimpse of her, I put Sister Agnes at no more than thirty. The thought of that motionless figure in the pew, waiting, remained with me as I fell asleep.

There was no doubt that the life of a nun was an unnatural one. At the age of thirty an attractive unmarried woman like Sister Agnes would be better employed meeting her married boss after hours from the office than keeping lonely trysts in a chapel. At the age of thirty, I myself had been doing just that. With the great Cy Fredericks himself, my married boss at Megalith. He had not of course been quite so great in those days. But he had been married all right. With all the heartbreak of the relationship, I doubt if I should ever have emerged as Jemima Shore, Investigator, without his help. It was not a case of string-pulling. He was just naturally infectious. You could not help catching confidence off him, like a cold.

There was no doubt that the life of a nun was an unnatural one.

I drifted into sleep.

'I expect you feel that we all lead unnatural lives here, Jemima,' said Mother Ancilla the next morning, in her tiny study. It was her no-nonsense, head-of-the-school tone.

'I wouldn't say that exactly, Mother,' I replied carefully. 'From my time here I respect the logic of your existence. Even if I don't share in it.'

'I assumed that to be so. Otherwise you wouldn't be here' – even brisker. 'But that wasn't my point. I was referring to the fact that our lives do have an order, an order of their own. Which is not the slightest bit unnatural, for two reasons. First it is an order dedicated to the service of God. We are convinced that as best we may, we are carrying out God's will for *us* on earth. Secondly, it is not unnatural because we are all here voluntarily. Of our own free will.'

I received a slight jolt.

'You look surprised, my child. But what I am saying is perfectly true. We are not living in the Middle Ages. A vocation is a difficult thing to assess of course. Only Almighty God can truly see into our hearts. But we do our best to choose the members of our community with care, even today when vocations are so much rarer. That is God's will too, and we must accept it.' (But I got the impression that Mother Ancilla might have a thing or two to say to God on the subject when the twain finally encountered each other.) Meanwhile, she was marching on:

'Sometimes of course, in spite of all our precautions, our long probationary period of postulancy and novitiate, we are just plainly mistaken. Or a nun is mistaken about her vocation. And then she is released from her vows and returns into the world. You may remember Beatrice O'Dowd from your time here. She was a nun for fifteen years, and left us last year. We regretted it but we did not try to stand in her way.' All the same I got the impression that Beatrice O'Dowd, like God, was not in Mother Ancilla's best books.

'And Rosabelle – Sister Miriam?' I was thinking of Tom. What, no incarcerated nuns, no immured and helpless victims, no white faces behind grilles?

'Exactly. Sister Miriam never asked to be released from her vows. Even when she had her nervous breakdown, she begged the community not to reject her.'

I had to believe all that she said.

'Tell me about some of the younger nuns here,' I replied, changing the subject. 'I must know everything possible about the community if I am to help you. Do they not feel, well, restless, with all the changes in the modern world? Someone like,' I appeared to search for a name, 'Sister Agnes, for example.'

Mother Ancilla's eyes met mine, level, watchful.

'Ah, I see you have noticed the resemblance then. I wondered whether you would.'

'The resemblance?'

'Sister Miriam. They were first cousins – although of course Sister Agnes is considerably younger. She was born a Campion, Agnes Campion when she was at school here. She did not change her name in religion, which is of course rare in our Order. In fact,' Mother Ancilla added rather crossly, 'it used not to be allowed. Our Blessed Foundress ...' She rolled her eyes to heaven, but so automatically that I felt her mind was distinctly on earth. 'Our Blessed Foundress commanded us to throw away all earthly things in her rule, including the names our parents had given us.'

'While keeping her own?'

'Royalty. That's different.' Mother Ancilla swept on without embarrassment. 'A symbol for leaving our own houses for the house of God. There was a technical relaxation of the rule last year' – Mother Ancilla managed to cram an extraordinary distaste into the word 'technical' – 'but I must say I was surprised when Sister Agnes took advantage of it.' After that Mother Ancilla's roving mind abandoned the subject of Sister Agnes's unexpected independence and returned to that of Rosabelle: 'The resemblance is of course much more marked in the religious habit. The eyes are so similar, don't you think? Sister Agnes had much darker hair, really jet black. Such a pretty child, her Spanish blood –'

I felt the subject of the ancestry of the Campions looming once more and said hastily:

'I did sense something familiar.' And so I had. 'But of course I never saw Rosabelle after she became a nun. I only heard indirectly that she had joined the community.' And that, in its own way, was true too.

Hadn't there been a letter? A long, long letter, all very earnest. In which Rosabelle examined herself and her problems in her small neat handwriting for page after page. She was in effect consulting me as to whether she should enter the convent. I knew it. Her father had recently died, she wrote, and she felt herself to be alone. Alone that is, except for the love of God. And – me. My friendship. An outsider. Not even a Catholic. I would be able to bring a fresh eye to it all: I had such a clear mind. And I would remember all our discussions on the subject in time gone by.

Yes, there had been a letter. And I had not answered it. Time gone by. It had arrived some time during my second year at Cambridge, when I was in the throes of enjoying that coveted place. Won with such grim concentration, it was now to be savoured. I had put the letter aside: Rosa and her problems seemed as remote as the time of the Blessed Eleanor.

Later I heard by chance from a cousin of hers at Cambridge, Celia Campion, a cheerful type, product of another convent school and rather improbably reading Maths: Rosabelle Powerstock had entered Blessed Eleanor's. Or as Celia put it, 'Cousin Rosa has taken the jolly old veil.'

'Mother Ancilla,' I said, 'I imagine that I am free to wander

47

as I please while I'm here, to talk to whom I please, to ask what questions I like.'

'But of course, dear Jemima.' Mother Ancilla threw up her hands. 'That's what you are here for. An outsider's eye to see clearly what perhaps we, so close to it all, have missed.'

'In that case I think I should try to talk to several of the nuns singly, on the excuse of my television programme of course, try and feel my way round a bit.' That seemed to Mother Ancilla an excellent plan. Why not start tonight? Nothing wrong with that either. It was, she pointed out, the Feast of All Saints and thus a whole holiday. This evening there would be Solemn Benediction in the chapel which I might like to attend? Yes, I would like to attend it, the music at Blessed Eleanor's being a speciality not to be missed. Afterwards the children would be watching a film – *The Sound of Music*, as a matter of fact. Such a lovely uplifting film. Had I ever interviewed Julie Andrews? No, what a pity – but any member of the community would be free for a chat.

In this way I had intended to ask to see Sister Edward. I thought I might just as well grasp the nettle of her hysteria at the beginning of my investigations, rather than let an unpleasant and fundamentally rather pointless interview hang over me. I shall never understand what impulse led me to substitute the name of Sister Agnes for that of Sister Edward. I certainly did not believe in such split-second decisions being manifestations of some divine plan. More likely it was something in Mother Ancilla's manner, a conviction that she was unwilling to discuss Sister Agnes, which prompted me.

Besides I was already falling half in love with my own cover story of a programme about women in orders. Why not, after all? Once I had cleared up Mother Ancilla's little problem for her. From the point of view of television, Sister Edward would be quite hopeless. But Sister Agnes now, so calm in a confused situation as I had already discovered. In her appearance, come to think of it, there was more than a hint of Audrey Hepburn in *A Nun's Story*. I should have remembered that I was supposed to be on holiday from my programme and not listened to the whisperings of the television devil.

Under the auspices of Solemn Benediction, the chapel seemed to be involved in some vast royal wedding service. The priests wore heavy white robes traced with gold and silver. Great golden tassels hung down from their copes. Candles filled the chapel, a series of bright tiers, which it must have taken the sacristan nun a laborious age to light. How different the chapel seemed from the menacing darkness of the night before! As the censers were swung gravely to and fro, first to the altar, then to the congregation, the heavy fruity smell of incense began to permeate the air. It would linger, I knew, in the still air of the chapel, long after those bridal candles were extinguished, and Sister Agnes knelt alone in the darkness before the sanctuary lamp, saying her novena.

> Sweet Sacrament divine
> All praise and all thanksgiving
> Be every moment thine
> Sweet sa-a-a-crament divine ...

People talk of the purity of boys' voices in a choir. But to me that evening there was a purity and an anguish about the female voices singing, which lingered in my mind long after the voices were still, as the incense lingered in the chapel. All that was missing was the bride: no doubt each lonely heart imagined that she was the bride in the centre of this superb ritual: the bride of Christ.

The nuns knelt or stood on one side of the chapel, the girls on the other. Visitors occupied seats at the back of the school benches. I glanced across at the nuns. It was no longer true that one nun looked much like another. I was beginning to be able to distinguish them again quite easily. Sister Damian the hedgehog, Sister Clare the plump coffee-bringer, and one or two nuns who had certainly been there in my day. That was Sister Elizabeth for sure, hardly changed, Sister Liz, the famed teacher of English, for whom Wordsworth and the lyric poets occupied roles in her pantheon not much below the saints. And Sister Hippolytus, the Hippo, who stood towards history as Sister Elizabeth stood towards English. Here the long history of the convent was the thing to conjure with, preferably in terms of the many documents and records perused by Sister Hippolytus in the convent library, to which no-one else paid any attention – foolishly, in the opinion of Sister Hippolytus. Many a history lesson had been hopelessly misrouted by a casual enquiry from Rosa or myself:

'Sister, is it true that the O.T.I. isn't really an English foundation at all? But Belgian.'

'Our Belgian sister house is a post-Reformation foundation' – Sister Hippo would begin fiercely, unable to resist the bait. Nevertheless, once concentrated on such matters as the Age of the Enlightened Despots, a strict teacher in contrast to the effusive Sister Liz. I owed a lot to them both, I had come to realise ... How could the younger nuns hope to compete with these established figures, who had enjoyed all the certainty of the old-style Church? Nuns in the modern world indeed. No wonder Rosabelle had collapsed under the strain. And Sister Edward looked like following her ... I really would have to talk to Sister Edward tomorrow. It was only fair.

My chat with Sister Agnes took place in the empty guest room next to mine, by permission of Reverend Mother. She told me that I could use it as a sitting room. The décor included the Assumption by Murillo and various other scenes in the life of the Blessed Virgin Mary. Sister Agnes did indeed have a Murillo-like air as she faced me across the mock fireplace with its single electric bar. She looked both demure and collected. She did not in truth greatly resemble Rosabelle, except around the eyes, but then, as Mother Ancilla pointed out, I had never seen Rosa in her habit.

And Sister Agnes, in response to my questions, remained demure and collected throughout. She gave the impression of a cricketer who has been instructed by his captain neither to score runs nor to let a ball pass by. Yes, these were difficult times for women in religion with so many new opportunities open to their contemporaries. No, she did not feel they were *specially* difficult times: for when had the life of women in religion been easy? You did not give yourself to God expecting an easy time. And so on and so on. Nothing I could not have written down in advance for myself.

So I was surprised that when our anodyne interview was concluded, Sister Agnes did not immediately leave the room. She stood, her hands clutching the top of the ugly guest-room chair, much as I had supported myself on the pew the previous night.

'Miss Shore, there is one further thing I should tell you,' said Sister Agnes in her well-modulated voice. 'You will discover nothing to your advantage here. Nothing. Do you understand me? Nothing.' Her voice was not raised a half-tone from our previous conversation and the words in themselves hardly sounded dramatic. But it was her eyes. She could not control her eyes. They were dilated, either in fear or anger. I did not know her well enough to say.

'Why don't you go home while you can?'

With this, Sister Agnes passed swiftly from the room. According to the noise of the swing doors she had gone directly to the nuns' wing. Not to the chapel this evening for her novena, unless she had taken the long way round by the nuns' staircase.

It was not until the next morning, the Feast of All Souls, that I learnt of the death of Sister Edward, suddenly in her cell, during the night.

The Black Nun

The Feast of All Souls, following All Saints, proved as doleful a day as I could remember. It even rained. The leaves in the drive ceased to scutter in the wind but congregated in sodden heaps. More leaves were driven off the dripping trees. Altogether it was a day of lamentation in the fullest tradition of the ancient faith. Now the black vestments of the priests matched with the black habits of the nuns. The girls wore short black veils over their hair in chapel in contrast to the flowing white veils of the previous feast day. The multitudinous flowers of the night before, great pyramids and obelisks of white chrysanthemums, had vanished. Whatever happened to them? A hospital, I wondered vaguely. But the nearest hospital was miles away and Churne Cottage Hospital had been shut down.

At least that question was answered a day later. I found it macabre that the same flowers, still in their festive pinnacles, were used to flank the plain wooden coffin of Sister Edward as it lay in the chapel in the days before burial.

The Commemoration of the Dead, I reflected bitterly, was a gloomy enough subject without the additional demise of a young nun from a heart attack following an asthmatic fit.

Dies Irae, Dies Illae, day of mourning, day of weeping. As the magnificent sombre words of the requiem rang out in the chapel, I thought of Mother Ancilla in savage terms. She, with the rest of the community, would probably consider it a happy coincidence that Sister Edward's poor weak heart had chosen November the second to give up the struggle for life. While her lungs still struggled for breath. Look how her coffin benefited from the flowers of the previous day's feast: Holy economy! I was in that kind of mood.

'Her medicines were all within reach,' Sister Lucy told me desperately. There were tears in her eyes. 'If only she had had the strength to take them.' Sister Lucy was the young nun who had recently succeeded old Sister Boniface as infirmarian. I was glad to see those tears in her eyes. She was human enough for that. Sister Boniface, on the other hand, sitting like an aged tortoise at the end of the dispensary, showed no emotion. I was unfair, I was being unfair, and I knew it. But I got the impression that Sister Boniface regarded the death of Sister Edward as a kind of defeat for modern stimulants.

She had apparently expressed considerable doubts as to the wisdom of dosing Sister Edward so consistently. But Dr Mayhew, who attended the convent, had been a great believer in the therapeutic power of such things.

'He said: with all these aids, there was no reason why she shouldn't lead a normal life,' Sister Lucy repeated. 'In so far as a nun's life *is* normal. I mean, that's what he said.' Sister Lucy was clearly in a state of great distress. Sister Boniface snorted and twitched her rosary. Her fingers were incredibly gnarled, like the roots of trees in an Arthur Rackham drawing. Arthritis: the endemic disease of ageing women living in damp conditions. Probably the nuns' quarters were not even heated – or only for one month of the year or something mediaeval like that. I shivered. Pain did not however stop Sister Boniface being as garrulous as ever.

My new mood of bitterness towards the convent and all its works had its origin in guilt. I could not rid myself of regret that I had not chosen to interview Sister Edward, as I had intended. It was not that I felt she had now taken her secrets with her to the grave or anything ridiculous like that. Just that something so chancy as a heart attack must depend on so many elements. My interview, the relief of talking to an outsider, might have even saved her from the fatal bout of asthma.

The dispensary lay just outside the infirmary which, like the convent itself, was divided into a nuns' and a children's section. Dr Mayhew had just left, after signing the death certificate. There was no doubt about it. Sister Edward had died from natural causes – if you could call anything about a nun natural, to echo the doctor's own words.

There would thus be no need for an inquest. No further tussles with the coroner, the unfriendly magnate of Churne, he who had criticised Blessed Eleanor's and Sister Edward herself so sharply after the death of Sister Miriam. That was a relief, at least. It would not have done to have the remotest suspicion of foul play or even suicide directed towards another inmate of the convent. Even supposing the coroner held his fire on this occasion – which was unlikely – the local population would not. The sidelong glances in shops to which Mother Ancilla had referred in her original letter would scarcely diminish.

As it was, Sister Edward could be placed tranquilly in her coffin – such a little coffin. But then Sister Edward herself had hardly been much taller than Sister Damian, the minuscule portress. On the whole the teaching nuns were considerably taller than the so-called lay nuns. These latter attended to the domestic duties of the convent. For the greater glory of God. And of course to free the other nuns from such menial tasks. It occurred to me how little I knew about the pathetic rabbit-like person who had escorted me that day by the statue of St Antony.

'What was her name – before?' I asked with sudden curiosity. I hoped that was a tactful way of phrasing it.

'Veronica O'Dowd,' Sister Boniface now added a sniff to a snort. 'She was in the school here since she was six years old. I knew all about her asthma. Many's the night I sat with her, choking her heart out. And soothed her. And said my rosary. She liked the click of the beads. We used to joke together. Sister Bonnie's rosary – the patent cure for asthma.'

Sister Lucy said nothing. Her silence suggested more that Sister Boniface must be allowed the licence of her great age than any form of agreement with what she said. From time to time Sister Lucy wiped her eyes surreptitiously with her handkerchief, large, white and rather masculine in type, the sort of handkerchief that all the nuns used. Then after a bit, to distract herself from Sister Boniface, she began to type up her medical notes.

Obviously as infirmarian she too must have seen a lot of Sister Edward with her chronic asthma. As a trained nurse – Sister Lucy had worked at a big London hospital before she discovered her vocation – she was certainly likely to be right in her notion of how to treat an asthmatic. Frankly, the remedies of Sister Boniface, prayers and so forth, struck me as not so far from the practices of a witch doctor. Or a witch.

Veronica O'Dowd. The name struck a bell. Hadn't the nun Mother Ancilla quoted to me as having left the convent so amicably, been called O'Dowd?

'Yes, they were sisters,' confirmed the former nurse. 'But Sister Edward was of course much younger.'

'The first and last daughters of a lovely Catholic family. Nine of them in all. Five girls and four boys – two boys priests and the first and last girls given to God. That's the way things should be,' muttered Sister Boniface. Given to God indeed: my indignation had not altogether left me. One sister had gone back into the world after fifteen years of wasted seclusion. The other sister was dead at the age of – what? her early twenties, I would say.

'Beatrice O'Dowd should never have chosen the name of John in religion.' There was no stopping Sister Boniface now. 'I told her. It may be the name of the disciple Our Lord loved, but He certainly doesn't love nuns called John in this convent. Sister John Brodsky died in a train crash before the war – an amazing thing to happen to a nun in those days. We hardly ever went in trains. Sister John had to have false teeth and she was on her way back from the dentist. She must have been so sad to have wasted the community's money. Being on her way back. When she got to purgatory, that is.'

Sister Boniface chomped her wrinkled cheeks.

'Sister John Megève died of diphtheria. She had never been immunised, being brought up abroad. And then Sister John O'Dowd getting all these newfangled ideas and leaving us. I warned her.'

'Edward wasn't a very lucky name, either,' I said, drily.

'Stuff and nonsense,' replied Sister Boniface. 'Sister Edward Walewska joined the Order when she was sixteen. And lived to be over a hundred. As a little girl in Poland she watched Napoleon dance at a ball with her aunt, from a balcony. I knew her quite well as a child here. What do you say to that, now?'

I had nothing to say to that. Except the obvious fact that nuns under the old order of things often lived to a ripe old age. Nowadays they often died young. Or left the convent.

Nevertheless the roots of the late Sister Edward's hysteria were beginning to be uncovered. Her sister leaving the convent after, presumably, a period of indecision and doubt would have been traumatic enough. Then there was Sister Miriam's secret, her ghastly death, the coroner's public castigation. It could all have added up to a pattern of imbalance in a much stronger person. But Sister Edward had been an asthmatic since childhood. While asthma itself was frequently of nervous origin.

Naturally I wasted no thought on Sister Edward's allegation that Sister Miriam had been deliberately killed. Not even the news that Mother Ancilla had been the last person to see Sister Edward alive sent my thoughts in any particularly sinister direction. Why should it? Sister Edward had felt faint during benediction, and later retired from the nuns' supper. It was quite proper that Mother Ancilla should pay a visit to her cell after supper. The younger nun seemed sleepy but the faintness had passed. She was certainly not breathing quickly.

No-one else saw Sister Edward alive.

Whether she called out as she fought for breath in the narrow cell could not be known. Whereas the children's wing and classrooms, together with the refectory, had been built in the late twenties in red brick, the nuns' wing and the chapel had been constructed in the throes of the Victorian gothic revival. From the outside the bland modern style contrasted with the heavily arched Gothic of the convent proper. I gathered that the nuns' cells, through their swing doors, had been re-created according to a Victorian notion of a mediaeval cloister.

The walls were thick. Not as thick as the walls of Blessed Eleanor's Retreat perhaps. But the intention was the same. Noise, human noise, was not intended to intrude into the great silence of God.

The Tower of the Blessed Eleanor was also an unexpected topic of conversation that night at supper. I had decided to eat my main meals in the refectory-cum-cafeteria with the girls. I did not fancy the solemn service of the Nuns' Parlour. Sister Damian continued to enchant me, but I found Sister Clare's portly figure, labouring along with her tray, an increasing trial. Besides, I was becoming interested in the girls themselves, the girls in general and Margaret Plantagenet in particular.

Tom would like Margaret. The thought came to me, unspoken, that evening in the refectory. She was not unlike one of his devoted acolytes at the W.N.G., a girl called Emily Crispin. Emily had come forward as a helper without pay—which was just as well as the W.N.G. were as fierce in their determination to keep all their funds for the poor as, say, the Powers Estate Projectors. It subsequently turned out that Emily could well afford the sacrifice, being the daughter of a rich man, although you would not otherwise have guessed it from her demeanour—or her clothes. Margaret had the same air of secrecy about her, an individuality which had nothing to do with her name or birth. It did have something to do with her physical appearance, the long crusader's face with its helmet of straight brown hair: and her silence. Emily Crispin, I once told Tom with irritation I did not bother to hide, sits for hours at your elbow without opening her mouth, like a dog asleep.

'That explains why I always get the impression she agrees with every word I say,' Tom replied.

Margaret Plantagenet herself never spoke much at meals. She left that to her chatterbox friend Dodo Sheehy.

It was Dodo, at supper on the Feast of All Souls, who enquired: 'I wonder if anyone saw the Black Nun last night?' Her tone was rather bright. Dodo was such a pretty plump little thing with fair curls and a Cupid's bow mouth, that nothing she said sounded completely serious. But I noted a wry expression on Margaret's face, a slight compression of the lips.

'Aren't all nuns black?' I responded lightly. The death of Sister Edward had not cast a notable shadow on their spirits: she was too young to have taught them. But I wanted to get the conversation away from the events of the night before.

'I'm talking about The – Black – Nun.' Dodo gave the three last words sepulchral emphasis. 'An apparition. Did you never see it when you were at the school?'

'No – wait, I do remember something vaguely. Doesn't it haunt the chapel? Or is it the tower?'

Margaret said: 'And the convent itself. Sister Miriam told us she actually saw the Black Nun when she was a girl at school.'

'She didn't tell *me*. It must have only bobbed up after dark. I was a day girl. You tell me.'

'Dodo, you tell.' Dodo was nothing loath. It transpired that the Black Nun was commonly held to appear shortly before or shortly after the death of a member of the community. Yes, of course, all nuns wore black, but the point of the Black Nun was that you suddenly came across a nun you didn't recognise, a nun you had never seen before. You imagined: a novice, a transfer from another convent. But the next day you heard of the death of a nun. And of course you never saw the Black Nun, that particular Black Nun again.

I burst out laughing.

'You don't believe us,' said one of the other girls at the table rather grumpily. 'But some of us saw the Black Nun three nights after Sister Miriam ran away. And that turned out to be the night she must have died.' Much chattering followed. Yes, a strange nun, a nun they had never seen before, a nun with a strange face, passing them at night, in the corridor, on their way to ... their way to where? Why, the chapel. To make a novena to Our Lady. And that night, they learned later, Sister Miriam had given up the ghost in the tower. Surely I had to admit it all added up.

On the contrary, it all sounded deeply implausible to me. Another enigmatic novena in the middle of the night: something I was fairly sure was not allowed by the rules.

When I was informed that the Black Nun had first appeared to Blessed Eleanor herself, goodness knows how many years ago, I scoffed openly. Six black nuns were supposed to have carried her to her tower, and at the last moment a seventh unknown nun appeared. Blessed Eleanor asked the stranger who she was, and the answer came back pat: 'I am Death itself, who comes before you as a Black Nun.'

'None of that delightful story appears in the Treasury of the Blessed Eleanor,' I commented in a fairly acid voice.

'Exactly. Sister Miriam told us about it. She used to tell us ghost stories after lights out.' I was glad to hear that in one respect at least my old friend had not changed. Ghost stories and ghoulish information generally had been Rosa's speciality.

'Anyway, somebody did see the Black Nun last night,' said the grumpy girl suddenly. Blanche, Blanche Nelligan, was her name. She did not look like a Blanche, being beetle-browed with rather a bad complexion.

'Tessa Justin, that girl with plaits in the Lower IVth. I was on prefect duty in the big dormitory and Sister Agnes was doing the rounds. Suddenly young Tessa appeared, shrieking her head off, plaits flying, saying a strange nun had interrupted her in the loo. That must have been the Black Nun.'

At this we all laughed. A minute later the chairs were scraping back for grace and supper was over. I decided not to give another thought to the Black Nun. I enjoyed my solitary tray of coffee after the girls' chatter. Then I climbed up the visitors' staircase to my own retreat. I really felt that I had quite enough problems on my hands without the question of a spectral religious haunting the junior school bathrooms. The Black Nun was scarcely likely to bother me.

Once I was installed in my room and had looked at the papers on my desk, I saw that I was wrong.

'If you don't believe in the Black Nun'—so ran a typed message on a sheet of plain paper placed on top of my copy of The Times—'why don't you come to the tower one night and see for yourself? Tomorrow night for example.'

There was no superscription and no signature. Jutting out from the paper, on the front cover of The Times I saw a photograph of Tom on the platform at his w.N.G. rally. That looked like Emily Crispin at his elbow with some papers on her lap. Neither of them looked particularly ghostly. The photograph gave me no consolation whatsoever.

7

Forewarned

In the night the wind got up. The change of noise from the steady downpour on the chapel roof to the gusts and rattling of my windows awoke me. Lying, somnolent, I was aware of some other noise quite close at hand. The guest room next to me – my temporary sitting room – was empty. Beyond that lay another guest room, also unoccupied. Beyond that the communal bathroom. If anything the noise was located in the furthest guest room, next to the bathroom. The walls here in the modern block were not particularly sound-proof. The vigorous sound of Sister Perpetua's broom scouring my bedroom regularly disturbed the peace of my sitting room.

I felt too drowsy to investigate. Besides, I needed my sleep. For I was always awake early in the convent, what with the chapel bells and the shuffle of the children going to early mass. In London I considered myself, and allowed the world to consider me, an early riser. I prided myself on my ability to take testing telephone calls at full strength from eight o'clock onwards. But I had to admit that the need to appear fresh and purposeful for a refectory breakfast at 7.45 was another matter altogether. As I drifted into sleep, I made a mental note to explore the convent grounds the next day. Such an expedition might be combined with a talk to one of the nuns. The tower above all presented an emotional problem. It might be better not to visit it for the first time after Rosa's death, at night – and alone.

In the morning I went into Churne. I had decided to buy a torch. Sister Lucy, on her way to have a prescription made up, offered me a lift. I accepted, wondering privately whether she wanted an escort to run the gauntlet of Churne. In the event, I had no time to worry about the local inhabitants. For Sister Lucy drove with a terrifying recklessness, amounting almost to innocence, which robbed me of all other considerations except for a desire for the safety of my own beloved Volvo. Down Churne Hill, a notorious winding black-spot, the battered Mini-Traveller driven by Sister Lucy was definitely the faster vehicle of the two.

One of my winces must have attracted her attention. I was recalling the old saying, repeated by my mother, that nuns made rotten drivers because they paid too much attention to St Christopher, too little to the Highway Code. In the car driven by Sister Lucy there was not even a St Christopher to aid us – hadn't he been demoted by the Vatican? Come back, St Christopher –

'Don't worry, Miss Shore,' Sister Lucy spoke quite calmly. 'I know this car like the back of my hand.' She did not mention the hill. Then she added rather shyly: 'As a matter of fact, though I really should not mention it, this car belonged to me once. In the world, I mean. Now of course it belongs to the community. It was my dowry to the convent. All I was able to bring them.'

'That, and your skill, Sister,' I said earnestly, trying not to look out of the window.

She blushed and looked genuinely pleased. On the way back Sister Lucy confided to me that Sister Elizabeth could hardly be trusted at the wheel of the Mini, having learnt to drive late in life. It was only then I realised she had taken my compliment as referring to her skill as a driver, rather than as a nurse.

The funereal rain had blown itself out by lunch-time. Only piles of sodden leaves and pools of water on the gravel drive served to remind us of the night's storm. But clearer sharper weather was on the way. My diary reminded me to expect a full moon that night. Surely the weather often changed around the time of the full moon.

After the previous day's *Times* had been properly perused, Tom received a quick note in my familiar style: 'Darling, your speech was *good*. I'm having a holiday away from everything, your world of the (political) poor and my world of the (television) rich, and that's good too. All my love, J.' I drew a heart at the end.

Yes, his speech had been good, full of honest compassion for the poor and honest indignation against the government. The poor, if they read *The Times*, would undoubtedly be pleased. The government, who undoubtedly did read *The Times*, would not. Tom could be proud of his intervention. I gave no address and allowed the letter to be posted with the rest of the children's mail. I doubted if the postmark Churne would mean anything to Tom.

The children's letters were put on a chest outside the refectory, as they had been in my day. It was amusing to note that the letters were now sealed, while the destinations could still be read by any inspector. In my day the boarders had their letters read by Mother Ancilla. According to Rosa it was a task she performed with lip-smacking thoroughness. According to Rosa, too, Mother Ancilla was not above making pointed allusions to the contents of a letter, if it suited her purpose. Rosa proceeded to organise my services as a postman; girls who wanted to write uncensored letters were urged to place them in my trustworthy hands.

'Is this quite *all right*, do you think darling?' asked my mother anxiously one day. She was enormously impressed by the whole convent set-up: and secretly adored the idea of the glamorous high-born girls with whom her own much lower-born daughter was mixing. Mother Ancilla's references to lineage found a ready audience in my mother. We had a couple of Italian princesses in the school, whose English mother had taken refuge here in the war. They were listed merely as Pia and Vittoria. And received scant shrift from us girls, as unpopular Wops, particularly when the Italian campaign was in full swing. But Mother Ancilla always gave the whole family, mother and daughters, the full rolling due of their titles. She also liked to practise the Italian learnt so many years ago in a visit to Rome as a novice. 'Principessa' was quite one of her favourite words, I decided.

'Fancy Princess Pia being descended from the Pope!' said my mother admiringly one day.

It was probably true, given the nature of early papacies. But I was already feeling a nasty instinct to put my mother in her place whenever she got a particular starry-eyed look.

'Popes don't have children,' I replied coldly. 'I should have thought even you knew that.' Fatally my mother gave way and tried to ingratiate herself with me.

'I do envy your opportunities here, Jem. You're learning such interesting things. Daddy and I sometimes wonder if you might even, well, think of *becoming* a Roman. I mean a Catholic,' she added nervously.

Either way she made it sound like a form of career like a teacher or a gym instructor. I did not deign to answer. I quelled my mother's objections to my clandestine postal service with equal use of intimidation by coldness.

Only Rosa never made use of my services. Did she *have* no boy friends, I wondered? I never enquired. Jealously, I preferred to cherish the fantasy that Rosa did not trust me to post her love notes. She told me other things about her holidays, casually, without emphasis. But the boys, with names like Marcus and Peregrine, all turned out to be cousins. On her mother's side. The Campion family, for all its ancient blood, turned out to be infinitely more prolific and thus capable of survival than the more plebeian Powerstocks.

I did ask once: 'Do you like him, Marcus?' I tried to keep the note of caring out of my voice.

'He's my cousin,' said Rosa in that blank voice she reserved for matters which she clearly felt were too obvious to need discussing. And that was that.

Looking at these letters now, laid out for inspection, I was pleased to see that some of them were boldly addressed to males. Robin Nelligan Esq., Ampleforth College, York. Jasper Justin Esq., Eton College, Windsor, Berks ... So perhaps freedom was on the march after all. It then occurred to me that Robin and Jasper were probably the brothers of Blanche and Tessa. So perhaps things had not changed so much after all. There was also an established safe ring about most of the addresses. Tom would have been full of scorn for them.

But of course it was ridiculous to suppose then as now that any really subversive letter would be left out on the chest. Rosa's letter to Alexander Skarbek for example. The nuns' letters could be distinguished by the quality of their paper—small and thin—often by the precise handwriting also, and always by the letters A.M.D.G. in the corner. That letter to Skarbek certainly did not lie out on this chest, open to curious eyes. The extent of Alex Skarbek's participation in Rosa's tragedy was still unknown to me. How had he taken the news of Rosa's death, for example, and the consequent collapse of her property hand-over scheme? The coroner's remarks had not dealt with that side of her life and death, mercifully: there had been no need to air in public the proposed handover, which had caused such pain in private. But Alex Skarbek had the reputation, at least in Tom's circles, for rigid determination. It always amused me to see how Tom and his friends of the W.N.G. derided in their opponents exactly those qualities which led to their own triumphs.

'An extremist ... quite ruthless in manipulating people ... thinks anything is justified so long as it advances the Project ...' So Tom muttered indignantly, with Emily Crispin, indicating agreement by her silence, close beside him. Yet Tom's brilliance in outmanœuvring the government on the subject of housing subsidies for one-parent families was generally acknowledged to be his greatest coup on behalf of the W.N.G. I knew all about that coup: it was the over-friendly young minister on my programme who had let slip the details of what the government was going to propose. I thought Tom's action – and my own – morally justified in view of the use we made of the information. But all the same, not too scrupulous.

Alexander Skarbek: had he simply accepted the loss of his new commune, on the verge of establishment, as one of the losses of war? In this case, the war being against society?

That was an area where Mother Ancilla might be gently probed further. After that it was tempting to contact the man himself in London. One advantage of having my own programme was that no-one with an axe of his own to grind resented my approach. He always hoped to turn my platform to his own advantage.

I walked round the hockey fields in the afternoon with my old friend and teacher Sister Elizabeth. She was not aware that I also had the key to the tower in my pocket – I had requested it from Mother Ancilla. The Reverend Mother had asked for no explanation, merely handed it to me.

'The only other key is on my belt,' she said, patting a bunch of keys. 'We don't want any more – mistakes, do we?'

Sister Liz and I paraded round the hockey fields. I watched an extremely energetic black figure hurtling towards the goal with a hockey stick wielded to deadly effect: Sister Immaculata. Surely she could not still be playing hockey after all these years. I remembered what a shock it gave me to find that nuns, at the sight of a hockey field, merely looped up their black skirts, and tackled the game with their usual brisk efficiency, veils and all. The maroon coloured figures of the girls were considerably more lackadaisical in their attitude to the game.

The only other participant showing any energy at all was wearing a short black skirt, black stockings, a black jersey with a white collar and a short black veil which revealed most of her hair – luxuriant hair. A postulant. I had to look up the word in the dictionary while I was at school. Postulant: Candidate, especially for admission into religious order. Tom I suppose was a parliamentary postulant at the general election. At least I was firmly on the side of his election. I wasn't sure what I felt about this girl's candidature. From the convent's point of view, however, it was a good thing that there were still some new vocations around: now that the Order of the Tower of Ivory was not after all to be dispossessed by the Projectors.

'She's Irish,' said Sister Elizabeth, following the direction of my gaze. 'Of course.'

Sister Elizabeth was a woman for whom I had a genuine affection, nun or no nun. Her generosity of spirit, her mad enthusiasm for literature in all its forms, endeared her to me. There was a Margaret Rutherford touch about her zest. With her flailing arms, springy walk (signally untouched by the passage of twenty-five years), and her earnestness, she really was not unlike my idea of Margaret Rutherford, supposing she had ever played the part of a nun.

Sister Liz was the only woman in the world capable of exclaiming: 'I thanked Our Blessed Lord on my knees this morning for making Wordsworth write the *Prelude* at such *length*.'

Of course as a schoolgirl I was attracted to her, just because her values did not seem totally permeated by those of the Catholic religion. We had corresponded in a desultory way after I left. 'I shall pray for you,' Sister Liz dutifully ended her letters. But I knew she prayed for sensible things like a proper understanding of *Paradise Lost* or a real appreciation of *The Waste Land*, not lost causes like my conversion.

Now we chatted easily on literary matters. The Christianity of King Lear was one topic; Sister Liz's determination to discuss James Joyce came as more of a surprise to me. Then I realised that she must have few opportunities to discuss Joyce's work. Of the two of us, it was I, not Sister Elizabeth, who shrank from discussing fully some aspects of Joyce's nature. I was uncertain where I should draw the line in order not to shock her. Sister Liz on the other hand had a kind of sublime frankness about her remarks which left nothing to the imagination. It sprang, I realised, from innocence. My own reticence was rooted in guilt.

Only the fact that our returning steps had led us to the entrance to the nuns' little cemetery made Sister Liz draw breath. We paused and, by unspoken agreement, entered through the low gate. It was an out of the way place. The girls did not come here. The seclusion was ensured by the high dark hedge surrounding the grass. Rows of plain stone crosses marked the last resting places of the community. The inscription on each was identical in form, and minimal. Sister John Brodsky O.T.I. 1900–1935. Below the name and dates: R.I.P. And that was all.

The last cross in the sequence was the one I feared. But it could not be avoided. Yes, here it was. Sister Miriam Powerstock O.T.I. 1932–1973 R.I.P.

At my side I noted that Sister Liz crossed herself. Then she held her rosary and her lips moved silently. I felt nothing, nothing at all. Then feelings did rush in, overwhelmingly, into the vacuum. I felt fiercely that there was no connection, none at all between this plain stone cross and the young girl who had once been my friend. My compassion, such as it was, was reserved for the memory of Sister Edward, who would soon lie in the neighbouring earth.

'I can't accept that this is anything to do with Rosa. I don't believe Rosa is *here*, you know.' My aggressive voice rang out in the quiet graveyard.

'Mother Church would agree with you about that,' replied Sister Elizabeth mildly. 'She's not here. Only her poor tormented earthly body lies here. May God have mercy on her soul.' And she crossed herself again.

Abruptly I asked Sister Liz if she would accompany me across the fields to the tower. I pulled the key out of my pocket. It was a bright new Yale key. The key to the padlock which now secured the tower, as Mother Ancilla had instructed me. Not the ancient rusty key which had broken off during Rosa's frantic struggles to escape her self-imposed fate. By now I needed to exorcise that tower for myself, and

Sister Liz with her warmth and compassion, her understanding of people beyond the narrow prescription of the convent, was the right person to accompany me. The evening's possible adventure had quite vanished from my mind.

As we skirted the fields, trying to avoid the squelching mire left by the rain, a late afternoon sun emerged from the barred clouds, illuminating the November landscape. Sister Elizabeth began to recite Wordsworth in her special faraway poetic voice, which like her walk, had not changed. Her eyes rolled in wonder as she spoke. It was as though she was receiving a direct message from the poet, line by line:

> It is a beauteous evening, calm and free,
>   The holy time is quiet as a Nun
>   Breathless with adoration ...

By this time we were in sight of the tower, black, square, shorter than I remembered – oh, the shrinkings brought about by time – the sun was beginning to sink behind it. I was reminded of a card in the tarot pack: the Tower of Destruction, depicted by a tower very similar in design, out of which spilled unhappy falling people in mediaeval dress. Yes, Tower of Destruction indeed and Rosa's destruction above all. It seemed quite inappropriate under the circumstances to contemplate a late night rendezvous with some prankish schoolgirls pretending to be ghosts. I would lay my own ghost and then depart.

> Dear Child! dear Girl! that walkest with me here,
>   If thou appear untouched by solemn thought,
>   Thy nature is not therefore less divine:
>   Thou liest in Abraham's bosom all the year ...

Sister Elizabeth's sonorous declamation was drawing to its close.

'Somehow those last lines rather remind me of you, Jemima,' she said afterwards. There was a charming note of hope in her voice. I realised that this literary reference was the nearest Sister Liz would ever get to probing my religious beliefs. I ignored the implied question. Besides, I had an irreverent desire to laugh at the idea of television in the guise of Abraham's bosom – Megalithic House. In any case, I was not untouched by solemn thought, rather the contrary. The sight of the Tower of Destruction was more upsetting than I had anticipated.

After a silence, Sister Elizabeth said simply: 'I love that poem. I first learnt it as a girl. I am not sure it did not influence me towards the Church, and later my vocation. The idea of a nun, breathless in adoration. So calm. So free. I'm a convert you know. I was received into the Church when I was twenty-one.'

'Quiet as a nun,' I repeated. To me they sounded ironic words. Where was the quiet in this seething community of neurotic women, many of them frustrated in one way or the other, quite out of touch with all that was good in the modern world? Many of them would do better to return to the world and find their own peace, than reside in this false quiet. As Beatrice O'Dowd had done. Only someone like Sister Elizabeth with her untouchable love of literature probably escaped a measure of frustration.

We unlocked the padlock – new, like the key – and entered the tower. The air was dank. Since the ground floor was windowless it was also dark. By the light of the open door we began to climb up the wooden ladder to the first floor. We went in single file. I let Sister Elizabeth lead the way. On the first floor there would be one window high up in the far wall, overlooking the farm lands beyond. You could neither see the convent from the tower nor be seen from it. A further window in the first floor, on the convent side, had been blocked up in the nineteenth century.

Although the tower was officially out of bounds, in my day at school it had been a fashionable dare to purloin the conspicuously large key from the portress, and pay an illicit visit to Nelly's Nest. I recalled some furniture, a wooden table, a large chair, a rocking-chair, I thought, an empty fireplace. Even in summer the thick stone walls gave off an unpleasant atmosphere of damp and chill.

'The community came and tended to the tower. After it happened,' Sister Liz observed over her shoulder as we climbed. She meant: you won't find anything distressing here, as in the graveyard. She said aloud: 'And no-one has been here since.'

I believed her. Once again my feelings had frozen. I gazed up at Sister Elizabeth's retreating black back, her neat black feet with their goloshes over black strap shoes, black stockings, black skirts looped up at the sides for walking the muddy fields. Sister Elizabeth panted slightly. The door banged to downstairs, removing our light. But at the same moment Sister Elizabeth reached the trap door and pushed it open. She poked her head through the trap door.

There was an audible gasp and Sister Elizabeth stopped quite still on the last rung of the ladder.

Then there was silence. She did not move.

'Sister Liz –' I said after a minute, anxiously.

'It's all right, my child,' she replied, rather heavily. 'Just that I had rather a shock.'

'What *is* it?' I could see nothing from behind her.

'Nothing really. It must be the children. A silly practical joke.'

I was going frantic. Much more slowly, Sister Elizabeth lumbered up the last rung and vanished into the room. I clambered up after her at speed. When I entered the room, Sister Elizabeth was leaning one hand on the table and panting.

The only other piece of furniture in the room was a large wooden rocking-chair. Just as I remembered, in fact. Draped in the chair and over it was a nun's black habit. Including a veil and rosary and all the other accoutrements you would need if you were to dress yourself up as a nun. Or to dress yourself if you were a nun.

At first glance there was certainly the impression of a black nun sitting there in the chair. A faceless nun. But the impression did not outlast the first second. We were looking at a set of empty and thus lifeless black clothes. Except—

'No shoes or stockings,' I thought suddenly, remembering my glimpse of Sister Elizabeth's stocking and goloshes.

'The children. It must be the children. They have an innocent sense of humour. They don't realise how distressing these things can be,' Sister Elizabeth muttered. She made no move to touch the clothes, I noticed. 'I'll tell Mother Ancilla and someone will fetch the habit in the morning.'

I thought: Yes. The children. The children—with their innocent sense of humour—had prepared some kind of reception for me tonight. A sort of religious scarecrow. And I, by my early visit, had sprung their trap.

I wrinkled my nose. In the damp air, another smell disturbed me. A smell which should not have been there. For a moment I could not quite place it, although it was one of the most familiar smells of my urban life. I gazed around and my eye fell on the empty fireplace. Not quite empty. At the back of the fireplace, carelessly thrown down, were a host of cigarette stubs. No attempt had been made to conceal them.

I wondered if the nun's habit which was to greet me tonight had after all been intended to be empty. Maybe I should have to pay a return visit to the tower. It was an unlikely ghost who smoked Gauloises. And in such quantity. My spirits rose. Forewarned was, traditionally, forearmed. The Black Nun, habit and all, could expect a somewhat cynical reception from me in the late hours of the evening.

Secret witnesses

Supper that night in the refectory was a subdued meal. I was getting used to the taciturn ways of Margaret Plantagenet. But Dodo's normally busy chatter was also absent. Alcohol did not play an enormous part in my life: I never drank spirits if I could help it, and I was not one of those who needed a drink or two to go on the television. In fact I avoided the pre-programme drinking as far as possible, leaving the traditional hospitality to my nubile aide, Cherry: 'Jemima's just on her way. And now won't you have another drink?' Consequently up till now I had not really noticed the total absence of alcohol from my life in the days at the convent.

Tonight I really felt the need for a drink at dinner. A carafe of wine, I reflected, would have loosened all our tongues. I remembered reading somewhere of American nuns in a newly emancipated Order who wore make-up and smoked and drank. How Americans exaggerated! Make-up did seem quite unnecessary in the brides of Christ, or perhaps that was just my Puritan streak. As for smoking – well, I had no particular feelings either way. As a non-smoker working in a profession of professional smokers, I felt more sorry for them and their addiction than anything else. But alcohol, now ... No doubt conversation in the American refectory (if they still had a refectory, that is, not a smart French restaurant) improved as a result.

Dodo and I exchanged polite news on the subject of my contemporary of the same surname, Dora Sheehy. Dodo turned out to have been named for her: 'Both of us Theodora,' she said, with a return to her old cheerfulness. 'But who could stick a name like that? She was Dora and I'm Dodo. Aunt Dora held me at my baptism, you know, she was my godmother. And why she didn't protest against another innocent child being lumbered with a name like Theodora I shall never know.'

'And Dora is now – ?' I enquired delicately. On the familiar form I expected to hear: married to a doctor, probably Irish like herself, and mother of five children. 'I haven't heard from her in years,' I added untruthfully.

I had never heard from Dora Sheehy. There had been a brief competition between us – in school terms – for the friendship of Rosabelle. When I arrived at Blessed Eleanor's, Dora Sheehy was allegedly Rosabelle's best friend. And when I left, Rosabelle was unquestionably mine. But Dora, as I remembered her, had been a dull and rather sycophantic girl, whose good quality from Rosa's point of view, had been her subservience.

I much preferred Dodo, blonde curls, giggles and all. She had confided to me that she had ambitions to get into television once she had left the convent. I was not a bit surprised. One of the odd things about Blessed Eleanor's was how few of the girls had that ambition. At visits to ordinary schools for lectures or brains trusts, to say nothing of encounters with my friends' growing children, I was quite used to the sidling approaches of pretty teenagers: 'Is there an exam or something I can take?' Dodo at least was conforming to that norm.

'But she was *Sister* Theodora,' said Dodo. 'We talked of her the other night.'

'Sister Theodora of the Angels,' put in Margaret. It was her first remark of the evening. 'Murdered in Africa.'

I felt curiously put down.

The plates were mainly empty. It would soon be the time for the traditional scraping back of our chairs and grace. Blanche Nelligan said, with a sudden very sweet smile, which lit up her heavy face:

'Would you come and have coffee with us for a change? In St Joseph's Sitting Room. We're allowed to entertain if we provide the coffee.'

'And we shall keep the odious Fourth Formers *out*,' added Dodo with a grimace. 'By fair means or foul.'

I realised that the restraint at dinner had been due to a genuine uncertainty as to whether I would accept the invitation. I was touched.

'Our coffee is much *much* better than Sister Clare's,' contributed Imogen Smith, blushing. I knew little about her so far except that she was Blanche's best friend, and always sat next to her.

'Immo brought it back from London on Sunday. Swiped from her mother's store cupboard.'

'But we'll pay her back of course –'

'Unless we decide that property is theft' – Margaret, with a rare grin.

'Oh, please let me –' I began feebly, feeling for my handbag. It was not there. Like the carafe of wine, that other accompaniment of life in a London restaurant, it seemed to have no place in the refectory.

'Actually the nuns don't exactly economise on things like coffee,' remarked Blanche later, pouring me an enormous mug right up to the brim with great care. It was made of thick grey china. There was no milk, and a plastic cup of white sugar had one plastic spoon sticking up out of it.

The coffee in point of fact was a great deal less nice than that provided by Sister Clare. I also thought rather wistfully of the delicate matching china in which her coffee appeared, white traced with green in a Chinese pattern. A beaker of hot milk, a jug of cold; coloured sugar crystals, tiny silver spoons – they were actually Apostle spoons, I was enchanted to notice. The tray was lined with a cloth embroidered, as only nuns could embroider, in an exact silk replica of the china's pattern. It was all no doubt arranged to the greater glory of God. But at the same time it was most delightful for mere mortals to behold.

'Yes, this is a pretty plush convent,' remarked Imogen. 'Basins in our rooms and carpets.'

'Those are your rooms,' I felt bound to point out. 'I doubt if the nuns have basins and carpets in their cells.'

'But we pay for them, don't we?' Blanche sounded plaintive. 'Out of our school fees.'

'Or rather our parents pay for them,' Dodo as usual put more energy into her complaints. 'And don't they let us know about it ... The last time Mummy came here she told me my room was more luxurious than the room in the hotel Daddy took her to in France for a holiday. And that was a hotel *très confortable* in Michelin. I said, if that was the case I would go to France, save the school fees, much nicer and she could come here for a holiday with Daddy.'

'We are *assez confortable* here, Miss Shore, you must admit,' Margaret interrupted. 'But that's not the point. The point is, how comfortable are the nuns? How comfortable should they be?'

Her voice, the intensity of her gaze, gave the remark considerable authority. The slightly frivolous conversation ceased. We all began to talk about Holy Poverty, at once and in different ways. Holy Poverty, and what that meant. Vocations, and what they meant. There was one insistent theme: surely nuns were better off nursing in Africa, refusing to abandon the sick, nursing to their last gasp (witness Sister Theodora of the Angels) than teaching a lot of upper-class brats in an over-plushy convent. The last vivid words were contributed by Dodo. I got the impression that she was repeating something once said by someone else. Before I could pursue the matter, Margaret stopped the conversation again.

'Your friend Sister Miriam didn't agree with all this luxury, Miss Shore. She wanted to leave the convent lands to the poor.'

I was quite astonished by her words.

To begin with, I was amazed that these girls knew of Rosa's crazy plan. Admittedly they seemed to have been her intimates, what Miss Jean Brodie would have called her *crème de la crème*. How many other people at the convent had known? It opened up a whole new field of enquiry. How many of the nuns had known? Wretched Sister Edward must have known something, hence her wild accusation of Mother Ancilla. The enigmatic Sister Agnes, she of the soulful Murillo eyes, had she known? A Campion cousin, too, according to Mother Ancilla. Although the property was inherited from the Powerstock side of the family, there could have been cousinly confidences on the subject.

But there was a second point. For all their intimacy with Sister Miriam, the girls had got hold of a slightly garbled story. Rosa, according to Mother Ancilla, was determined to give away the convent lands. As soon as possible. No question of waiting for her own death. As for the question of a will, it had been the existence of Sister Miriam's unaltered will, made at the time she entered the convent, which had ensured the receipt of the property by the community.

Was Margaret testing me in some way? My instinct was at work again. I felt myself on the brink of a piece of valuable knowledge. If I trod carefully enough, I might arrive at it.

'But she didn't. She didn't leave the convent lands to the poor,' I said.

'How do you know she didn't?' Margaret, smooth, definitely up to something.

'Here we all are. Her will, I gather, for what it's worth, carried out her father's intentions, and automatically entrusted the land to the community.'

'That was her original will,' said Margaret. She let the words sink into the air of St Joseph's Sitting Room, with just enough emphasis on the word 'original' for her meaning, also, to sink very slowly but surely into my mind. I bent to my coffee, fastening my lips reluctantly to the thick edge of the china. It was by now cold and rather disgusting. But I wanted time to think. I therefore treated the rite of drinking Blanche's coffee with all the respect that would have been due to Sister Clare's superior brew.

I looked round. The furniture of St Joseph's Sitting Room did not offer much for inspection. A battered record player was the chief sign that it was a room for girlish recreation. There was a large sofa, equally battered, pushed to the back of the room, as though no-one ever sat on it. Otherwise with its pictures – Leonardo's Virgin of the Rocks, Botticelli, Fra Angelico? – I was beginning not to distinguish them in their heavy gold frames – it might have been a nuns' sitting room. The girls' notion of the unfair luxury in which they lived suddenly seemed a little pathetic to me. Once again, I got the impression that someone outside had been at work influencing their notions concerning poverty and distribution of wealth. It could have been Rosabelle herself, of course. Then Rosa had changed. I could imagine Rosa as a secret fanatic – mysterious Rosa as I used to call her – but not as a proselytiser.

At least copies of the *Daily Telegraph* and one copy of the *Daily Express* – banned in my day – were to be seen, indicating progress. The fact that they were several days old was less encouraging. Just as letters to males on the chest had seemed encouraging, until I discovered they were mainly to brothers. The *Tablet* was still the most prominent magazine displayed. Did they read the liberal press? It would have been good to have found a copy of the *Guardian* or even the *New Statesman*.

'Sister Miriam told us she was going to make another will,' confided Dodo in a rush. My long silence had had the desired effect.

'And then she died. And it was too late.'

I caught Blanche looking at Imogen. There was a nervous intensity about Blanche's normally rather impassive gaze. I thought I saw Imogen give her a very slight shake of the head. I was not quite sure. Margaret said nothing. Like me, she was contemplating her coffee cup.

'I don't think you should exaggerate all this,' I said carefully. 'If Sister Miriam wanted to give the lands to the poor, there was really nothing to stop her.' As Mother Ancilla had found – or very nearly found – to her cost.

'But if she was going to, well, put an end to it all, then she might want to leave the lands straightaway to the poor. In her will. No time for handing it over' – Dodo again.

I was in a quandary. On the one hand the girls had the whole matter ridiculously upside down. Rosabelle had unquestionably intended to hand over the lands. Rosabelle had not intended to die. It was the latter tragedy which had frustrated the former plan. The will, so convenient from the point of view of Mother Ancilla, was a rogue element coming out of the past. On the other hand, there was clearly more information to be gleaned from the girls about Rosa's state of mind shortly before her death.

Margaret's remark had been calculated, I was sure of it. I was beginning to think a great deal more about Margaret Plantagenet was calculated than met the eye.

'The sick, the mad if you like, don't always act very consistently,' I went on. 'I shouldn't worry about Sister Miriam's will if I were you. She probably told another lot of girls that she was going to leave the land to a lot of cats and dogs –'

'Sister Miriam was fond neither of cats nor of dogs, Miss Shore.' If Margaret had not sounded bland, she would have sounded rude. I was reminded a little of the stone-walling technique of Sister Agnes in my interview with her. 'And she did not talk to another lot of girls. We were her girls –' Ah, the Miss Brodie touch. 'Because she knew that we shared her concern about the way wealth is shared out. For the real poor.'

All the girls started talking at once:

'The third world –'

'As much food in a *day* –'

'No running water –'

'The convent grounds alone would house a whole estate

of workers' families, hundreds of them.' It was Dodo's voice which won out. 'Instead of which upper-class drones like ourselves play hockey on them.'

I had a ghastly feeling during this cacophony that the girls were indeed great fans of my programme. Just as Mother Ancilla had said. And not only the Powers Estate investigation, the so-called Powers Mad programme. What on earth was the title of the programme on starvation at home and abroad? Food for Thought – And Nothing Else. I had interviewed Tom in the course of it to give the work of the W.N.G. in that area a deserved little puff. Now this conversation Tom would enjoy. No established complacency here.

The evening bell put an end to these thoughts. I suddenly realised that Sister Agnes was standing at the door of the sitting room. I had no idea how long she had been there. Unlike most of the nuns, her progress did not seem to be marked by either a rustle or a jangle. No doubt it was the graceful nature of her movements which enabled her to pass from corridor to classroom so quietly. Time for night prayers in the chapel. With the exception of Margaret who was on prefect duty and could say her prayers in private as a result. Later she would join Sister Agnes in patrolling St Aloysius's dormitory. St Aloysius, the patron of youth. Not a saint for whom I had ever had much affection when at school: I suppose even then I had had not much sympathy for youth as such. The sort of young I admired were those like Margaret and Dodo, who showed some signs of thinking for themselves.

For me, it was time to make ready for the night's expedition. Through the high windows of St Joseph's Sitting Room, curtainless, I was glad to see the moon shining full and reassuring over the chapel, as promised in my diary.

'Who's got my veil?' cried Imogen in anguish, 'I know I brought it down here.'

'Sister Agnes, do let her off her veil. It's only night prayers,' said Blanche. 'Two minutes flat in the chapel; as if God cared about a veil –'

'Mother Ancilla is most particular about your veils in the

chapel. You know that.' Sister Agnes's tone was strictly neutral. It was impossible to tell whether she felt that Mother Ancilla and God were on the same side as regards veils or not.

'Come on, Immo, here's a veil for you,' said Margaret kindly. 'One of the Fourth Formers must have left it behind.' She pulled a rather dusty looking black veil from behind the sofa. It was caught. There was a sharp tug, the veil came away, then the noise of a scuffle and a loud cry.

'Christ!' exclaimed Margaret. It was a strictly unreligious monosyllable. 'Tessa Justin, what the hell are you doing here –'

A smallish girl, with abnormally long and thick plaits was being hauled out from the sofa. Sister Agnes made one of her rapid darts across the room and pulled the child to her feet, away from the furious grasp of Margaret. She proceeded to dust her down with her handkerchief, with little clicks of disapproval, though the convent floor was so spotless that one could not imagine even a sojourn behind a sofa resulting in much contamination.

'Tessa Justin! You were supposed to be in bed half an hour ago. I'm afraid Mother Ancilla will have to hear of this in the morning. Come along now.' Sister Agnes swept the child, by now managing a few anguished sobs, out of the sitting room.

'Those bloody Fourth Formers!' Dodo's language too was degenerating. 'They dare each other to do that sort of thing. She must have heard every word we said.' Margaret said nothing. It was the first time I had seen her look really nonplussed.

After they had gone, I tried to watch television in the sitting room. Some modern drama or other, in which adultery, offices, and adultery in offices, all featured prominently. It was no good. It failed to grip me. My mind was too closely involved with the dramas here in the convent. And the prospective drama, tonight, outside. Finally I went to my own room, both excited and jangled.

The Treasury of the Blessed Eleanor was just the thing to

set me right, I decided, catching sight of it lying on my desk. I opened it at the marker:

'Within the Tower of the Church dwell many witnesses to the Word of God,' I read. 'Some of these witnesses lean out from their Tower and cry out: Here be the Tower of God's Church, to all who have ears to listen. Others of these witnesses dwell secretly within the Tower and their words are never heard in the outside world. Nevertheless the prayers of these secret witnesses are their words. These secret witnesses are most acceptable to God.'

As I finished the passage, I realised that the marker was not of my own making at all, but a typed slip of paper. Exactly similar to the first slip which had suggested the rendezvous with the Black Nun. Even the wording of the message was reminiscent.

'If you don't believe Sister Miriam made a new will,' it ran, 'why don't you look for the will yourself? And you might ask Blanche Nelligan and Imogen Smith about a certain piece of paper they signed.' And the words 'secret witnesses' at the bottom of the passage were underlined in pencil, in case I had missed the point. But I had not missed the point.

Secret witnesses ... most acceptable to God in the view of the Blessed Eleanor. Not so acceptable perhaps to Mother Ancilla and the more conservative section of the community. Grimly I wondered who else in the quiet convent might be looking for the will.

9

To the Dark Tower

As I made the preparations for my nocturnal adventure, I wasn't so much full of courage as lacking in fear. I did not believe in ghosts. As a child I had been unaffected by ghost stories. When Rosa loved to entertain me with her ghoulish tales, it was her face I watched, rapt with her own horror: I hardly listened to her words.

Night-time. I wondered what the Black Nun's interpretation of night-time might be. Eleven o'clock? Ten o'clock?

Nor was I worried by the prospect of the solitary journey. Darkness of itself had never frightened me: my terrors were all within my own breast, regrets and guilts long buried, potentially more powerful than predatory creatures of the night. Besides, I had lived on my own to all intents and purposes since I was eighteen years old. Solitariness, even loneliness, had become a condition of my life.

Boots, a thick coat and my new torch were the necessary preparations for my expedition. And the bright little key which I had 'forgotten' to return to Mother Ancilla. Whoever else had acquired the spare key to that padlock, it seemed wise to bring my own. Beside my bed lay a candle and some matches.

'For emergencies, isn't that now?' said Sister Perpetua on

the first day, in her soft Irish voice, arranging the candle and matches with care on the table as though they were sacred objects on the altar.

'You like candles?'

'Ah sure candles give comfort where torches never do.' So it was more as a tribute to Sister Perpetua than with any practical intention of using them that I also slipped the candle and matches into my pocket.

My self-confidence, or perhaps in retrospect arrogance would be the right word, was complete. Like Childe Roland, I would come to the Dark Tower, and sort out at least one of the mysteries which enmeshed the convent. Where Sister Liz had attempted to win converts to Saint William Wordsworth, I had always preferred plain Robert Browning. I could make Browning's melancholy my own, and also his sense of drama. As a poem, 'My last Duchess' was far more to my taste than what I privately considered Wordsworth's holy ramblings. Just as I rated the romantic marriage of Elizabeth Barrett and Browning way above the pious Wordsworth family life – as described by Sister Liz. It was years before I discovered that the relationship with Dorothy was not necessarily all it seemed: and then it was too late, the pattern was set. So now, with Browning's Roland, I murmured to myself: 'Dauntless the slug-horn to my lips I set and blew ...' I might have no slug-horn but there was a strong possibility I would be able to make some sort of report to Mother Ancilla in the morning ...

It was therefore in a mood of positive optimism that I padded down the visitors' stairs, ignored the left turn to the chapel and found myself facing the small side door to the gardens. It was a door sometimes used by outsiders to enter the chapel. There were certain neighbours who treated the convent as their parish church and came to mass there regularly on Sundays and feast days. Blessed Eleanor's chapel was not strictly speaking a parish church. The bishop disapproved of the practice, which was also much disliked by the parish priest proper of the diocese. Outsiders at the chapel services

84

were supposed to be confined to parents visiting their daughters.

Mother Ancilla however turned a resolutely blind eye to both episcopal and parochial disapproval. Blandly, she assumed that it was the most natural thing in the world that everyone round Churne should wish to worship in the chapel of the Blessed Eleanor. Parishioners had been known to receive coffee and convent-baked biscuits at feast days after mass. No such hospitality was available in the chilly parish church of St Gregory.

Mother Ancilla fended off the attempts of the parish priest, condemned to serve the convent masses as well as his own, to spot errant parishioners among bona fide parents. She was once overheard assuring the caustic Father Aylmer that an old lady of at least seventy, mobled in chiffon over sparse white hair, was 'one of our dear parents'.

In my day there had been two or three priests attached to St Gregory's. Nowadays, with the universal decline in vocations, the strain of providing a regular mass at the convent must have risen considerably. No doubt the parish priest at St Gregory's, whoever he might be, loved Mother Ancilla's empire-building no better than old Father Aylmer had done. It was understandable under the circumstances that some of these errant worshippers preferred to slip in through a side door.

I had noted that at night this side door was fastened merely by an inner bolt. Now I drew the bolt back and slipped out into the convent grounds.

My moon was still shining brightly, no longer quite so high over the chapel. I hoped that its light would see me at least as far as the Dark Tower. Preferably there and back again.

Apart from the moon, casting its own eerie light, the journey across the fields was remarkable chiefly for the variety of life I saw. In theory I was alone. But I never once felt myself truly alone throughout my journey. In practice every hedgerow, the furrows of the newly ploughed fields, seemed alive with life. Small animals scuttered hither and thither. An owl hooted somewhere. And the occasional bird – were they not supposed to be asleep? – stirred in the hedges. I came to the conclusion that the so-called silence of the night was a poetic misnomer.

I was quite happy to plod on across the furrows, in my stout boots. The only person I would have been happy to have at my side at that moment was Sister Liz. Her great voice, ringing out over the dark fields, would have provided the correct musical accompaniment. I could almost hear her now:

> Great God! I'd rather be
> A pagan suckled in a creed outworn, ...
> Or hear old Triton blow his wreathèd horn ...

Another of her favourite poems. Not one, however, which could have pointed the path to Rome. Was there something pagan abroad? Ancient gods and goddesses stirring under the sod. If so, I did not feel it. As a rationalist, I was if anything closer to the God of Mother Ancilla, the authoritarian religious system of the Church of Rome with its own precarious logic, than to whatever earthly creatures were shaking the old soil. I had no beliefs, I told myself, and thus no fears.

And that sharp, hoarse sound was, I guessed, a fox barking. Somewhere in the distance. Not even the unexpected nature of the noise caused me apprehension. There was the exhilaration in my independence, to which at that moment I was convinced that nothing, not the loneliness of the night, not nature's marauders, not even the human powers of mischief, could shake.

The owl hooted again and I stumbled over something heavy in the darkness. A log or heavy fallen branch. My boots prevented me from suffering too much damage. I declined to regard the incident as a hubristic reminder of my own mortality.

By the time I reached the tower, I was confident that nothing and no-one could check me, cause me true affright. The tower loomed up above me, quite dark. The moon was now quite far down behind it.

On my principle of being forewarned, I decided to pad softly round to the other side of the tower and see if some glimmer showed there out of the solitary window. Glimmer. The west still glimmering with some trace of day. Banquo's murderers, another nasty late-night rendezvous. No, that was not the parallel I sought. I would stick to Childe Roland and his Tower. Around the back of the tower there was no glimmering whatsoever, only the darkness was more eerie, with the moonlight stronger and more diffused, reflected against the thick walls.

I returned with slightly more haste to the tower entrance. I hesitated, and felt for the sharp little key. Then I groped my way for the padlock, and switched on the torch. I had my first surprise. The padlock was still firmly shut. That seemed to suggest that no-one else had yet entered the tower. Even with a duplicate key, it was difficult to see how they could have relocked the padlock from the inside. Unless they were possessed of superhuman powers. Only a ghost would pass successfully through a padlocked door and leave it locked ... That was another nasty thought like the stupid recollection of Banquo's murderers. My impregnable spirits wavered a bit.

For the first time, I had the impression of being watched, watched by something or someone other than the owls and the foxes. This impression was extremely strong and growing since my visit to the far side of the tower; and yet I had absolutely no rational grounds to support it. Instinct. My journalistic instinct, that famous instinct, at work? Sheer suggestibility, more likely, the culminative effect of the journey and the moonlight on even the toughest spirits. I had overestimated my own hardihood. I jumped sharply at the crackle of a twig near me, and nearly dropped my little torch.

Prayer would have been nice in a situation like this, I reflected wistfully. A quick crossing of oneself as Sister Liz would have done, or Mother Ancilla. My guardian angel would come in handy at a moment like this, supposing I believed in such a thing. That prayer Rosa taught me, which little Catholic girls muttered at night time, something invoking their guardian angel to sleep not while they slept. My guardian angel, or perhaps some stout saint. Was there a Saint Jemima? Hebrew for dove, one of the daughters of Job, it all seemed a little far back and Old Testament for the saints. Perhaps Job would protect me, a most suitable patron, a man who knew a thing or two about life's rough edges ...

Hesitating still, occupying myself with foolish thoughts, I finally resolved to put an end to my fears and enter the building. Unquestionably, my trip round to the other side of the tower had filled me with a morbid reluctance to go further. As though I was gradually being surrounded by unnamed terrors, a tide of terror lapping round me, rising. Here be monsters ... as they used to write on unknown seas on the edges of antique maps. Here be the Tower of God's Church. That reminded me: secret witnesses. Blessed Eleanor, protect me. Were there indeed secret witnesses all round me, in the darkness? Secret witnesses, friends to the owls and foxes, lurking there beside them?

Come on, Jemima, I addressed myself aloud, come on, daughter of Job. I had not talked to myself like that since I was a child when I used to rally myself for an unpleasant task by talking aloud. Once again the ground crackled near me. But it was nothing. Absolutely nothing.

I opened the padlock quickly and competently. I pushed open the thick door into the chasm beyond, remembering the geography carefully from my visit with Sister Elizabeth. I pushed the door hard, and took care to leave it wide open.

I stepped firmly over the threshold of the tower, and clutching my torch firmly in one hand, picked out in its small precise light the wooden rail of the ladder. The rail supported me.

'Is there anyone there?' I called, looking upwards, in the most calm and masterful tone I could muster. Complete silence followed my words. The dampness which surrounded me was marked and most unpleasant. We did not seem to have aired the tower at all by our afternoon's foray. 'Is there anyone there?' Why, that was De La Mare's Traveller. 'Tell them I came and no-one answered–'

Nothing moved.

I put my hand more firmly on the rail. The next moment there was the most appalling feeling of physical assault. With a hideous noise, all the more ghastly for the contrast of the silence only seconds before, I was being attacked on all sides, beaten, murdered. Screaming, screaming unashamedly I dropped the torch and tried to beat it off, beat them off. In vain. The hideous noise, the whirr and whoosh continued.

Finally I turned and fled back outside.

Panting, dishevelled, my hair mussed, half crying, it took me some time to realise that I had been attacked, if that was the right word, by bats.

I recovered my breath slowly; on the one hand I felt idiotic at my panic, on the other hand the waves of terror had been slightly diminished by the upset.

Come on, Jemima, indeed. A few bats were not going to put me off, having come so far. The existence of the bats, my temporary breakdown, only confirmed my resolve. No doubt it was the bats, poor blind benighted creatures, who were responsible for my fears of a new hidden presence.

I stepped over the threshold once more and scrabbled on the ground for my torch. The odd thing was that I could not find it. It must have rolled away. It could hardly have rolled very far on the solid pressed earth floor. It was also odd that it had gone out when I dropped it: perhaps the bulb was broken. In which case, I decided after a moment, there was no point in bothering with it further; leave it to the bats.

The only problem was: how was I to illumine my ascent of the ladder? As a non-smoker, matches were out of the question. Now if Tom had been with me, forever slapping the pocket of his worn jacket for cigarettes and/or matches and never seeming to have them both together – matches. I dug into my own pocket. But there *were* matches here, matches and a candle. In my panic I had forgotten. The percipient words of Sister Perpetua came back to me: 'Ah, candles give comfort where torches never do.'

I found the candle, strangely soft and thin in my fingers. It had broken and bent, but when the first match flared, it was still indubitably a candle. Sister – or Saint – Perpetua, many thanks. I lit the candle, despite its droop, and began rather gingerly to climb up the ladder.

Then I heard a distinct sound above my head. This was no creature of the night. And it was no familiar sound heard during my evening's travail. Not exactly a human sound either. A scrape on the floor, an irregular jarring on the floor above my head, like something rocking above my head ...

Rocking.

Christ, the rocking-chair.

My cry was every bit as irreligious as Margaret's had been. It was no wonder. Someone, something, was gently rocking to and fro in the rocking-chair above my head. I still plunged on up the ladder, holding my unsteady candle: at the time, it was sheer instinct not courage; there seemed no other choice but to go on upwards. Unlike my terror of the bats, my urgent instinct was to confront the danger, not to flee it. As I reached the last rung of the ladder, I think I was aware of another different sound behind me. Not the door shutting. Some new movement in the darkness of the tower's windowless ground-floor chamber. But there was no time to analyse it.

Pushing open the trap-door above my head with one hand, I prepared to make the last of the ascent. My candle flickered and almost died so that I entered the first-floor chamber into what seemed like darkness, except for a square grey light – the far window. The chair was still softly, remorselessly, rocking in its corner. The candle flame righted itself. Heart thudding, I held it upwards.

I saw, unquestionably I saw, a nun sitting there in the chair. A nun waiting for me. Gently rocking to and fro.

But that was not why my heart stopped in my breast.

Equally unquestionably the nun in the rocking-chair had no face. The faceless one. That old nightmare of my childhood, the faceless one who waited for you, whose face you could never recognise, because it had no face. Everything in my world had to have a face, because then it was human and ordinary and you could understand it and control it. But this black shape had no face. Even in the candlelight I could not be mistaken. There were white hands, long bony hands rocking on the edge of the chair. And a black habit stretching to the ground. And a veil and a wimple and a rosary. Even the faint rustle of a nun's skirts joined to the rocking of the chair.

But beneath the white band of the wimple there was nothing, blackness, the void.

I know that I screamed loudly, starkly. Quite different from the brief frenzied panic of the bats' attack.

And then I must have fainted. I hope I fainted. Or perhaps not immediately. Just before I fainted there were jumbled strange impressions. A blow, a sharp blow from somewhere behind me. Or perhaps I merely fell and hit my head on the ladder. At any rate the light seemed to explode and vanish, and the Black Nun whirled round in the spectrum of my eyes, white hands still clenched on the chair. Then she seemed to rise up. A voice in my gathering dream said 'Now,' very clearly. As the voice of an anaesthetist before an operation. I felt the nun's habit enveloping me, her black skirts muffling my eyes, my head, my senses sinking. After that, everything was totally black and there was no light at all and no sound.

Much, much later, I felt the habit being gently pulled back from my eyes like a bandage. The total blackness had gone, there was a little subdued light, and something white near to me.

'Miss Shore,' I heard a gentle urgent voice saying as if from a great distance. 'Miss Shore, Miss Shore.' My name sounded beautiful, like the sound of the sea heard inside a shell.

Bending over me, her wimple so close to my face that it constituted the bar of white in my darkness, was Sister Agnes.

'Miss Shore, Miss Shore.' The sibilants receded and stopped. What she was saying was: 'Miss Shore, are you all right?'

'Of course I'm all right,' I said. 'What the hell are you doing in the tower, Sister Agnes?' I added, struggling unsuccessfully to sit up.

'In the tower, Miss Shore?' replied Sister Agnes, leaning forward again, and soothing my forehead with the ubiquitous nun's white handkerchief.

'But this isn't the tower. This is the chapel, Miss Shore.'

10

Particular friendships

'Poor Miss Shore,' said Sister Agnes softly, pausing in her ministrations. 'You have quite a nasty lump here on the back of your head.' Her fingers explored my skull gently. Then she took my hand and guided it to the back of my head. There was indeed a vast lump there. Sister Agnes's fingers had not hurt me, but my own clumsier touch caused me to wince violently. And that in its turn made me realise that my whole head was in the power of a huge headache, dormant, except that, as I lay on one of the chapel's pews, the faintest movement brought it to ferocious life.

'How in God's name did I get here?'

'I think you must have fallen and hit your head. Here on the edge of the pew. See how sharp the wood is.' Once more Sister Agnes guided my fingers to the bevelled end of the pew. Her guidance was rather a pleasant sensation. But I really had to sit up. Reluctantly I did so. The effort certainly aroused all the devils of the headache inside my forehead. And I felt rather sick into the bargain. Sister Agnes also appeared to be dusting off my coat and boots – what an abnormal amount of dust for the spotless chapel to contain – they were really filthy.

Nevertheless –

'I mean, how did I get here? Into the chapel?'

93

Sister Agnes did not answer immediately, but performed a few more little soft efficient dabs.

'You're not quite yourself yet, Miss Shore,' she said, her face turned away. 'You've probably forgotten just how you came to be here. A blow on the head can do that, you know.'

As a matter of fact, she was right. Or had been right. Up till a moment ago, the precise circumstances preceding my unconsciousness had eluded me. But now they came back, flooding back, along with the headache. And now I felt the shape of my torch – once more back in my pocket.

What was I doing in the chapel indeed? Yes, but what was Sister Agnes doing in the chapel for that matter? I had no idea of the time. It was still dark outside. No hint of grey showed through the stained glass windows which surrounded the altar.

Under the circumstances I decided that Sister Agnes had as much explaining to do as I did. I was not disposed to make her my confidante.

'You're right. I must have fallen and hit my head,' I replied vaguely. 'I can't remember anything else.'

'That's right, Miss Shore,' replied Sister Agnes sweetly. 'Relax. Don't you try to remember. Don't strain yourself.'

She helped me to my feet. I staggered and nearly fell on her. But Sister Agnes was unexpectedly strong and wiry to the touch, for all her professional gentleness and grace of movement. She managed to support me. Then, in a passable imitation of a frog-march, Sister Agnes helped me up the visitors' stairs.

At the outer door to the chapel we paused for breath. It was bolted. Once more bolted.

'At first I thought there was an intruder,' said Sister Agnes. 'Then I heard a noise – it must have been your fall – I'm sleeping in the cubicle at the end of the big dormitory, with the door open. I came down here. That door was open. Perhaps you opened it, Miss Shore? Then I heard a groan in the chapel. And I found you.'

It was quite a long explanation from the enigmatic Sister

Agnes. Particularly in view of the fact that I had not asked for one.

'Perhaps you had opened that door, Miss Shore?' she repeated, as we mounted the stairs.

'I'm afraid I can't remember *anything* just before the accident,' I said firmly. 'The last thing I remember is watching some rotten play on television in St Joseph's Sitting Room.'

I got the distinct impression that Sister Agnes relaxed. I added: 'I really think I should go to the infirmary.'

'You wait here and I'll go and wake up Sister Lucy,' was all Sister Agnes said by way of reply.

Sister Agnes deposited me on my own bed and departed, almost noiselessly. While she was away, I wondered rather groggily why she hadn't called Sister Lucy in the first place.

Time passed, or perhaps I dozed.

But it did seem an age before Sister Agnes returned. There was a frown, or something as near a frown as I had yet seen on that marble face.

'Sister Lucy wasn't there,' was all she said. 'I'll take you to the infirmary myself.' She lifted me up by my elbow, cushioning it, setting me on my feet again.

'You're surprisingly strong, Sister,' I said, 'I'm sure I'm no light weight.'

'It's not a question of strength, Miss Shore. Just how you use your body. I learnt that of course in my profession in the world.'

She made it sound extremely mysterious. We were whispering as we passed down the passage to the infirmary.

'What was your profession, Sister?' I asked her jokingly as she tucked me into a clean bed in the end cubicle of the vast – and apparently empty – lay section of the infirmary. 'Weight lifter?'

'I was trained as a dancer, Miss Shore,' replied Sister Agnes, pursing her lips slightly. 'And later I became an actress.'

'A *dancer*?' I cried.

'Shhh. I'm sorry, Miss Shore. But I don't think you should excite yourself. Before Sister Lucy takes charge, that is.'

It explained many things, her grace, her strength. Even her looks, the huge doe eyes seemed to owe something to the style of the ballet. At that moment, Sister Lucy bustled in, out of breath.

'Ah, Sister, I found your note.'

The two nuns conferred together outside the cubicle in low voices. I couldn't hear what they said. Besides, I was beginning to feel sleepy. I wasn't even able to appreciate fully Sister Lucy's night costume, the neat little muslin cap over her head, just as Rosa reported. But she did seem to have quite a lot of hair under it, no shaven head here. Pleasant auburn hair. In fact she looked a great deal more like the nurse she had been, than the nun she was.

The strain of the evening was beginning to tell, and my head ached. I felt secure and safe in Sister Lucy's care. Sister Agnes must have left because when I opened my eyes again Sister Lucy was sitting composedly by my bed, reading her little black prayer book. It was her office, I supposed, the prayers every nun had to say daily. Composed no doubt by the Blessed Eleanor herself. I continued to feel safe in her care.

The next day I was officially cleared of concussion, although commanded to spend the day in bed. Everything seemed to be back to normal – including strangely enough my clothes. I had a distinct, if groggy memory, of Sister Agnes brushing off quantities of dust from them in the chapel. Yet Sister Lucy denied finding any dust at all; it would be fair to say that she positively bristled at the idea of any contact with the chapel, however unplanned, resulting in the contamination of dust. I had another glimpse of the nurse Sister Lucy had once been, in her own way fairly formidable. I composed myself by concocting an official explanation of my fall for any interested enquirer.

The need to keep my own counsel for the time being was underlined by a discovery I had made in the pocket of the brown overcoat I had worn to the tower. Inside the pocket I found a typed note, exactly similar in appearance to the note which had summoned me to the Dark Tower. 'If you really want to avoid any further nasty bumps on the head,' it read, 'why don't you go back to London and television where you belong? You have been warned.'

An interested enquirer was not slow to manifest herself. Quite early in the morning, Mother Ancilla swept in at her familiar fast pace. Whatever her problems of health, they were not visible in her walk or her bearing.

'Jemima, my child, what's this I hear?' She clutched my hand fervently. 'When I asked you to help us, I certainly did not ask you to get hit over the head, did I? We must take better care of you—'

'I'm afraid I was very silly, Mother.' It was impossible not to feel twelve years old again. I was almost hanging my head.

'We prayed for you at mass of course. No, don't look cross. Naughty girl. We feel God should take you under His special protection since you are doing His work here.'

I was not, strictly speaking, displeased to hear I had been prayed for in the chapel.

I had not rejected Sister Lucy's urgently proffered tranquillizer either. In my philosophy, such activities came under the heading of 'Will probably do no good, will certainly do no harm.' Tom would have had a much stronger reaction to both suggested remedies; he had a personal horror of tranquillizers—having seen their effects on Carrie—and would have felt positively contaminated by the mention of his name in a Roman Catholic chapel. I was made of softer stuff. But it did not do to give Mother Ancilla an inch—

Sure enough: 'Maybe a little visit of thanksgiving?' she enquired hopefully. 'For your safe deliverance?'

'I'm sorry, Mother Ancilla,' I said very firmly. 'As far as I am concerned, I owe my deliverance to Sister Agnes.' I gave her my official story: a sudden noise in the night, an investigation in the chapel, stumbling in the darkness, hitting my head hard on the back of the pew. It was all so ridiculous, I exclaimed. My story gained unexpected plausibility from the fact that there *had* been a sudden noise in the night. It transpired that Sister Lucy had rushed through the nuns' corridor to the aid of Tessa Justin.

As Sister Boniface observed gruffly: 'That Tessa Justin causes nothing but trouble. Nightmares about the Black Nun indeed! Screaming her head off and saying a nun had tried to put a pillow over her head. And there's Sister Lucy trying to make out she's emotionally disturbed and needs talking to! Showing off I call it. Calling attention to herself. Her mother was just the same. Always showing off. When we were children here, anyone who even mentioned the subject of the Black Nun had to say all three mysteries of the Holy Rosary as a penance. Trying to get out of going to early mass. Or not done her homework ... Showing off, I call it.' And so Sister Boniface rumbled on.

It occurred to me that Sister Lucy's position as infirmarian was not totally enviable with this old religious war-horse breathing down her neck. How different the healing of the sick must seem to her in the convent, compared to a great London hospital. Was she quite satisfied with ministering to the needs of 'upper-class brats' – to quote Dodo Sheehy's evocative if possibly second-hand phrase? At least Dodo's aunt, the late Sister Theodora of the Angels, had died nursing black babies ... How did nuns decide on the exact expression their vocations should take anyway? I supposed I should really have to ask them: it would make a fascinating part of the television programme I was still valiantly contemplating.

Not so much 'Why the Cross?' – and hadn't that been done before anyway? – as 'Which Cross?' ...

'My recent experiences simply prove to me that I should keep to my self-imposed rule and not pay stray visits to the chapel –' I told Mother Ancilla cheerfully.

'You're incorrigible!' Mother Ancilla, throwing up her hands, almost roguish, at her best. She looked better than on the day of our first interview. Her cheeks were still white. But I had the impression that the deep lines at the edges of her mouth had softened somewhat. The frightened look had gone. I wondered what had happened to make Mother Ancilla look more cheerful.

One bell sounded. One bell for Reverend Mother. It sounded curiously loud. But then in the infirmary we were bordering on the nuns' wing. The infirmary was a kind of limbo. I had never liked the definition of that term during Religious Instruction at school – ('But Jem, you *must* go to Divinity Lessons, whatever they call them,' my mother had insisted. 'You don't want to be different from the other girls.' She meant: more different than you are already.) Limbo: a place for unbaptised babies. It had a punitive sound to it, like an orphanage for outcasts. I much preferred the easy modern usage of my own world. I used it all too often in my investigative interviews:

'So, Mrs Poorwoman, the social security services have left you in a kind of limbo, have they not?' There being a strong suggestion that something could and would be done about the matter.

Perhaps I could make some use of my own stay in this limbo. There was one untapped source of information about life in the convent close at hand ... if I could lure Sister Boniface from discussing her personal grudge against Sister Lucy and her methods. An on-going limbo, to combine two jargons.

'My bell.' Mother Ancilla sighed. 'Just when we were having a lovely talk, dear Jemima.' She sounded almost happy. Was that possible? Her serenity was particularly surprising in view of her next remark: 'It's the day of Sister Edward's funeral. Had you forgotten? Quite natural in view of last night's events,' she went on. 'That bell is probably to tell me of the arrival of the family. Mrs O'Dowd is such a dear woman and Sister Edward was her youngest. I ought to go and greet them.'

She marched away. A happy warrior. A general whose troops had just won a skirmish. But what was the victory?

'Mother Ancilla –' I called after her.

She did not stop. Perhaps she did not hear me. Nuns like

ordinary women were capable of growing deaf around seventy and Mother Ancilla would be further handicapped by the head-dress blocking her ears.

Later in the morning Sister Lucy and I watched the funeral procession together out of the high thin Gothic window of the infirmary. The line of nuns, strung out, single file, paused silently under our gaze out of the chapel door in the direction of the cemetery.

'What a tiny coffin!' I exclaimed involuntarily. I had forgotten the touching smallness of that rabbit-like figure.

'Sister Edward herself was not much more than five foot.' Even wood was not wasted at the convent.

The tall male figures – her brothers? – behind the coffin looked enormous in contrast to the nuns. The nuns' eyes were downcast. The men were looking about them. But they were not carrying the corners of the coffin. Like the Blessed Eleanor, Sister Edward was being carried to her grave by six black nuns.

'How do they choose the six nuns to carry the coffin?' I enquired idly. 'The six strongest? Or particular friends of the deceased?'

'Not particular friends,' replied Sister Lucy primly. 'Nuns of the O.T.I. have no particular friends. The rule of our foundress is most specific on that point. Particular friendships within the community are not pleasing in the sight of God since they distract the religious from her work in God's holy cause and can give scandal to other godly women.'

I couldn't help laughing.

'Oh come on, Sister Lucy. You know that I didn't mean that.' Particular friendships – but had I not meant that? Wasn't a particular friendship what Rosabelle and I had enjoyed: but then Rosa had not been a nun in those days. Nothing against particular friendships at a school, surely.

'I'm afraid I over-reacted,' responded Sister Lucy. She sounded flustered by my teasing. 'As you can imagine, communities have to be very strict about that sort of thing. Even the very innocent sort of particular friendship, as we call it, can cause disharmony. And disruption.' Seeing that I looked still unconvinced, she went on: 'To the participants themselves, I can assure you. As well as being displeasing to God. Think of, well, you were a friend of poor Sister Miriam,' Sister Lucy coughed and stopped.

'I should investigate the topic for my programme.'

'Miss Shore, please—' Now Sister Lucy looked frankly horrified.

'Oh please don't misunderstand me,' I soothed her. We turned our attention back to the procession.

At a distance the noise of the singing was thin, a little sorrow, not a mighty lament as it had sounded in the chapel on All Souls' Day. In keeping with the small size of Sister Edward's coffin, the short span of her life. Even the procession itself from our lofty vantage point was like something seen at the wrong end of a telescope. The little black figures became formalised. That veiled and bowed figure between two women wearing black hats must be Mrs O'Dowd, mother of the lovely Catholic family. No Mr O'Dowd, as far as I could make out. He presumably had died years ago, worn out. Of the four men, two were in priests' cassocks and two in equally priestly long black coats. Doctors, had Sister Boniface said?

On the dull November day, no sun, trees black, there was only a single splash of colour in the procession. One of the women mourners was wearing a bright purple coat. Purple of course was a colour of mourning in the Catholic Church as pink was a colour of rejoicing. Purple vestments in Lent, purple coverings for the statues in Holy Week. But there was something about this coat, its cut maybe, its swagger, which did not speak of the funeral. It was also remarkable that of all the mourners, this little purple figure was wearing neither a hat nor a veil. She was wearing shiny black boots—again not particularly funereal—but her head, a head of bubbly fair hair which made it the more noticeable, was not covered.

'Blondes really should not wear purple.' It was a judgement from another world. I said it aloud.

'I agree. Beatrice O'Dowd could have spared Mother Ancilla that at least.' The contained Sister Lucy sounded quite venomous.

My interest quickened sharply. 'So that's the ex-nun. The former Sister John.'

'That's Beatrice O'Dowd.'

A return to the flatter tone. The more you looked at the procession, the head of which was now vanishing down the soggy path to the cemetery, the more flaunting the costume of ex-Sister John appeared. A gesture against Mother Ancilla, so Sister Lucy interpreted it: yet it was hardly reverent to her mother, the priests her brothers, the corpse of her dead sister, if those were your values.

I decided that it was time to talk to Beatrice O'Dowd. In the interests of my programme, as I put it to Sister Lucy: who received the request with an impassivity which entirely failed to conceal her violent disapproval.

I did not exactly relish the idea of that flaunting purple in the white calm of my little cubicle. But Beatrice O'Dowd proved a pleasant surprise. Close to, detached from the black procession, the purple did not look so garish. Her hair was naturally sandy rather than blonde. She had the long upper lip and slightly prominent front teeth of her younger sister. It was true that the hair-style was over-bouffant and the lipstick an unbecoming bright pink. Years in television had given me an automatic eye for such things. For the same reason, I could see through to the homely woman in her late thirties visible within the slightly old-fashioned trappings of glamour.

After all, fifteen years of sombre black under Mother Ancilla's eagle eye was enough to send anyone towards all colours of the rainbow. Under her coat Beatrice O'Dowd wore a tight purple polo-necked sweater (she really did like the colour). Whether nuns wore bras or not – and what a perfect opportunity to find out, from an ex-nun – Miss O'Dowd was certainly wearing one now.

Clothes apart, Beatrice O'Dowd seemed to be a straightforward, even down-to-earth sort of woman. It was interesting how completely she lacked the demeanour of a nun: there were no cast-down eyes here à la Sister Agnes, no evidence of hysteria à la Sister Edward. She crossed her legs—rather stocky legs in their black boots—as though to the manner born, twitching down a skirt which was once again just slightly too short for the current fashion. Yet you never saw a nun crossing her legs. Rosa once told me that it was a mortal sin for a nun to cross her legs. It was more likely that nuns sat with their knees together because to cross them under the thick folds of the habit would be a difficult manœuvre.

How odd it must have been for Beatrice O'Dowd to learn such necessary feminine accomplishments as sitting in short skirts after fifteen years' freedom from these cares. Whatever it had cost her, how completely this woman had thrown off the trappings of a nun. Of course it could have been the other way around: perhaps Sister John had never properly adapted herself to them. Hence her desire to leave.

'I wanted to talk to you anyway, Jemima,' said Beatrice O'Dowd conversationally. I did not know that we were on Christian-name terms. Still, television intimacy is a phenomenon which all successful performers have to endure. 'So I was glad when you sent for me. In a way it does make more sense seeing you in here.'

'In here?' I thought she meant: sick, in the infirmary.

'Here at the convent. We had discussed contacting you in London. I said: yes. The others said: wait a bit. And then lo and behold you turn up here. As young Ronnie told us. And of course that made absolute sense to us all. We realised that you were one jump ahead of us in your thinking—'

'You're going much too fast. I've been ill you know,' I said desperately. 'Why did you want to talk to me? Please begin at the beginning.'

Beatrice looked momentarily nonplussed. Then she leant forward again and said in her conversational style:

'But of course I wanted to talk to you, Jemima. Seeing

that Rosabelle Powerstock was such a particular friend of mine.'

It was not, I feared, a phrase that a former nun of the O.T.I. could use by accident.

11

Will

My first reaction to the words of Beatrice O'Dowd was a sudden sharp pang. Irrational annoyance – jealousy would really be too strong a word – seized me. What had this rather plain woman with her fat legs – she *was* plain and her legs were bulging over the tops of her boots – to do with my Rosa? The ridiculousness of my reaction struck me almost immediately. My Rosa was long since gone to her Tower of Ivory. Many years later a middle-aged nun called Sister Miriam had formed a particular friendship with another woman, then a nun:

'Particular friendships can cause scandal to other godly women in the community' – Sister Lucy's observation. I quoted it aloud.

'Particular friendships! Absurd phrase –'

'But you just used it.' Beatrice O'Dowd paid no attention.

'Did you know,' she enquired warmly, 'that this convent was founded on a particular friendship? Do you think that an upper-class woman like Princess Eleanor would have stuck around in this dump without the particular friendship of Dame Ghislaine le Tourel to cheer her up? And yet we were denied even the simplest of human relationships, and taught to consider them wrong. With your understanding of people, how society really works, you must know what I mean.'

I ignored the compliment.

Dame Ghislaine. She had certainly featured in the life story of the Blessed Eleanor. A devoted *Dame d'Honneur*. One of the six black nuns who carried her in her coffin to the tower. The nun who was chosen as the next Reverend Mother by the dying wish of the foundress (no nonsense about democratic election in this community). Eleanor and Ghislaine. As Mother Ancilla would say – royalty, that's different.

It was all a very long time ago. Rosabelle and Jemima. Like Eleanor and Ghislaine that too was a very long time ago. Ancient history. Not so Sister Miriam and ex-Sister John. Beatrice's language of denunciation had a strictly contemporary ring. As contemporary for example as the passionate phrases of Dodo Sheehy on the subject of the poor. And not altogether unlike them.

'From the first moment I saw your programme,' continued Beatrice as though giving me a prepared lecture, 'I was with Rosa all the way. I like to think I may even have suggested the handover. Be that as it may.' Poor Rosa, was she not even to have the credit of her own generous idea? 'Certainly Mother Ancilla always thought so.'

She managed to get a great deal of dislike into the name of Mother Ancilla. I recalled Sister Lucy's venom in pronouncing the name of Beatrice O'Dowd.

'That's when she decided to get me out at all costs. Nothing and no-one stands in the way of Mother Ancilla when she decides to have her own way.'

'But surely you went of your own accord? You didn't want to stay – I mean, listening to you –' I really wanted to say: looking at you. In your boots with your make-up and your crossed legs and your bouffant hair.

Beatrice O'Dowd sighed.

'Oh in a sense, yes, of course. I was in a state of crisis about the whole thing for years. My vows, I mean. I would have gone sooner or later. I was way ahead of Rosa in *that* way. Although of course she would have left in the end. If she had lived.'

She sighed again.

'Poor Rosa. No, I wanted to stay here to see the thing through. Go in my own time. The handover of the land— well, you know all about that. I could have supported Rosa through it all, the lawyers, Mother Ancilla, the lot. I was so much stronger than her. She *needed* my strength. And then they took me away from her.'

A voice from the past. A letter still remembered:

'How strong you are, Jemima. Not needing any props to support you. No religion or belief or anything like that. I need so many props. That's one of the reasons I had to become a nun. To be propped up by God.'

Even in the convent Rosa had still needed strength.

'There wouldn't have been that ghastly upset,' Beatrice went on, 'that nervous breakdown—that's what it was of course, but the nuns would never admit it. Even her terrible plan to shut herself up in the tower. That would never have happened if they hadn't sent me away, using the excuse of a particular friendship. It was deliberate victimisation.' Another phrase from the modern world.

'Mother Ancilla told me Rosa had been very ill,' I put in mildly.

'Oh she told you that. Too late. And wrapped you round her little finger, I'll be bound. The charm of that woman when she wants to use it. But she didn't fool little Ronnie, my sister Veronica, she knew the truth about Mother Ancilla.'

Beatrice O'Dowd's tone changed abruptly.

'There was another will, you know.'

'Ah.'

'You knew?'

'No. But—a hint was dropped.'

'Who by?' Sharply.

'The girls: nothing specific, just gossiping.' I did not intend to be more explicit until Beatrice O'Dowd showed me a few of her own cards.

'Which girls?' Even more sharply. 'There are over eighty girls here. Counting the junior school.'

'I haven't met anyone from the junior school,' I replied pleasantly. Which was true – except for a brief glimpse of a weeping Tessa Justin, in St Joseph's Sitting Room. 'Some of the girls who were friendly with Rosa. They seemed to know all about her plans – your plans – to give away the lands. And they as good as indicated to me that there was a second will. Leaving it to the poor and away from the convent, after all.'

'Oh, them. Margaret and Dodo and Co. Oh yes, Blanche and Imogen even witnessed the will. That's how we knew about it in the first place. They didn't read it, but Rosa told them quite frankly what it was. But I hoped –' She stopped. 'You see, there is a girl here who knows where Rosa *hid* the will, and Mother Ancilla knows that too –'

It was at this point that Beatrice O'Dowd and myself became aware that Mother Ancilla was standing there at the entrance to the cubicle, watching us. She had appeared with a silence worthy of Sister Agnes herself. One of the reasons for this silence might well be the fact that she was holding her black rosary crushed in her hand. So that it would not chink. So that it had not chinked.

'Speak of the devil,' was all I could think of saying in a bright voice. It was, under the circumstances, a singularly inappropriate remark. Mother Ancilla showed no signs of having heard it.

'Dear Beatrice,' she cried. What an actress the woman was. I honestly could not have told the difference between the affection with which she clasped the former nun's hand and the love with which she mantled, say, a princess. 'We're all so pleased you came down to see us, even on this sad occasion. The community are longing to see you.'

I really believed her. I turned towards Beatrice to see how she was taking all this. After fifteen years of Mother Ancilla's sway, I wondered how easy she found it to face her.

The answer was: not easy at all. Beatrice O'Dowd was gazing at Mother Ancilla, fascinated, as a rabbit gazes hopelessly at a snake. Gone was the forceful downright woman who had been instructing me only minutes before. Beatrice O'Dowd, purple jersey, black boots and all, looked frankly terrified. The resemblance to the late Sister Edward was suddenly marked. I remembered that fateful encounter in the school corridor.

'Thank you, Mother,' she mumbled. 'I'll be glad to see them all again.' She picked up the purple coat.

'And how is your work going, my child?' enquired Mother Ancilla, even more tenderly.

'Splendidly, Mother, thank you,' replied Beatrice with an increase of spirit. 'In spite of recent setbacks we think we have found a way round our problems.' She actually gave the Reverend Mother a challenging look. Mother Ancilla tucked in the corners of her mouth. If Beatrice could look like a rabbit, Mother Ancilla could certainly resemble a snake. Her gaze was watchful, cold. But her next words still sounded benign:

'I'm very pleased to hear it, dear Beatrice. And I mean that most sincerely. Just because your – er – plans did not work out one way, it does not mean they are displeasing to God in every way.'

'Thank you, Mother.' Beatrice sounded sardonic.

'Often Our Blessed Lord comes to our aid in the most unexpected ways.'

'I will bear in mind what you say.'

'I take it that although your project cannot go ahead in its original form, it will nevertheless go ahead in a different way?'

'You can take it that our project will go ahead, Mother Ancilla,' returned Beatrice with something of the older nun's bland sweetness. 'Rosabelle Powerstock's will shall prevail.' That sounded like a text. 'And now if you'll excuse me, I'll go and look up some of my particular friends in the community. Miss Shore, we'll be in touch.' There was no doubt of the deliberate provocation of her last remarks. And she went, I noticed, in the direction of the school wing, not the nuns'. I waited till the purple coat had disappeared from view.

'What is her project, Mother Ancilla?' But I had already guessed the answer to my own question. It was really no surprise to me to learn that Beatrice O'Dowd now worked for the Powers Estate Projectors. Directly under Alexander Skarbek: his aide.

Alexander Skarbek. I suspected strongly that there had been some contact between Skarbek and that little Sixth Form group. Possibly through Rosa, certainly through Beatrice. How many others? And what orders had he given Beatrice O'Dowd? I might have to swallow my pride, ring up Tom, and make a few more enquiries about Alexander Skarbek.

'I wonder just what Beatrice O'Dowd intends to do now?' said Mother Ancilla meditatively. 'Poor Mrs O'Dowd was telling me that she's still completely under the influence of that dreadful man. She was always so easily led. And oh *dear* that coat and that jersey! Nuns never have any taste in ordinary clothes, you know. That's why it's so disastrous when they put themselves into short skirts.'

How strange to think that at her age in the world Mother Ancilla would now be dressed as an old lady. In her black habit on the other hand she still appeared as a dominating and formidable figure. A woman of iron will.

Will. It all seemed to come down to a question of will. Will and the will.

Will. There was a great deal of it about. Not only the will of God but a great deal of other wills including the last will and testament of Rosabelle Powerstock. The will of Mother Ancilla to preserve the convent and its work at all costs. The will of a good many other people – including Beatrice O'Dowd, the outsider Alexander Skarbek, the girls of the Sixth Form – to bring that work in effect to a halt by installing a housing project at the convent walls. The will of the Black Nun, or the sinister forces represented by that phantasmagoric figure. The will of the Black Nun was the clearest of the lot: that Jemima Shore, Investigator, should drop her investigations and get out. Her note in my overcoat pocket had made that amply clear.

I concentrated for a moment on the will of Rosabelle Powerstock, the late Sister Miriam. Or rather the two wills of Rosabelle Powerstock. One, a simple testament made at the time of her final vows, which all the nuns made, leaving her effects and modest possessions to the community. The vast Powerstock Estate, of course, long ago placed in trust and excluded. The other, written many years later, the product of an anguished mind.

The missing will.

A will leaving the lands to the poor, Margaret had hinted. But even a mentally distressed nun would hardly phrase her intentions in the language of the Bible – 'Give all to the poor' in this day and age would probably end up by giving all to the government, not the same thing at all. Or at least not in the way Rosa had intended. The poor in this case were therefore ably represented by the Powers Estate Project. I could safely assume the Project to be the beneficiary of the missing will.

Yet even here there was a mystery within the mystery. Why had Rosabelle bothered to conceal her new will before her death? Who did she wish to conceal it from? A will was there to express her intentions when she was no longer there to make them clear herself. Yet she had apparently gone to great pains to hide this will. Unless of course someone else had hidden it – after her death.

The will. Will. I continued to propound to myself these problems.

'Wilful,' said Sister Boniface. She was handling her rosary by my bed. Her chest wheezed and the fingers clutching the beads were as twisted as ever. I thought of Keats: 'Numb were the Beadsman's fingers . . . and while his frosted breath etc., etc.' St Agnes's Eve: Sister Elizabeth was beginning to have an effect on me. But Sister Boniface's tongue was still vigorous.

'Wilful. That's Tessa Justin for you.' Sister Boniface seldom let a subject go. 'Now she wants to have a private interview with you, Jemima. Those were her exact words. If you please! The little madam. Says she has some private information to tell you. I said: be off with you and don't bother Miss Shore when she's sick. Besides, you were sleeping. She said: but I've got to tell her what I know. I said: you can tell her tomorrow, all in good time. And off she's gone, sulkily, to bed.'

For once I was listening with rapt attention to Sister Boniface.

'I could see her first thing tomorrow,' I suggested quickly.

'Oh she'll keep, she'll keep,' replied Sister Boniface. Her tone was comfortable. 'You still need to take things easily. Besides, she's got a busy day tomorrow. We all have. Her mother's coming down to open the school bazaar. Why don't you wait and talk to her when the excitement's all over?'

At the time I saw no great harm in the delay.

12

Worse than death

It was characteristic of the prudence of Mother Ancilla that
Blessed Eleanor's Christmas bazaar took place in early
November. That way, she reckoned, no-one of any decency
could possibly have begun their Christmas shopping. The
parents' entire financial outlay could therefore be plunged
into the giddy whirlpool of the school bazaar. Mother
Ancilla was in no doubt that given a choice of Harrods and
the school bazaar, any sensible parent would choose the
latter.

The school hall, when I poked my head rather nervously
round the door, did for a moment resemble Harrods in the
pre-Christmas rush. Exhausted adults were milling to and
fro, many with small children attached to their hands. In
other ways, however, it was remote from the great Knights-
bridge store. The nuns, unlike shop assistants, spent most of
the time exclaiming and clucking over the old girls, particularly those with babies.

Mother Ancilla was everywhere, kissing and clasping
hands, until her fingers finally became permanently
entangled with those of a handsome, rather plump, middle-
aged woman with black hair in a knot, and a great deal of
gold jewellery. I was surprised. She had surrendered the hand
of another well-dressed parent, rumoured to be an Austrian

baroness 'related to absolutely everybody in Europe'. But when she pounced on me, hand in hand with her new protegée, the mystery was explained:

'Jemima, you remember the dear princess, you remember Pia.' How satisfied my mother would have been to learn that Pia had allied herself in marriage to an Italian prince of even more exalted birth than her own!

'Geemima! So wonderful! I'm telling you.' Pia embraced me ecstatically, taking me into her warm bosom, where the softness of her cashmere jersey contrasted with the sharp imprint of her myriad gold chains. She smelt delicious. She was charming.

'Gianni! Gianni! 'Ere, 'ere.' Pia's English had not improved. And Gianni, whoever he was, husband, lover, son, chauffeur, was not attending. 'Look 'ere, last night I'm sitting in Claridge's and I'm watching television, because we don't go to Annabel's, really so boring every night, and I *see* you!'

She was a fan. I wondered just which repeat she had seen in her luxurious suite: not the Powers Estate Investigation, that would be too ironic. Yet it was due to be repeated sometime. I was beginning to think of that as a lethal programme. Perhaps Princess Pia would now become infected and sell all that she had? Looking at her chains I decided that like the centurion she probably had a great deal to sell.

Mother Ancilla beamed.

'Isn't it wonderful to think of dear Pia watching you on television?' she cried. I only wished my mother could have survived to hear the news. She too would have thought it quite wonderful.

I edged away in the direction of Sister Elizabeth. At least she remained sublimely indifferent to the occasion in hand. We managed to have a quick exchange on the nature of Christian pantheism as expressed by Shelley in 'The Skylark' before a parent claimed Sister Liz to discuss the somewhat lesser literary matter of his daughter's essays.

At the secondhand book stall Sister Hippolytus was presiding grumpily. The books comprised a mixture of lives of the saints and extremely worn paperback Agatha Christies. The Agatha Christies were doing a brisk trade. I could see no way of avoiding my former history mistress; Sister Agnes, whom I wished formally to thank for rescuing me in the chapel, was nowhere around.

'You haven't bothered to come and see *me*, Jemima, with your questions about convent life,' said Sister Hippolytus, who made no pretence of being other than cross at her exclusion. 'Yet no-one else here knows anything at all about the history of this place. No-one else here even *cares* about history.'

'Tomorrow, Sister Hippolytus,' trying to sound as apologetic as I could.

'Tomorrow, tomorrow. Today belongs to God, tomorrow may well belong to the Devil. As Blessed Eleanor said to Dame Ghislaine when she was dying and Dame Ghislaine wrote it down. I've written it down too, you know. A new life of our foundress is sadly needed, don't you agree? Besides, I'm making a major historical revelation –'

I began to edge away to another stall. I could not honestly regard a new life of the Blessed Eleanor as one of the crying needs of modern publishing.

'God granted me an extra long spell in the infirmary last winter,' said the old nun, deserting crossness temporarily for complacency, 'and I was able to get on with it wonderfully well. I was able to help one or two of the Sisters to a speedier recovery by telling them stories of bygone times at Blessed St Eleanor's. They had never heard such tales before.'

I believed her, including the miraculous recoveries of those Sisters condemned to the Hippo's historical revelations ...

'Anyway history makes much the best television.' That was Sister Hippolytus's parting shot. 'The past. Towers, ancient foundations, secret hiding-places, old buildings, that's what the public likes. You'll see. Not a lot of foolish women talking about themselves.'

The implication was: to another foolish woman. But for

all her crotchety temper, Sister Hippolytus had cleared up at least one matter in my investigations.

I helped myself to some of Sister Clare's excellent coffee. Sister Clare was presiding behind an urn, aided by Blanche Nelligan and Imogen Smith. Blanche rolled her eyes to indicate how far this coffee would fall below my standards.

At a nearby stall Sisters Damian and Perpetua had arranged a series of bottles ranging from Worcester sauce to something mysterious and unlabelled in a vast black bottle. For a handsome sum of money, people were entitled to throw hoops over these bottles in an attempt to secure them. As I arrived, the little hedgehog was plucking nervously at her companion's sleeve.

'Sister, Sister,' I heard her say. 'One of these bottles is alcoholic. What happens if a child wins it?'

'Ah, never worry, Sister,' replied Sister Perpetua happily. 'They won't win anything at all, and that's a promise. These hoops are all far too small to go over the stands. That's the way we used to do it at home in Ireland,' she explained to me, without a trace of shame. 'You make so much more money that way. After all, it's all for charity isn't it? The poor little black children.'

The other stalls were run on rather less ruthless lines. The prize goods – clothes and napkins exquisitely embroidered by the nuns themselves – quickly vanished. Whereas a quantity of logs and leaves and ferns sprayed in silver by the junior school still lurked to trap the unwary visitor.

I even bought one of these festive pieces of nature myself.

'Miss Shore, can we have your autograph?' A group of giggling juniors, bored with the rest of the proceedings, surrounded me. Some proffered autograph books, others scraps of paper. The last girl lingered. She was tiny, with huge goggling eyes and hair scraped into a thick pony tail.

'Will you put: For Mandy, Miss Shore?' It was done.

'And that's my toothbrush holder.' She pointed to a large besilvered log, in which three very small holes had been bored. 'Nobody's bought it. And I took so much trouble –'

A frightful expression of woe which did not convince me for a moment: I bought the toothbrush holder. After all, there were unlikely to be two like it in existence. Triumph succeeded woe on the small face.

'Mandy Justin,' said the voice of Mother Ancilla sharply, 'you should be getting ready to hold the bouquet. Your mother's just going to make her speech. And if you see Tessa tell her to go to the platform too.'

So yet another member of the Justin family was an adept at improving the shining hour. My attention was caught by a cortège of what were evidently more Justins, shuffling uneasily onto the platform. Another prudent move on the part of Mother Ancilla was to have the so-called opening ceremony performed as a closure when the stalls were more or less empty. This meant that the distinguished visitor, in this case Lady Polly Justin, had to stay to the bitter end, buying for all she was worth. And so did all but the most brazen of the other visitors. It was a bold parent who ran the gantlet of Mother Ancilla's disapproval by leaving before the speech.

I studied the Justins.

I recognised Sir Charles Justin. He was a Conservative M.P., enormously stout, very much looking the part of authority. He had once given a drink to Tom and myself on the terrace of the House of Commons when his right-wing and Tom's left-wing views had somehow brought them into agreement over some matter of individual liberty (Tom), freedom from state control (Sir Charles Justin). He looked remote and intensely gloomy sitting there on the platform.

I deduced that the proximity of Lady Polly Justin was responsible for much of this catatonic state. Lady Polly looked pretty as a picture in exactly the right furry hat and soft frilly blouse. Her looks, strong nose, heart-shaped face, reminding me of Romney's Lady Hamilton, gave one hope for her daughters. Perhaps Mandy and Tessa would one day turn into swans like this. Nevertheless Lady Polly succeeded in making a speech of quite exceptional incompetence. As a Tory M.P.'s wife, she must surely have become accustomed to such things. Of course the ever-protective Tom never forced his constituency on Carrie – her nerves would never allow her to make a speech. But he was Labour. Tories were known to be different and demanded far more from their wives.

Yet Lady Polly not only read her speech but lost her place and dropped her notes. She even made a hash of that hoary old play on words – 'a fête worse than death'. This came out as: 'I am sure this is not a death worse than a fête, even though my fate may be, trying to open it, I mean close it.' Quite. Perhaps she did it on purpose to try and gain her husband's attention? If it was a manœuvre, it failed. Sir Charles showed absolutely no interest in the proceedings whatsoever.

The lanky young man yawning beside Lady Polly was, I guessed, Jasper Justin of Eton College, Windsor, Berks. There was a miniature version of him sitting beside Sir Charles, equally spindly, in the uniform of some doubtless impeccable prep school. It was difficult to believe that Sir Charles had ever looked quite like that. But perhaps Justins put on weight, with responsibility, as they got older. Mandy Justin duly presented the bouquet to her mother, looking like a little doll, and giving a truly magnificent display of bashfulness. There was no sign of Tessa Justin.

'You must come and meet Polly,' purred Mother Ancilla in my ear. 'She's such a dear.' Like Lady Polly herself, Mother Ancilla was quite unabashed by the platform performance.

Not so every member of the audience.

'Honestly, Miss Shore, did you ever hear such rot?' hissed an indignant voice beside me. It was Dodo Sheehy. Dodo and Margaret had not been much in evidence during the bazaar. No doubt they disdained such things as being both time wasting and class ridden. It was a point of view one could share.

'Sir Charles Justin is a fascist beast,' she went on. Blanche and Imogen, standing rather languidly by, having abandoned the coffee stall, nodded as though well versed in the horrors of Sir Charles Justin's politics.

Margaret Plantagenet was standing by herself, over by the door. Her arms were folded. Her face wore its habitual stern expression in repose, what I called her crusader's look. Lady Polly, platform surrendered, stood quite close to her, twittering away and gesturing. I could not hear what she was saying, but the two of them could hardly have presented a more complete contrast in style and looks. I could not imagine Margaret opening a bazaar such as this in ten years' time, any more than she might marry a Conservative M.P. That for her would truly constitute a fate worse than death. I had long ago abandoned my fantasy of Margaret among the brides in the Nuns' Parlour arrayed in white.

I decided to greet Margaret. But on reaching her, I was sucked into Polly Justin's orbit.

'I can't understand it,' she was saying with great indignation. 'Where is Tessa? I mean where is she? Why isn't she here? Why didn't she come for my speech?' It was tempting to suggest that Tessa Justin might have heard her mother speak before, and decided to keep clear. I resisted the temptation. But as the other parents melted thankfully away, a great deal of agitation was revealed among the remaining nuns. Mother Ancilla, like Lars Porsena, was sending her messengers forth, east and west and south and north, to summon Tessa Justin.

Mandy Justin was hopping to and fro at her mother's skirt sucking one finger.

Jasper Justin continued to yawn, while eyeing Dodo Sheehy. Master Justin, evidently a precocious youth, eyed a Fourth Former.

'I told you the girl wasn't here,' said Sir Charles Justin, fixing me with a belligerent and slightly bulbous eye. 'The trouble with Polly is that she's like a bitch in a thunderstorm when trying to make a speech. No sense at all.' It was the solitary remark I heard him make.

For all Mother Ancilla's enquiries, for all Lady Polly's fluttery demands, by the time the last parent had vanished, the last girl had returned to the children's wing, the Justins' silver

Daimler still sat empty at the front door. By itself it seemed to constitute a great gleaming reproach to the institution which had so carelessly mislaid a member of its precious cargo.

Tessa Justin, the fact had to be faced, had utterly disappeared.

An hour later it transpired that she had not after all disappeared without trace. It was Mandy, weeping, who finally disgorged a typed note from her pocket.

'From Tessa,' she said, between sobs.

'Dear Mama and Papa,' it read. 'If you really want to know where I am, I have gone to stay with Aunt Claudia. Because I am unhappy here and she won't make me come back. I have got plenty of money. So don't worry. Your loving Tessa.' It was all typed, including the signature. Lady Polly continued her hysterics.

'Oh isn't that just typical of Tessa? Claudia Justin isn't even on the telephone. She's Charles's mad sister. Yes, Charles, don't contradict me. She is mad. Living in the Lake District and thinking dogs and cats can speak. You know the sort of thing.' But Sir Charles showed no signs of interrupting. He just looked more furious than ever.

'Why did she do this to me?' ranted on Lady Polly. 'We'll have to drive up there. No, we can't. It's much too far. And we've got the Spanish Ambassador coming to stay. Oh it's too bad of Tessa—Charles, what shall we do?'

Sir Charles Justin said nothing. He strode forward and got to the wheel of his Daimler. It seemed as good an answer as any.

It was Jasper Justin who was left saying placatingly: 'Come along, Mama, we'll send a telegram. Mother Ancilla will iron it all out. I'm sure Tessa's perfectly all right. She always is.'

As I watched the departing Daimler, into which the remaining Justins had piled like the family of Louis XIV going to Varenne, I wished I shared Jasper's confidence. I myself was much less sure that Tessa Justin was perfectly all right. For one thing, I had recognised the typing of the note.

And its style. I was positive that the same unknown source had provided all four typed notes; they had certainly been done on the same machine; three to me, one now to the Justins. Unless a ten-year-old had deposited two of the notes on my desk and secreted the third one in my overcoat pocket (which did not seem conceivable), then Tessa's note was a fake.

In which case, where was Tessa Justin? Kidnapping, I reflected with a sinking feeling, was one of the few experiences which really did justify that overworked phrase, a fate worse than death. Unless it turned out to end in death itself.

With a heavy heart, I took myself back to that room, the guest room, which I was now beginning to consider as my own personal cell. I tried, as calmly as I could, to consider the possibilities.

I was interrupted by a knock on my door.

There were few people I wanted to see at that particular moment. Certainly not Mother Ancilla, nor Margaret and Dodo for that matter. I desperately needed peace for thought before I talked to any of them.

I went to the door.

It was Sister Boniface. Her expression was almost as troubled as my own. And she was wheezing hard as she came in: she must have just climbed the visitors' stairs.

'Jemima, I'm worried,' she began without preamble, sinking down in a chair, a sign of exhaustion. Nuns rarely just sit down like that. 'I've been praying about it in the chapel. Taking my troubles to Our Lady, who lost the Infant Jesus when He went to the temple. And she's told me to come and talk to you.' More hard breathing.

'That child. Disappearing like that. Leaving a note. I don't like it one bit. She can't type for one thing. They don't learn typing till the Sixth Form. That note was beautifully typed. Sister John couldn't have done better herself, Beatrice O'Dowd I mean, when she was here she taught them typing. She was a trained secretary.'

The old nun drew breath.

'Besides, it's not like Tessa Justin. She's a show-off, you know. If Tessa was unhappy, we'd all know about it. She'd paint it on the chapel roof if she could. Not disappear. No fun, that, not seeing all the fuss for herself.

'Sister Lucy won't listen to me. Talks about a situation of sibling rivalry, I think that's what she calls it, all to do with Mandy presenting the bouquet. Hence Tessa's choice of her father's sister as a refuge. I told her that was all rubbish. But she won't listen. So I prayed to Our Blessed Lady, and she told me to come to you.'

'What about Mother Ancilla?' I had to ask that.

'I see you haven't heard yet. Poor Mother Ancilla. The strain of it all, the bazaar, the child vanishing. She's had one of her attacks. A bad one. She's lying in her cell now. They don't even want to move her to the infirmary.'

So potent was the aura of Mother Ancilla that for a moment, at the prospect of its removal, I felt quite helpless.

'I'm acting Reverend Mother. As the oldest member of the community.' Sister Boniface at least did not feel completely helpless. That at least encouraged me.

'And then – she wanted to tell you something, didn't she? Urgently. A private interview, she said. And I stopped you, Jemima, I'm sorry about that. And now I'm a frightened old woman.'

Not so strong after all. Another frightened old woman. As Mother Ancilla had been in our first discussion. No, merely that Mother Ancilla had collapsed and the burden had fallen on Sister Boniface's even more ancient shoulders.

I took a deep breath. It was time to take someone into my confidence. It looked as if my confidante, directed by the Virgin Mary or otherwise, was destined to be Sister Boniface.

As briefly and unemotionally as possible, I told her of Mother Ancilla's request to me, to uncover whatever might be evil or discordant at the heart of the convent. I did not burden her with the murkier ramifications of the whole affair. And I did not go further into the mystery of the Black

Nun and my own terrifying encounter in the tower, beyond saying that there were forces of evil at work in the convent, and forces of good, in which some use was being made of the legend of the Black Nun, and I was not quite sure as yet which was which. God willing (oh fortunate phrase, that came to my tongue) I intended to find out.

But there was one vital question I had to ask her.

'Sister Bonnie,' I said, 'you know this place. You've been here, how long? Since you were a small child at the school – seventy years! Then you know everything there is to know about it. Is there any way known to you in which the tower, the old tower, Blessed Eleanor's retreat, could be linked to the chapel?'

An extraordinary look crossed the old nun's face. It was neither fear nor astonishment. It was a kind of illumination. For one instant she even looked young again. I had seen a glimpse of the young nun she had once been, not the gnarled old creature who confronted me.

'So many years ago,' she murmured. 'So many years have passed. That you should ask me that now.'

'Please, a life may depend on it.'

Sister Boniface gave me a more straightforward look, a return to her old self.

'When I was a novice,' she began gruffly, 'we knew that a secret passage joined the tower to the mediaeval chapel. That the chapel, our modern chapel, had been built over its foundations, so that the passage came up somewhere lower, into the level of the old chapel, into our crypt as a matter of fact. The idea was that the Blessed Eleanor, making one of her retreats, used to come by night from her tower to pray privately in the chapel. But no-one ever talks about that now.'

'Why not? You must tell me.'

Another straightforward look.

'Because many years ago, when I was young, still a novice in short, a historian came here and talked a lot of nonsense about the Blessed Eleanor. He had been researching in some

mediaeval sources he said. And he had come to the conclusion, or so he told Reverend Mother, right to her face,
can you imagine it, well, you didn't know Reverend Mother
Felix, but anyway he told her right to her face that the secret
passage hadn't been for that at all. That it had been for Dame
Ghislaine le Tourel to visit Blessed Eleanor at night, and for
no good reason ... And then, he asked if he could see the
entrance to the secret passage!'

After all these years, indignation still burned.

'He wasn't a Catholic of course,' she added. 'Hardly. He
was a *heathen*, in my mind. And I'll tell you what Reverend
Mother Felix did. Straightaway she summoned us all and she
told us that henceforth the secret passage did not exist. That
we were never ever any of us to speak about it again, according to our holy vow of obedience. That we must protect the
reputation of our Foundress from the attacks of the ungodly.
And he went away defeated. And we never did speak about
it again. And the others who knew about it then are all dead,
years ago. Why, I believe I'm the only person alive who
knows how to find the entrance.'

'Sister Boniface,' I said slowly. 'I'm afraid you're wrong.
There is someone else still alive who knows how to find that
entrance to the secret passage. Will you show me too? To
the greater glory of God.' I don't know what made me add
that last phrase. Convention. The convention of the situation
in which I found myself.

13

Come to dust

It was nine o'clock. Looking out of the window I saw nothing but darkness. No moon tonight. It might have been the small hours. I was waiting for my rendezvous with Sister Boniface. She was adamant that she had to complete the ordained ritual of night prayers before joining me. I did not look forward to what we – I – had to do. I felt not so much fear, or the false exhilaration of my previous expedition. More a great sadness.

Whatever I discovered, whomsoever I might rescue, the status quo of the convent could not be saved entirely. But perhaps that was destined for disruption in any case. Mother Ancilla was still lying in her cell, too ill to be moved to the infirmary. She had suffered another heart attack, I learnt from Sister Lucy. The convent doctor had been and gone. That too cast a pall of sadness over us all.

I wrote a note to Tom.

I had decided to do that in case anything happened to me. It would be brief, and for once impersonal. The sort of note that he would not destroy. He could even show it to Carrie.

'Dear Tom,
Just in case. Check up on Alexander Skarbek in London. And ask Sister Boniface where to find the secret passage in the convent. That's all.

J.'

I addressed the envelope: Tom Amyas M.P., House of Commons. I left it lying on my desk, right on top of the Treasury of the Blessed Eleanor, where it could not be overlooked.

A soft knock at the door interrupted my preparations. This time I would take two torches – Sister Boniface would provide me with a second – and in honour of Sister, otherwise Saint, Perpetua, two candles. A piece of rope (purloined from a child's trunk in the store room) and a good sharp knife (purloined from the cafeteria where it had vanished from under Sister Clare's eyes. Or so she put it. She was still making ineffectual noises of loss when I discreetly left the refectory).

Another soft knock. Clearly not Sister Boniface.

It was Sister Agnes.

'Miss Shore, please excuse me.' How polite she always was, deferential. Yet she always gave the impression of trying to put me at my ease, rather than the other way round. 'I know it's late. But I can't get little Mandy Justin to go to sleep. It's hardly surprising with all the upset of her sister running away. But she keeps saying that she has something to tell you, the television person, as she calls you. And she won't tell it to anyone else. I don't like to fetch Sister Lucy. So I wondered if you would perhaps consider coming along to St Aloysius's dormitory – '

I agreed with alacrity. Experience had taught me that it did not do to keep the Justin family waiting when they had news to impart.

Mandy Justin was presented for my inspection in Sister Agnes's own sleeping-quarters: a kind of extra cubicle on the outside of the big dormitory. That gave her freedom of movement to supervise the older children, who slept in double rooms, without disturbing the juniors in the dormitory.

This time Mandy's tears and suffering had, I fancied, been genuine. The first thing she said was:

'I'm not going to tell it to her,' and she pointed to Sister Agnes. 'I'm just going to tell it to *you*. Because you bought my silver toothbrush holder. And I've seen you on telly. Besides, I'm frightened of nuns.'

She started to sob. I touched her rather gingerly. Over her head my eyes met those of Sister Agnes.

'Sister?' It was only tentative.

'I'll go, Miss Shore,' she replied. Her expression was impossible to read. 'There, Mandy, don't cry,' she added kindly. 'You tell your story to Miss Shore, and then you can go to sleep.' She sounded even gentler than usual.

Sister Agnes withdrew. But she did not go very far. I could see her shadow outside the cubicle, the elongation of the shadow, its formlessness making her look much taller than she was.

Mandy's story was about a nun too. A strange nun, a nun she had never seen before, who had handed her the typed note. That note which she subsequently presented as being from her sister Tessa. Having been threatened that if she, Mandy, so much as opened her mouth on the subject, or produced the note until exactly one hour after the bazaar ended, the strange nun would come and take her away too. Like Tessa. The story of the Black Nun had clearly not reached the infants at Blessed Eleanor's. Otherwise Mandy Justin would have been not so much tear-stained as hysterical.

'Don't worry, Mandy, don't worry. It'll be all right.' How did one console a seven-year-old child whose ten-year-old sister had been kidnapped? I needed Sister Agnes. But there was one question I had to ask.

'The voice, Mandy; the voice. Did you recognise the nun's voice?'

'I told you I didn't know her. She was a horrid great nun. Besides, she was whispering—'

A horrid great nun who whispered. Was that what lay ahead of me in the Dark Tower? I surrendered Mandy to Sister Agnes.

'She'll sleep now.' I hoped that was true. I left Sister Agnes and the child abruptly. I went back to my room and tore open my note to Tom. I added in a scrawl: 'That isn't all.

I love you, my darling. Till – death – but I do hope it won't happen. J.' I ended it with the outline of a heart. It was no longer the sort of note he could show to Carrie. But that would be his problem. I addressed another envelope and replaced the white note on top of the black Treasury.

Down the visitors' stairs, quiet as possible. Into the chapel, checking that the outside door was bolted on the way. It was. The red sanctuary lamp winked and glinted from the altar. The candles at the shrine of the Sacred Heart had burnt low since my first visit there. The statues, like living people, seemed to be making beckoning gestures in the gloom. Sacred Heart of Jesus, pray for me. Heart, my lucky symbol. St Joseph, father of the Holy Family, pray for me. Our Lady Tower of Ivory, pray for me. All the saints, pray for me. I could hear the litanies chanted in my imagination. But I did not pray myself. I merely adjured all possible saints to pray for Tessa Justin, or at least to try and guard her from on high. Tessa, Teresa – St Teresa, pray for her. No, not the great St Teresa of Avila, a woman for whom, beliefs apart, I had a great deal of sympathy. Reading a biography of her once, a composite with the other St Teresa, I had always felt that we should get on. I addressed myself not to that Eagle but to the Dove, the lesser St Teresa, the Little Flower. Sainte Thérèse, protect your Tessa Justin.

A dark form rose slowly up from the front pew.

Sister Boniface, bending and moving with difficulty. Her agility these days was all in her mind – and her tongue. She gestured me to follow her into the sacristy, to the left of the altar. The oak door was already open. But there was no light. Sister Boniface's heavy breathing was the only noise in the chapel.

Once we were safely in the sacristy, Sister Boniface shut the door firmly. The heavy sound made me jump. But Sister Boniface spoke naturally in the dark:

'I'll switch on the light for a moment. To find the door to the crypt staircase. Only for a moment. We mustn't alarm the whole community.'

There was an instant of extreme brightness. Sister Boniface felt her way round the oak panelling which lined the sacristy. I saw the priest's robes, already laid out for the next morning's early mass. How elaborately they were embroidered, how minutely, when you saw them close! Even the vestments for an ordinary weekday mass, representing so many hours of nuns' labour. Still, it was labour voluntarily given. A.M.D.G., as I had quoted to Sister Boniface.

The furthest panel had a little iron inset. It contained a ring. Sister Boniface twisted the ring and pulled it sharply. The panel swung back and a narrow but well-turned stone staircase was revealed.

'I'd better turn out the sacristy light now,' said Sister Boniface. She sounded quite cheerful about it all. I switched on my torch. 'Here's the second one. You take that too.' She handed it over.

'When I come back, I'll leave the panel open of course. You'd better come back before early mass. Otherwise whoever serves mass tomorrow might go and shut it. And then where would you be? No windows in the crypt. And *very* deep down –'

'Sister Bonnie, please!'

We descended.

The crypt was indeed very deep down. And not a very salubrious atmosphere when we got there. At least I was allowed to switch on the light: a rather dim bulb dangled in the centre of the arched ceiling from a wire. But the floor was stone, unlike the floor of the tower, so that we were spared that prevailing smell of damp. The crypt was also, so far as I could see, extremely clean. The convent cleanliness extended even underground. There were various niches in the stone walls, containing more statues. And one large alcove, with a wooden *prie-dieu* in front of it. A kind of shrine, it appeared. The alcove above contained a life-size statue. I inspected it: a queen with a crown on her head – Mary, Queen of Heaven, presumably. The features were idealised, soulful, and reminded me of Sister Agnes. Victorian, I supposed.

'Blessed Eleanor herself,' said Sister Boniface. 'She was briefly Queen of England, you know. Wouldn't it be lovely if we had a Catholic queen again? Do you think Prince Charles—'

It was no time for this Mother Ancilla talk.

'I should think the statue is about 1860, wouldn't you?' I said hastily.

'Oh no, it's a portrait from the life,' said Sister Boniface reproachfully. 'Very, very old indeed. Anyway there are coffins here. Dame Ghislaine and quite a few of the early nuns. And they certainly are old. They stayed here undisturbed all through the Reformation, thanks to the mercy of God and the protection of Our Lady. Blessed Eleanor herself, I regret to say, was taken to Belgium. Although to be fair she did perform several miracles there in the last century. Which she might not have felt inclined to do here . . . Being on her home ground.'

I was not disposed to discuss the finer points of miracle-making either. Besides, I did not like the reference to the other inhabitants of the crypt.

'I can't see any coffins,' I said nervously.

'There's a grille. Look behind you.'

I turned round. The far wall was not in fact made of stone. It consisted of a series of shelves, on which stacked coffins could be vaguely discerned. I had no idea how many of them there were. Or how far back they extended. A large iron grille stood between us and the coffins. Nevertheless I found the sight extremely creepy. But it did not seem to worry Sister Boniface at all. Perhaps it was her own strong faith, perhaps it was her inevitable nearness to death. But Sister Boniface was really quite unconcerned at her presence here among the bones of the dead.

The dust of the dead by now. They had all come to dust. Dame Ghislaine had been dead for over five hundred years. Even her dust had vanished.

'When was the – er – last?' My gaze was still riveted on the grille.

'Reverend Mother Felix. No, Reverend Mother Xavier and Reverend Mother Louise must both have been buried here after her. At my age, one gets muddled. You see only Reverend Mothers are placed here now. The rest of the community are buried in the cemetery. The grille is only opened on the death of a Reverend Mother.'

'So Mother Ancilla –'

'In God's good time, Mother Ancilla will rest here too.'

It was in both our minds that God's good time for Mother Ancilla could not be far away.

'I'm glad they're still behind a grille. The coffins. They can't get at me.'

'But, my child, it's behind those bars that you have to go,' said Sister Boniface. 'That's where the entrance to the secret passage is. Hidden by the coffins.'

14

The power of darkness

I felt quite sick. Bones, dust, what did it matter? The fact
that the last corpse must have been laid here over thirty years
ago? All the same, this was a charnel-house. A grisly trap.
I wanted to escape—

'Sister Boniface,' I answered in a shaky voice. 'Please show
me now.'

She motioned to the grille.

'It was on the right. You should find the door in the wall
on the right. It may be very dusty there. You may have to
move a coffin, several. And that grille is probably very stiff.
It hasn't been used for a generation.'

But it wasn't stiff at all. I tugged the handle. The grille
swung back with ease. There was no dust that I could see.
The door was very clearly delineated in the wall. And none
of the coffins was blocking it. In short, there was no reason
why the door to the passage could not have been in regular
use lately. No reason at all.

I felt the door. And found another inset with a ring inside
it, similar to that of the sacristy. I turned it and pulled sharply.
The door opened. Another exit not to be shut against my
return. Blackness yawned, complete blackness, and this time
a heavy, disgusting stink of damp. Sister Boniface and I
peered into the chasm.

'So it's still there,' she said after a while. 'Do you still want to go, Jemima?'

'I don't want to. I must.'

'I'll pray in the chapel till you come back,' said Sister Boniface.

'Take your torch back.'

'No need, nuns can see in the dark, didn't you know? I'll find my way back to the chapel. God bless you, my child, and preserve you from harm.'

Harm. What is it that would harm me? That evocative phrase, the powers of darkness. Darkness had no powers, I told myself savagely as I stepped into the black chasm. Come on, Jemima. The only power of darkness lay in the use that clever, unscrupulous people made of it to frighten and waylay the innocent. Darkness would have no power over me, because I would not permit it to do so.

I began to feel my way along the passage, watching the ground in the light of my torch. The passage was narrow, and the walls at the bottom crumbly. I could now understand how my coat, covering my unconscious body, had gathered dust. It struck me that I must have been carried, not dragged. There had been no bruises on my body when I was recovering in the infirmary.

But if carried – another inescapable thought assailed me. That meant two people. Two people of considerable strength. I was taller than average. It was not a conclusion to cheer a lonely traveller.

I hoped I would not find two people – two people of considerable strength – at the end of my journey.

The ground was surprisingly even. And above my head was a well-worked stone roof. It was inconceivable that this passage had been constructed in this form in the Middle Ages. Like the statue of the Blessed Eleanor, I suspected a much later date. It all had the workmanlike look of a well-put-together Victorian folly. Obviously whichever Reverend Mother had been responsible for building the Victorian chapel had had the passage thoroughly overhauled as well.

The existence of the passage had been common knowledge in Sister Boniface's youth: which brought us to a period before the first war. Then the threat of the historian's revelations had induced Mother Felix to impose her vow of silence. But knowledge did not die away so quickly. Sister Hippolytus, for example: did she know about the passage? Was that the revelation she promised us in her manuscript? More than likely. Poking about in the convent records, she could easily have made such a discovery.

I have no idea how far I travelled before the ground began to rise. I had the impression of walking at least half a mile, but the darkness robbed me of a sense of time and distance. As the crow flew the tower was not really so far from the chapel. It was tramping the fields which took the time to get there. No doubt the passage followed the most direct route.

The incline grew more pronounced, the ground was cut into steps. Then there were formal steps of stone, and those in their turn led to a winding staircase. Finally I found myself in front of a door. It was exactly similar to the door at the other end of the passage. The door was shut.

She who hesitates is lost. Come on, Jemima. I twisted the iron ring which held it, extinguished my torch, and pushed the door open. I stepped forward.

Immediately something very hard indeed struck me sharply on the top of my head. I ducked. Instinctively I put up my hand. It felt like stone. A broad smooth stone surface with a sharp edge. Then I heard a noise which sounded like a cat or perhaps a kitten mewing.

There was no other sound at all.

I felt upwards again. I had hit my head on a piece of stone. It was in fact the mantel of a stone fireplace. I recognised where I was: standing bent inside the fireplace of the first-floor chamber of the tower. The fireplace where I had originally spotted those tell-tale Gauloises stubs. The winding stair must have come up inside the thick walls of the tower. Boldly, I switched on my torch.

The rocking-chair was still. And empty. There was no sign of a black habit there. Or a black nun.

Tessa Justin was lying on the floor in the corner. In the small light, she looked as if she were asleep or perhaps drugged. But it was she who was responsible for those sounds, the mewings of a kitten. The trap-door to the ground floor was closed.

I walked across to her. She was not asleep. Her eyes were open. I didn't think she was drugged. She was in fact sobbing, but so tiredly that only these tiny sounds emerged.

'Tessa,' I said softly, 'Tessa, don't cry.'

She didn't look up. Her body – still in its school uniform but the maroon heavily marked with dust – froze.

'It's me, Jemima Shore.' No move still. She didn't look at me. I touched her shoulder. It was quite rigid. Maybe after all she had been drugged.

'I've come to rescue you.' No move. I had an inspiration. 'I've come to hear the story you've got to tell me. Look, look at me, Tessa.'

Slowly Tessa Justin lifted her head off the floor. Her thick plaits were dusty too, whitened. Her eyes looked enormous. I shone the torch onto my own face.

'See, I'm not a nun.'

She gave a loud cry, said something like: 'Oh, oh, take me *home*.' And scrambling off the floor, flung herself at me.

At least Tessa Justin, the missing Tessa Justin, was neither drugged nor damaged. And for the time being at least she was safe. I didn't know how long that happy state of affairs would last. How soon before the powers of darkness who had kidnapped her and dumped her here, planned to return? As once they must have come to find the imprisoned Rosa in her Tower of Ivory. And seen that she never escaped from it ... It didn't do to think of such things.

We had to get back. But first I had to soothe the incoherent Tessa. I doubted whether I could carry a ten-year-old girl all that way down the passage. By myself.

'Tell me later,' I kept saying, patting her and trying to

disentangle myself. But she wouldn't let me go. I longed for the calm strength of a nun, any nun. The gentle authority of Sister Agnes, the businesslike ways of Sister Lucy.

Tessa Justin would not be stopped from pouring it all out, as we sat there on the wooden floor in the dark tower. And we each held one torch. Eventually I pulled her onto my lap in the rocking-chair. And cuddled her there as best I could. The feeling of closeness grew on me. I couldn't remember when I had last held a child of any age in my arms.

'There, there,' I kept saying, and other things, endearments and tender words, until the choking finally stopped.

Like her sister Mandy, Tessa poured out a story in which there was the now familiar feature of a strange nun, a nun she had never seen. Except that Tessa, being in the Lower Fourth, knew all about the Black Nun; and readily identified her as the persecutor. Mandy had spoken of a horrid great nun who whispered. Tessa described the Black Nun herself, speaking in a low hoarse voice, the Black Nun who for some time, for ages, forever, had been out to get Tessa Justin.

How the Black Nun had come to her at night and whispered to her – and nobody had believed her. And how on another night the Black Nun had threatened to put a pillow over her face and nobody had believed that either. How Sister Lucy had just given her medicine and Sister Boniface had threatened to give her a good smack. And even lovely Sister Agnes had not believed her. That's why she had tried to talk to me about it. And Sister Boniface had stopped her.

But it was true, all true. The Black Nun was out to get her. And then, the worst thing of all, just before the bazaar, as she was getting tidy, she received a message to say that her parents were waiting for her in the sacristy. She thought it was a bit odd –

'But everything about nuns is a bit odd, Miss Shore, isn't it?' she said rather pathetically. So along went Tessa to the sacristy. And the next thing she knew, the strange nun, the Black Nun, pulled her down some stairs and into a dark place and through a long smelly tunnel. And then –

'And then?'

'Well, these questions,' she cried. 'All the time these questions. And if I didn't answer I would never see my parents again, or Mandy, or Jasper, or Charlie or anyone.' More sobs. I cuddled her again.

'Questions? The will, then, Sister Miriam's will –'

'Oh yes, the will, the beastly will. Oh if you know where it is, can't you tell them, Miss Shore? I told her, I told her what I knew. But she just wouldn't believe that was all.' The head buried in my coat. I smoothed the plaits, all I could see of her.

It transpired that what Tessa Justin knew about the will was this: it was not much, I had to admit. Except that she did know more than anyone else about it. There had been this odd conversation with Sister Miriam, on what turned out to be the very day Sister Miriam disappeared. Tessa had just come back from seeing off her parents at the front door when she found herself grabbed by Sister Miriam who looked, as she put it, 'awfully odd, even for a nun'. In Tessa Justin I detected already the beginnings of an anti-nun prejudice to rival Tom's.

There was nobody much about. Sister Damian, the portress, was not at her post, and there were no other nuns visible. Sister Miriam had much surprised Tessa by suddenly putting her thin face very close and whispering to her:

'I've made a new will, you know.' Or something to that effect.

'Of course she *was* a little batty,' confided Tessa – oh Rosa! – 'We juniors knew that. Batty but rather sweet. We all liked her. So we never teased her on anything horrid. And then she said something about it being quite safe and I must remember and tell nobody. Then I think her bell rang – a bell rang, hers or someone else's, and another nun came round the corner. I don't remember who. And she started and let me go and ran off. You don't often see a nun haring along, do you?' she ended.

But Tessa hadn't really understood what Sister Miriam was

talking about. Even when she was found dead. Till that day in St Joseph's Sitting Room where she had hidden for a dare and had been discovered. And after that Margaret Plantagenet and Dodo Sheehy had suspected something. Because she had foolishly boasted to her best friend, who was Cordelia Smith, Imogen's sister, that she knew where the missing will was. Then Cordelia told Imogen. And the big girls had questioned her. And she didn't tell them anything of course. Horrible bullies. But she had told everything to the Black Nun, and now to me. And please would everyone leave her alone?

'But where, where was it safe?'

But that alas was exactly where Tessa's childish memory became vague. All she could tell me was what she had told the Black Nun so many times, and not been believed for her pains.

'It was something to do with brides,' she said. 'Brides and nuns, or the other way round, nuns and brides.'

'Nuns and brides – nuns, the brides of Christ? That's what they're sometimes called.'

Yes, that was it. The brides. The brides of Christ. Being safe among the brides of Christ.

Safe among the brides of Christ, I thought. Safe indeed. But that might be anywhere in the entire convent ... No wonder the Black Nun had shaken Tessa till her teeth rattled and still got nothing more out of her. And gone away and threatened to come back soon. And how Tessa must then tell her more or else ... Yes, it was time for us to be going.

There was no point in dusting the child down. We should get dirty enough on our return journey, if not worse. I urged her to cling onto her torch at all costs –

'Tie your plaits round it if necessary.' A wan smile. 'It belongs to Sister Boniface. She's waiting for us in the chapel.' That did cheer Tessa: obviously Sister Boniface was to her, as to me, a symbol of security.

We made our way back through the fireplace. I made no attempt to close the door behind me. That was for others to clear up. Down the winding stair, stone giving way to earth, then back the way we had both come through the tunnel. The return journey seemed to take aeons of time. It was not that Tessa dragged behind. On the contrary, she was incredibly staunch considering her ordeal. The Justins had spirit, one had to hand it to them. Show-off she might be, Tessa was also full of proper courage as well.

But I was waiting and listening all the time for some noise ahead of us. The signal of the return. Even now was the Black Nun abandoning her nightly search for the will? And going back for a fresh examination of her victim? Who could tell? Perhaps she had at last found it, and would return in triumph...

A whole age of nervous footsteps had passed before we saw the crypt door ahead of us. God be praised, it was still open. And praise all the saints too. And St Teresa – both St Teresas. I was in a mood to be generous. I had not admitted to myself how much I had been dreading to find our exit barred.

'Come on, Tessa, not much further,' I said in a low voice.

She went through the door first with her torch. I followed, stooping. We were once more beside the coffins, in the charnel-house in fact. The grille too was still open. Swung back as it had been before. The dim light still burned in the crypt. I could see that the outer door to the sacristy was still ajar. Everything was just as it had been. We were safe. Safe indeed. Once more under the roof of the brides of Christ.

It was a piercing scream from Tessa which told me, violently, that I was wrong. Not everything was just as it had been before.

There, there behind the marble statue of the Blessed Eleanor, lay the difference. A black shape, a long shadow, now stretched out from behind the statue. Tessa's screams rang in my ears as the black shape, now growing in size, stepped out from the protection of the alcove and began slowly, purposefully, to move in our direction.

15

A crypt is for coffins

'Run, Tessa, run,' I shouted. 'Find Sister Boniface'. The little girl, still obediently clutching her torch, did not hesitate, and bolted in the direction of the open door.

She reached it. The last I saw of Tessa Justin was her thin legs scampering up the stairs to the sacristy. Then the crypt door clanged to. She must have banged it behind her.

I was alone with the Black Nun.

Black not only from head to foot in her habit but also black and faceless. In the electric light of the crypt I could see clearly that the so-called Black Nun was wearing a black mask. That made me feel no better. At that moment I would have preferred to face a ghost than this silent figure, hands folded under her cape. The characteristic gesture of nuns by which they hid their hands. I knew all about these particular hands. I had already glimpsed their long bony fingers in the candlelight of the tower.

I touched the knife in my pocket.

The Black Nun now stood quite close. Between me and the door. The odd thing was that I could smell her: a strong human smell of someone who is excited. It gave me quite a different kind of jolt: I don't think I had ever consciously smelt a nun before. Whatever the austere nature of the cleansing materials allowed to them, every nun I had known had been as immaculately clean as if no body whatsoever existed inside the habit. And there was another smell, too, a different smell...

I was taken quite unawares by the next action of the Black Nun. Suddenly she extended one long arm from beneath her cape and with those same strong fingers, swung down the iron grille in my face. Iron bars now separated us; on the one side of them, the Black Nun, hands once more folded under the cape. I was imprisoned with the coffins.

The Black Nun continued to face me. Then with another rapid movement, she whipped up her hand and removed the thick mask.

'Jemima Shore. We've met before,' said the Black Nun. 'That rhymes. How charming.'

It was the roll of the 'R' on the word rhyme which reminded me that Alexander Skarbek had a faint foreign accent.

When I last saw him on my television programme, I had noticed it. I thought it part of his attraction. Now it only confirmed my worst fears, and still more fearful anticipations.

He removed his other hand from under the cape. I saw that he was smoking. A Gauloise. The second familiar smell I had noted. The first smell had, of course, been that of a man. Looking down I saw that the floor was littered with cigarette stubs. He must have been waiting here for me for some time. Knowing where I had gone. Knowing that the tower was locked and that I had to come back this way. Into the crypt.

The crypt with its coffins, amongst which it seemed likely that I would stay.

'A bad habit,' said Skarbek. He flung down the cigarette and stubbed it out impatiently with his foot. I noticed that he was wearing black boots, ordinary Kings Road type of boots as I would normally have termed them. With chunky heels. His feet – for a nun – looked enormous. Yet he was hardly much taller than I was. That explained the absence of shoes and stockings when Sister Liz and I first discovered the empty habit. For one idiotic moment I recalled all those wartime stories about German paratroopers dressed as nuns and how you could tell them by their boots.

'You look quite charming surrounded by coffins,' said Skarbek. 'Are you fond of coffins, Jemima?'

'Not particularly, Mr Skarbek.' My frigidly formal tone was the best I could do under the circumstances. I suddenly had to hang on to the grille. I was shaking.

'But a crypt is for coffins, Jemima.' Another roll of the 'R'. I wondered how I could ever have found his accent attractive. Or him.

Yes, in a way he made a plausible woman, or nun at least, because of the regularity of his features: yet his light eyes and sharp straight nose, his wide mouth, had not struck me as particularly feminine when we met. More wolfish. But he seemed slight to me then. Physically it was odd how a slender man became a towering woman – or a horrid great nun, in the words of Mandy Justin. A nun who whispered, who spoke in a hoarse tone: that was to conceal the man's voice. The wimple to conceal not the signs of age, but the man's throat, the prominent Adam's apple. Then the black mask to hide the man's face to anyone who might recognise it, such as myself. But there would be no need to disguise his face to children. Especially to little girls, late at night. So Skarbek the Black Nun had been able to roam as he wished through the convent, looking for the will which eluded him. The will leaving the lands to the Powers Project.

His relief at hearing the news that this will did exist after all must have been profound. Otherwise why not let Rosabelle hand over the lands herself and endure the long battles with the lawyers?

It only remained to find it. The missing will. And then the property for which one woman had already died would belong to the poor. Or rather to the Powers Project.

'Do you think I make a good nun, Jemima?' Skarbek interrupted my frightened searching thoughts. His voice was still light, almost caressing, through the grille.

'I don't think you make a nun at all, Mr Skarbek,' I said with all the spirit I could muster. 'Nuns are dedicated to the service of God. If I believed in his existence I would say that you on the contrary were dedicated to the service of the devil.'

'Harsh words, Jemima. But like you, I don't believe in the devil. All the same, the devil and all his pomps is a good phrase. Certain pomps are quite devilish, aren't they? Places like this. Wasting money, parasites on society.'

He was playing with me. There was no point in joining in the sport.

I rattled the grille.

'Mr Skarbek, are you going to let me out of here?'

'But of course, Jemima. If only because I want to come much closer to you.' With a courtly gesture towards the grille. 'Perhaps you will like me better if we are closer to each other. Or is it the habit which troubles you? That can easily be arranged. At least part of it.' Rapidly, as if born of long practice – which I suppose it was – Skarbek removed the black veil, fixed by its tiny black pins, then the stiff white wimple and white cap beneath. He placed them on the *prie-dieu*. Beneath it all his hair was unexpectedly long. Instead of a nun he looked now like a young priest, standing there in black soutane. Then he swung back the grille.

I stepped out. It was a relief to be free, free at least from the coffins.

'I'll have your torch if you don't mind.' He took it. I made no resistance. I did not want him to know about the knife. Till I was ready. Then he offered me one of his cigarettes from the blue packet. I had not smoked since I was fifteen, when I puffed out of bravado with Rosa. But I took one and lit it clumsily and drew on it as I had watched others do, as I had watched Tom do, so many times. It was an odd feeling having Skarbek's face so close to mine, now free of its habit, as he held the match. Odd. Intimate. Distasteful.

'Mr Skarbek –'

'Alex, please. You don't mind if I call you Jemima. After all I was on your programme. We're friends.' A roll of the 'R'. I wondered if he was putting the accent on. What new friendships television brought me to be sure – Pia recalling me with delight, who had hardly known me at school, Tessa and Mandy Justin, who both thought of me as their ally for no better reason than because they had seen me on the box, and now Alexander Skarbek. 'I know you especially well because I saw you again last night on the programme, our programme. I thought how pretty you were all over again.'

It was sickening to think of this kind of compliment actually winning the hearts of Rosa and Beatrice O'Dowd. For myself, I had always lived in the world, and was scarcely susceptible.

'You know, Jemima,' went on Skarbek, 'I thought last night that you would make a good nun. I don't mean all that –' he gestured to the veil and wimple with his cigarette. He looked so masculine to me now that I wondered even the children had been deceived. 'But your spirit. There is something nun-like about you, something pure, withdrawn, dedicated to service.'

'The nuns you have known may have started pure and dedicated to service,' I retorted with an angry puff of my cigarette, 'but they soon became dedicated to something quite different.'

'Nun, what nun?' he said sharply. 'Put that thing out. You have no idea how to smoke it.' He took the cigarette from my fingers and threw it on the floor to join the others, crushing it with his boot.

'Rosabelle Powerstock, Sister Miriam, and Beatrice O'Dowd, Sister John, when you first knew her.'

'Ah yes. Those most sincere ladies. I certainly changed the direction of their dedication, that is true. Or rather we changed it between us, did we not? Our programme, as I call it. From the service of God in heaven to the service of the poor on earth. Not a bad swap, I would say.'

I said nothing. I was wondering, now that he was more relaxed, whether I could make a dash for the door. I put my hand casually into my pocket and closed it on the knife.

Immediately Skarbek threw down his own cigarette, grabbed my wrist and pulled it out of my pocket, knife and all. He continued to hold it up, gazing at the blade. Then he laughed and with a twist made me turn the blade towards myself.

'Don't be frightened, Jemima. A dagger to your heart? No, no, too crude. I don't work like that. Everything is natural that happens here. Natural – if unfortunate. A key breaks off in a lock. A sick nun starves to death as a result. It's all a mistake. Who is to question that?'

'So – Sister Edward too?' I said bitterly. 'Her medicines out of reach. Struggling for breath. Natural if unfortunate.'

'I did not kill Veronica O'Dowd,' replied Skarbek. 'I can assure you of that. That was – how shall I put it – purely unfortunate. She would not have lived long in any case. Asthma had weakened her heart. Her family knew that. For you, perhaps, another unfortunate incident in the tower. Jemima Shore, Investigator, is the victim of her own adventurous spirit. She investigates the passage, a door slams, too late. She can't get out. Like her friend Sister Miriam, she dies in the Tower of the Blessed Eleanor.'

'Who told you about the passage? You can satisfy my curiosity about that.'

'Ah, the passage. That was a bit of luck, wasn't it? The reminiscences, which would otherwise have been intolerably dreary, of a bad-tempered but historically-minded old nun.'

I had no difficulty in recognising the description ... Sister Hippolytus. I wondered when he had met her: how he had fooled her. It would not be so easy to pull the wool over Sister Hippolytus's eyes.

He opened my fist and the knife clattered to the floor. Then he put his hands in my pockets and brought out the rope, the candles and the matches.

'How very thoughtful of you, Jemima, to bring your own

rope. I was wondering what I was going to use to tie you up. Perhaps you might be wearing an exciting belt under that thick and rather unexciting coat? Or perhaps my rosary? Quite thrilling that.'

'What are you going to do?' I could not stop the apprehension from creeping into my voice.

'I'm going to tie you up. To this convenient grille I think. Inside it or outside it? Shall it be inside with the coffins? Or outside with the statue of the Blessed Eleanor? Boring woman. I've looked at copies of her Treasury once or twice, searching for the will. Incredibly tedious, don't you think? I do hope her ghost doesn't come to call on you. For your sake. She might bore you to death. Forgive me, I didn't mean to make quite such a bad-taste joke—'

'Not inside. Please. Not with the coffins.'

'Surely you don't seriously believe in ghosts? They're all dead, you know. Bones and nothing else in those coffins.'

'What are you going to do?' I said again.

'Just tie you up for a little while. That's all. Not forever. There's someone I have to go and see. And I don't want you to get away.' He busied himself with the rope, tying me deftly, quickly, to the outside of the grille. At least I was thankful for that. Perhaps this small mercy was some kind of good omen that he did not after all intend to deal too harshly with me. It was better to hope.

'You might try saying a few prayers if you're lonely,' he said. 'You're not a Catholic, I know. Then I could teach you a few. A Hail Mary or two works wonders for the nerves.'

'Are you a Catholic?' I asked incredulously.

'My parents were. I was brought up as such. Until I saw the error of their ways—very early indeed in my existence, I can assure you. The country where I was born is one of those where ignorance and superstition is so deeply rooted in the hearts of the stupid peasants that nothing, not even communism, can get rid of it. Poland.'

'Poland. I didn't realise you were Polish.'

'I came here as a refugee when I was very young, ironically

from the new state after the war. Because I was officially a Catholic, the do-gooders here even sent me to a convent school at first – until I ran away.' It explained many things.

'So you see I know what I'm talking about when I say that you would have made a charming nun. By the way, what a pretty colour your hair is.' He put out his hand and touched it. I flinched. 'And your face. There is still something child-like, untouched, about your face. In spite of that incredibly severe expression you are trying to assume.'

He held my chin and looked at me. I turned my head away. The light, almost yellow eyes were like those of an animal. A hunting animal. Not an animal in the zoo. Of the two of us, I was the captive animal. I saw him glancing at the veil.

'I wonder how it would be –' he said suddenly. 'Do you fancy dressing up as a nun?' And he bent his head and pressed his lips hard to mine. I struggled and tried in vain to press myself further back into the grille. I was profoundly horri-fied.

'No,' I cried, when at last he released me.

'Blasphemy? Sacrilege? You can't believe that,' he said, smiling.

'But *you* do.'

'I must remind you that there is no God. Hence no blas-phemy. All the same, it might have been interesting. For us both. I assure you, Jemima, I'm not interested in unwilling victims. No-one was unwilling.'

'Pathetic sex-starved women,' I said. 'What splendid con-quests!'

'Oh, quite. Conquests weren't the point. Surely you understand that.' He lit another cigarette. 'That was all purely for the good of the cause. It meant nothing to me whatsoever. Beatrice O'Dowd is a nice woman but an awful fool, not at all my type. In any case it was not necessary to seduce her, she simply exchanged one love or passion for another, in both cases strictly platonic. As for those girls, that fat little blonde with the absurd name, Dodo, and Blanche and Imogen.' He mimicked their enthusiastic upper-class voices. 'Working for the poor in the holidays from their smart fee-paying school. Writing us eager letters, imagining they have actually joined us on the other side of the barrier. Hero-worship was what they wanted, not sex.'

'And their leader, Margaret?'

'She's different. At least she knows how to keep her mouth shut. An interesting girl. She's more like you.'

'And Rosabelle?' I had to ask.

'Ah, your friend. The heiress. A strange woman. Even for a nun. So many different impulses: no wonder she had a nervous breakdown.'

'Beatrice O'Dowd thought all that happened because Mother Ancilla got her away. They were of course great friends.' Even now I refused to use the term 'particular friends'.

'Nonsense. Rosabelle had many secrets from Beatrice, I can tell you. Including where she hid her will. Beatrice always exaggerates her importance in every situation. It makes her hell to work with at times at the Project. The others complain. It was Rosabelle Powerstock who first contacted us, I can assure you. Afterwards–' He seemed to have nothing more to say on that subject. I did not know whether to be glad or sorry. Just as I did not altogether know whether to be glad or sorry at the unexciting truth about the relationship between Rosa and Beatrice. Glad that it had been innocent. Sorry that Rosa had not even been granted the comfort of one real confidante in her last months.

'The brides of Christ indeed!' he went on angrily. 'Most of them would be a great deal better off as proper brides, bourgeois white finery, veils, orange blossom and all. At least they would perform one useful function in society; wife followed rapidly by mother. I prefer the intelligent,' he repeated. 'That's why it's a pity that you're not more accommodating. Tom Amyas is your chap, isn't he? Oh, don't worry. We make it our business to know that sort of thing about M.P.s who don't exactly love us. Just in case the information comes in useful. An awful ass, isn't he, always grinding on about his conscience. Does he bleat about it in bed as well?'

I did not deign to answer. Skarbek fished something out of his pocket.

'Which reminds me. We can't have this hanging about, alas. That would never do.'

It was my note to Tom. Skarbek lit a match and put the flame to the corner. The black fragments floated down to the floor to join the cigarette stubs.

I was no longer so hopeful that nothing terrible was going to happen to me. Skarbek was robing himself in the wimple and veil again. Then he took up my two candles.

'Your candles I'll leave you,' he said. 'Out of reach. But alight. No funny stuff burning the ropes. You will be like a saint, Jemima, with two candles burning to you. Your own particular shrine.'

So saying, he moved the *prie-dieu* across the crypt until it faced me. He placed one candle on either side. Then he switched off the crypt light.

'Very charming.' An elaborate roll of the 'R' again. I was certain he was putting it on. 'Saint Jemima of the Coffins.' To me the whole crypt, now lit only by the flicker of two small candles, looked less charming than horrifyingly eerie.

And roped to the grille, in my own particular shrine as he called it, I no longer believed Skarbek in his protestations about blasphemy. In some corner of his being, however remote, he still believed in the possibility.

'I promise I won't be long,' he said, 'we have so many interesting things to talk about. Later. But there's someone I just have to see. Another intelligent female, as a matter of fact. I really do have a taste for them. And I must deal once and for all with that wretched child. Something natural, what was it I said, something natural but unfortunate.'

Tessa! In my fear and confusion I had forgotten all about Tessa Justin. And what on earth had happened to my old but stout-hearted sentinel, Sister Boniface, last seen departing to pray in the chapel? Why had Sister Bonnie not raised the alarm? Tessa Justin, in her filthy and hysterical state was surely sight enough to promote a dozen search parties.

'Tessa will have woken the whole convent by now,' I answered. 'I doubt if you will find it quite so easy to deal with her.' My words were bold. But I was worried by the lack of extraordinary sounds from above. In fact, no sound at all. 'Sister Boniface was there and –'

'Oh, she's been dealt with already.'

Not Bonnie –

'Nothing sinister in this case. Purely natural, dear Jemima. Not even unfortunate. Lured away from the chapel. A story that Mother Ancilla needs her. After that she will be given an assurance that you are safe. That Tessa is safe too. That you both returned through the chapel while she was absent. She won't interfere with our plans.'

Our plans. That was it. I had to face the fact – that Skarbek had an accomplice within the convent itself. A highly efficient accomplice or as he himself described her, an intelligent female. Someone who had nightly opened the crypt door to let in the Black Nun. Not Beatrice O'Dowd, who was no longer an inmate of the convent, free to come and go as she pleased. Besides, I believed Skarbek when he said that Beatrice, foolish clothes and all, was still in her own way animated by love, or at least idealism. 'Very easily led,' Mother Ancilla had said. In more ways than one, I was beginning to think that the Reverend Mother's opinions represented the most solid canon of common sense in this unquiet convent.

'And so, Jemima, I must leave you. I must go once more among the brides of Christ.'

I watched the Black Nun depart. His figure in its habit soon melted into the darkness of the crypt staircase. At least he left the lower door open. The candles flickered. I prayed – yes, prayed to something or someone – that they would not go out. And leave me alone and helpless in the darkness. No smoking, no praying, where now were the principles of a lifetime, I asked myself. Come on, Jemima. It was a grim attempt at humour. At least it might help me to survive.

I had many reasons to wish to survive. For one thing, I now knew where the last will and testament of Rosabelle Powerstock was hidden.

16

Healing hands

He was gone. I was alone in the crypt with the coffins – and
the statue of the Blessed Eleanor – for company. I heard the
upper sacristy door shut. I was entombed.

There was silence.

Only minutes later, it could not have been more, there was
a noise. It sounded like that same sacristy door opening. Yes,
and now footsteps down the stairs again. Why? Had Skarbek
forgotten something, or had he perhaps thought better of
leaving me in the crypt? Was I destined for the tower straight
away ... All these questions thronged through my mind,
none of them arousing very pleasant images, as the light footsteps descended the stairs.

A nun stood framed in the doorway. It was not, I thought,
Skarbek. So far as I could be sure against the limited light
of the candles. The crypt light flicked on.

'Why Miss Shore,' said a familiar voice. 'Whatever are you
doing here?'

It was Sister Agnes.

A lesser woman might have screamed. Or amplified her
question. At least she might have cried out: whatever are you
doing there tied up with ropes, with two candles beside you,
confined to a grille in a crypt, backing onto a multitude of
ancient coffins. Not so, Sister Agnes.

'Oh dear, oh dear,' was all she said, moving swiftly across the crypt to my side. 'Poor Miss Shore. Poor dear Miss Shore.' From her tone she might have been sympathising with a child who had fallen over and cut her knees.

'Free me, Sister Agnes, free me please.'

'Of course, Miss Shore, of course I'll free you.' Her delicate strong fingers were already plucking at the rope.

'There's a knife somewhere. On the floor over there.' Sister Agnes bent down and came up with a cigarette stub. She wrinkled her nose. Then she found the knife. She straightened and held it towards me—for a moment, I even thought—

But Sister Agnes quickly and competently cut the rope. I was free. Dusty, stiff, still terrified, but free. She put the knife down on the *prie-dieu*.

'You must have help,' she said.

'We must both have help,' I replied earnestly. 'Tell me, first of all, is Tessa all right?'

'Tessa? But she ran away. You remember—'

'No, no, she didn't run away. Anyway she's back. Oh, God, don't tell me he's got Tessa—'

'There's no sign of Tessa Justin upstairs in the dormitory, I assure you. But we can deal with that later. First, I must help you upstairs. Why, you're in the most distressing state.'

Once more Sister Agnes began to cluck, and dust my clothes. I felt her healing hands cross my brow for the second time; she had rescued me before, and was experienced in how to soothe me. Then carefully and I thought disapprovingly, Sister Agnes blew out the candles which had constituted my shrine.

'How dreadful,' said Sister Agnes. It wasn't clear whether she meant the whole enterprise or just the candles themselves.

'Now I shall help you back up the stairs.'

I thought: we've done this before too, as the young nun put her arm round my shoulders and began to aid me back up the winding stair to the sacristy. Once inside, there was no light on. That was odd. Perhaps Sister Agnes, like Sister

Boniface, had not wanted to alarm the whole convent. But in my opinion, growing rapidly in urgency, the sooner the whole convent was alarmed, the better.

Where was the switch? I felt round to the door, found it. The sacristy flooded with light. Sister Agnes moved quickly round after me and switched it off again.

'Please, Miss Shore,' she said. 'Not yet. Here's your torch. I found it on the floor. Use that if you like. We nuns can see in the dark, you know.' As Sister Boniface had observed to me earlier. Sister Boniface. Surely the old nun would have sent someone by now to my rescue.

'I left Sister Boniface here in the chapel–' I began.

'Hush, hush, Miss Shore. Don't worry about Sister Boniface. If she was praying here, and has gone, she was probably needed by Mother Ancilla. Our Reverend Mother is gravely ill and Sister Boniface is by convent tradition her deputy. Until the new Reverend Mother is chosen.'

She sounded amazingly matter-of-fact about the prospect of her superior's imminent death. But one expected nuns to be matter-of-fact about death. It was Sister Agnes's calm approach to my own predicament which confused me. To say nothing of the missing child.

'But Tessa Justin, I *found* her. And now what's happened to her? You don't understand what's going on here, Sister Agnes.'

By way of answer Sister Agnes opened the sacristy door to the chapel. We were once more in the religious light of the sanctuary and its candles. Candles in their proper place in front of a proper shrine. It was a great relief to me to find myself back in the ornate Victorian chapel, away from that mediaeval nightmare of crypts, secret passages and towers.

The chapel, so far as I could see, was empty. I devoutly hoped – not quite the cliché the phrase usually was – that no-one was lurking behind the far pillars. No Black Nun within the distant shadows.

Sister Agnes paused by the first pew.

'No, Miss Shore,' she said. 'I think it is you who doesn't

understand quite what is going on here.' Then she guided me out of the chapel by the visitors' door. 'Come, we must go to your room.'

There was great authority in her low voice. I felt mesmerised by her. Far more mesmerised than I had felt while in the power of Alexander Skarbek. Her personality was hypnotic. In her mixture of tranquillity and strength, combined with her physical resemblance to my dead friend, I found all the qualities I had once sought, and sought in vain, in Rosabelle.

I tried once more a feeble protest.

'Don't you think the infirmary – Tessa –'

'No.'

We went in silence up the stairs. Sister Agnes opened the door of my room. She settled me in my chair, taking my coat, dusting the skirt of it again, and finally placing it on the bed. It look dishevelled, and as I felt, forlorn as a result of its experiences in the passage.

'Listen to me, Miss Shore. I have to leave you here for a while. There is something I have to do. Someone I have to see. Please stay here.' She paused and placed one hand on mine. It was a clasp whose warmth and firmness reminded me not so much of Rosabelle as of Mother Ancilla.

'Promise me that whatever you do, you won't leave this room until I return. Is there a key? Good. Then lock your door. And don't let anyone in.'

I was only too delighted at the idea of locking my door. I had absolutely no wish to admit any of the sinister nocturnal ramblers at Blessed Eleanor's. Above all, not the Black Nun. Still roaming somewhere loose in the corridors, the rooms, the passages. Maybe even in the empty guest room next to mine. I shivered. I would lock my door all right.

'Trust me, Miss Shore,' concluded Sister Agnes solemnly. 'It won't be for very long. I shall come back. Later. We have so much to talk about.' She was the second person that evening to use those same words.

I ought to warn her –

'The Black Nun—' I began desperately.

'Later. Lock your door.' Sister Agnes departed. I was abandoned to the three holy pictures on the walls, where the Botticelli Virgin still looked at me with her expression of detached pity, the Titian Madonna still offered cherries to her child, and an Angel was, as ever, arrested in mid act of announcing impending pregnancy to the maiden Mary. Then there was the Treasury of the Blessed Eleanor, described by Alex Skarbek as intolerably dull. I could do with a little dullness, I decided. I picked it up. No white marker this time to mark my place. I turned a few pages, was guiltily inclined to agree with Skarbek, then went to the brief life at the back of the book.

'Of all the holy women under her care, Dame Ghislaine le Tourel was the one for whom our foundress had the most tender love,' I read. 'Blessed Eleanor loved in Dame Ghislaine le Tourel the blessed reflection of Our Saviour Jesus Christ, which she loved in duty bound wheresoever she found it, and most of all she found it in Dame Ghislaine le Tourel.'

The reflection of Christ—who was I to say that was not the truth of their relationship? It was, as we all agreed, a very long time ago. The anonymous author of this charitable nineteenth-century life was just as likely to be right as a later historian. A non-believer. And a man. His insights into the mentality of mediaeval nuns were as likely to be limited as mine were. The relationship of Rosabelle and Beatrice O'Dowd had turned out to be an innocent one. Why not then give the benefit of the doubt to Blessed Eleanor and Dame Ghislaine?

I read on.

Then I saw the handle of my door turning. It turned and did not give. There was a little rattle. My visitor seemed to be disconcerted to find the door was locked.

I heard a voice, very low but not whispering, outside the door: 'Miss Shore, Miss Shore, are you there?'

'Yes, I'm here. Who is it?'

'Oh thank God you're all right. Thanks be to God. I've

been so worried. I didn't know where you were. I didn't know what to do. Tessa Justin came rushing to the infirmary in the most ghastly state—'

It was Sister Lucy.

With a great sigh of relief, I jumped up and unlocked the door. Sister Lucy was outside, panting. She came in, and recovered her breath.

'You're safe. Thank Heaven. I haven't known what to think. You see, Tessa Justin reappeared a while ago, running to me with some extraordinary story about Black Nuns and secret passages and the tower, and kept saying "Save her, save her" meaning you—'

Admirable little Tessa Justin.

'We were all upside down from seeing to Mother Ancilla. And then Sister Boniface came along from visiting Mother Ancilla's cell and said that it really seemed too much to have Tessa Justin calling attention to herself with a pack of lies when Reverend Mother might be dying—'

'Sister Boniface said *that*—' I was bewildered.

'Yes. And of course I knew what Tessa was saying must be nonsense. Tessa is really a most emotionally unstable child.' Sister Lucy was recovering something of her normally competent manner. 'Just the sort of story she would tell—the concept of the tower for example and the passage—full of psychological significance. I agreed with Sister Boniface to that extent, that she had made the whole thing up. At least we were as one about that. Then Sister Boniface suggested corporal punishment, a good hiding was her exact phrase. As you can imagine, I didn't go along with that. Tessa was simply mixed up in herself. So I gave her a nice soothing sedative, something strong but appropriate to a child. And she went down like a baby. Sleeping the whole thing off now.'

'But Sister Boniface knew—' I began. I stopped.

'Yes, please do explain,' said Sister Lucy. 'What is going on? Where on earth have you been, Miss Shore? I looked in here a while ago and the room was empty. Sister Agnes is missing too; her cubicle is empty.'

I hardly knew where to begin. But Sister Lucy was a nurse and must have heard some strange tales in her time, tales of humanity twisted between good and evil. Nurses, even nurses who have become nuns, knew all about the dark side of human nature.

'Oh, Sister Lucy. I've had the most terrible time.' The strain of it all was beginning to tell on me.

'Sit down again, Miss Shore. Yes, you do look – well, exhausted is hardly a strong enough word. I'll get you something. A good tranquilliser is what you need. In fact I think I've got something right here in my pocket. I was going to ask the doctor if any of these would help Mother Ancilla.'

She dug in her capacious black skirts with her healing hands, and produced a small pink box.

Sister Lucy held it out towards me with a happy smile at having solved my problem.

'I'll get you a glass of water.'

I did not take the pink box.

My eye had followed Sister Lucy's gesture automatically downwards as her arm went towards the pocket of her habit.

And stopped there.

Sister Lucy's skirts, the whole length of the hem, very deep, eight or nine inches of it, were covered in tell-tale white dust.

The crumbly particles of the secret passage showed up particularly strongly in contrast to the black of a nun's habit. More strongly, for example, than they had shown up on my brown coat, now lying on my bed, or on Tessa Justin's maroon uniform.

After a moment Sister Lucy followed the direction of my eyes. It was too late to avert them.

But Sister Lucy did not stop smiling. Nor did she withdraw the small round pink box.

'Why don't you take one all the same, Miss Shore?' she said pleasantly. 'It'll save trouble in the end.'

17

Trust

'You,' I said without moving.

'Yes. Me,' replied Sister Lucy. She remained as normal in her manner as before. The only moment of discomposure she had shown throughout our entire interview was at the beginning and then I suppose she was not totally sure of the situation. Where to find me. What I knew.

Casually she put her hand into her pocket and took out a knife – that same knife from the cafeteria which Sister Agnes had used to free me. She might have been a surgeon contemplating my body for an operation.

Her self-possession was now completely restored. With Tessa Justin heavily sedated – was she intended to survive? – and myself at the receiving end of what was doubtless a lethal pill, Sister Lucy had very little to worry about.

The accomplice. The intelligent female praised by Alexander Skarbek. Sister Lucy: the new infirmarian, the trusted nurse. Sister Lucy: the accomplice of the Black Nun. Someone who believed in medicines and pills and potions. Who argued with Sister Boniface and described her methods as old fashioned. Oh Sister Bonnie, with your rosaries and your penances, what injustice had been done to you! Sister Lucy who believed in science and psychiatry, whichever suited her book better at the time. Or did she believe in any of these things? In the end it seemed that she merely believed in power over others, and power was what these remedies had given her. And I had considered Mother Ancilla to be the power-mad member of the community...

'Tell me one thing, Sister'. The title sounded ironic. But I could think of no better way to address her. I didn't even know her other name. Or anything about her at all. Except that she was both a nurse and a nun. Two categories in combination that made me trust her absolutely: whereas in the past I had always been too canny to trust any nurse altogether – they're human beings like ourselves I was prone to observe; and I had certainly not trusted every nun.

'Tell me what will happen to Tessa?' I asked her.

'Nothing. Nothing at all. She'll sleep it off, just as I told you. Nightmares. Tales of Black Nuns and towers. Who will believe her, a highly strung child like that? Her parents are angry enough with her already for making herself a nuisance: they are hardly likely to listen now. Nothing will happen to her. And gradually she will forget. Especially when you yourself are no longer here to support her and feed her mind with – lies.'

'So what will happen to me?'

'Nothing. Or rather I should say: nothing more. An over-dose – how tragic, such a promising career! How sad! But of course she was hopelessly involved with a married man, wasn't she? We may even type a little note of farewell to your friend Tom Amyas – rather differently phrased from your own note, though. The death of Jemima Shore, Investigator, the television star. A headline in the evening paper. A tribute on television news. And then – all forgotten. Television is so ephemeral, Miss Shore. It's quite forgotten the next day. As you will soon be forgotten.'

I felt the depths of her hatred beneath her agreeable if slightly prim voice. I kept a watchful eye on that knife. In her own way Sister Lucy was far more frightening than Alexander Skarbek, because she was mad. He was evil, but in a horrible way within the bounds of reason. She was mad, and therefore outside them.

'Television is not always forgotten the next day. Have you quite overlooked the effect of the Powers Estate programme on Sister Miriam and Beatrice O'Dowd? We shouldn't be here now if it hadn't been for that programme.'

'That wasn't television,' cried Sister Lucy. 'That was Alexander Skarbek himself. His wonderful strength and his beliefs reached out to them ...' And so on and so on. Raving, calmly raving. With death facing me, in the shape of a small round pill box, I did not feel disposed to argue the logic of her case.

'Sister Edward?' I interrupted her. 'That was you, I suppose.'

'That was a mistake. More of an accident. He was angry about that. But she was beginning to suspect that Sister Miriam had been deliberately shut into the tower by a nun. She had seen something. She was asking questions.'

'Actually she suspected Mother Ancilla,' I pointed out. Sister Lucy did not seem noticeably regretful about the mistake.

'She was dangerous, I tell you. Sister Edward was in the infirmary when Sister Hippolytus confided to me about the secret passage and where the entrance was to be found. And I passed it on to Alexander – with everything else that happened to me in the convent. Nightly,' she said proudly. Almost with pity, I remembered Alexander Skarbek's disdain – the intolerable reminiscences of an old nun, he had termed Sister Hippo's historical revelations. And after all, he had not received them first hand. I was glad that Sister Hippo at least had not been taken in by the Black Nun. Her reputation for sharpness of character, matching that of her tongue, survived.

Then Sister Lucy added: 'If Sister Edward hadn't been such a ninny, she could have gone and found the passage for herself. As it was, she might have passed on the story at any moment. To her sister Beatrice for example.'

'You hate Beatrice O'Dowd, don't you? Why? When you both work for the same cause. The same man.'

'The same man! Beatrice O'Dowd doesn't even *know* the Alexander Skarbek that I know. Any more than those stupid Sixth Form girls knew him. Margaret and Dodo and Blanche and Imogen – he used them all. How exciting they found it: a man dressed up as a nun roaming the convent ... so perfect for their adolescent fantasies wasn't it?' And how was it for yours, Sister Lucy, I wanted to ask, but she was continuing in the same vein: 'Playing up the legend of the Black Nun for all they were worth. Believing they were in on the secret. But they never knew the truth about him. They weren't in the *real* secret at all. Any more than Beatrice O'Dowd was. Beatrice O'Dowd is a foolish spinster who wants to do good in the world.' She made it sound the most ridiculous objective. 'What could she know of the delights, the visions, the travels of the mind and spirit which we two have experienced?'

I thought: Alexander Skarbek. He had succeeded in corrupting Sister Lucy. But the innocent he had tried to corrupt and failed. In their own way Beatrice O'Dowd and Rosabelle Powerstock had held him off by innocence. Margaret and Dodo were still innocent because they were young: long might that innocence last and protect them. Particularly Margaret. But Margaret was clever. After all, her reserve did not conceal a lack of balance. 'More interesting,' Skarbek had said. 'More like you.' All that meant was Margaret would probably end up working for someone like Tom: her resemblance to the dedicated Emily Crispin still tantalised me. I was glad that I too had held him off, although in my case it was knowledge not innocence which had protected me from corruption.

Sister Lucy was visibly controlling herself after her outburst. The surgeon's knife had begun to shake. The knife stopped shaking. Finally she succeeded in presenting to me once again that pleasing visage which, in spite of everything, I still associated with her.

She rattled the pill box gently.

'So now, Miss Shore, why don't you take one of these?'

She stood between me and the door. I was sitting down. Even a maniac armed with a knife could not, I fancied, force me to swallow a pill. At which moment Sister Lucy bent forward, grabbed my throat in a grip of extraordinary strength, and pushed me viciously backwards. She had dropped the knife. As I flailed about feeling for the knife, I felt the pill being placed roughly on my tongue. She fastened my jaw with one hand. At the same moment my nostrils were grasped and pinched so that I could not breathe. The temptation to swallow was ghastly —

The loud noise of the bell startled us both. A nun's bell quite close. One loud clamour. Then silence. Then another toll.

'My bell,' said Sister Lucy automatically. Two bells for the infirmarian. The slight release in pressure gave me my chance. I spat the pill out into my hand, and then threw it to the floor. Whatever it was, I wanted it to be no nearer to me than I could help.

'Mother Ancilla! Sister Boniface must be looking for me.'

'On the contrary it is I who am looking for you, Sister Lucy,' said a gentle voice. 'That's why I sounded your bell.' We both turned round. It was Sister Agnes who stood there, in the doorway, eyes level and steady as ever. She had a large bell in one hand. And a small pistol in the other. She really was making a habit of rescuing me. One of these days I should really have to do something for her.

'Do be careful, Miss Shore.' Sister Agnes was as ever polite. 'This pistol is bound to be loaded. I have just persuaded Mr Skarbek to hand it over to me. And I don't think he is the sort of gentleman to carry an unloaded gun around with him, do you?'

'Where is he?' asked Sister Lucy hoarsely. 'Where is Alexander?'

'He's in the car, under the trees, Sister. In the Mini-Traveller. He's waiting for you. Don't you think you should join him?'

'My car!'

'The car you brought with you when you joined the community,' Sister Agnes corrected her. 'The community's car!'

Sister Lucy looked uncertain. But she did not look nearly so uncertain as I felt. I could not believe my ears. Unless Sister Agnes was also in the plot, it made no sense to allow Skarbek and Sister Lucy to make their escape like this. In their different ways, they were two dangerous people: too dangerous to be set at liberty as if nothing had happened.

Sister Agnes still had her mesmeric effect on me. And she hypnotised Sister Lucy too, or else it was the gun. The infirmarian walked towards her as in a dream, and still in the same state turned towards the visitors' staircase. The outside door was unlocked. She walked through it. The last we saw of Sister Lucy was her black habit in the light thrown from the porch, passing towards the drive.

We could not see her face. She might have been anyone. Any nun, that is.

'Why, why, Sister Agnes?' I burst out. 'Why let them go? You're as crazy as they are.'

'He's changed back into his own clothes.' Sister Agnes did not answer my question. 'I'm glad of that. I found them in the sacristy, hidden under the priest's robes for tomorrow's mass. The insolence of it: his jersey and anorak beneath the vestments embroidered by Sister Perpetua to celebrate her twenty-five years in religion.' Sister Agnes, I noticed, was too delicate even to mention the subject of his trousers in the same breath as a priest's vestments.

Then she put her hand on my arm.

'What could I do, Miss Shore? Think about it. The convent in uproar, our work all undone. Mother Ancilla is dying. We don't want her to die like this, do we, with the good name of the Blessed Eleanor dragged through the newspapers? We went through it once with Sister Miriam, and

Mother Ancilla suffered so much. What would our foundress have thought?'

Oh these nuns! Their unworldliness. The good name of the convent; had she no sense of reality at all?

'He had a gun! I know you took it away. But he's still dangerous.'

'Oh this,' said Sister Agnes, looking down at the pistol in her hand. Casually she gave it a little click. Nothing happened. 'No, this wasn't Mr Skarbek's. He didn't as far as I know carry a gun. Not the type. Preferring his own methods.' She wrinkled her nose and did not enlarge on the subject. 'No, this comes from the children's acting cupboard. We did *Murder on the Nile* last term: Agatha Christie. Really delightful – you would have enjoyed it. We needed a gun for that. I didn't think Sister Lucy would notice the difference, with the state she was in. All those pills she was always taking.'

'You're quite an actress,' was all I could think of saying.

'I was an actress once: I told you,' replied Sister Agnes with a smile. 'Not a very good one. Then I became a nun.'

'You're quite a nun, then.'

'Thank you, Miss Shore. Now that is a compliment I really value. Even though I know myself to be unworthy of it.'

Sister Agnes cast down her eyes with a modesty wholly worthy of the Murillo I had once fancied she resembled. It had been a foolish notion. Or rather Sister Agnes's appearance might be that of a Murillo, but her spirit was made of sterner stuff. Another Spanish painter, Goya, would have made a better job of Sister Agnes.

Sister Agnes bent down and picked up the knife which Sister Lucy had abandoned. 'I must give that back to Sister Clare first thing in the morning,' she said. It was evident that her sense of order was outraged by the presence of the knife so far outside its natural habitat of the cafeteria.

She was indeed quite a nun. If not so quiet as the poet Wordsworth and her own demeanour would have one believe.

The suspicions of Sister Agnes had, ironically enough, first been aroused by the prevalent nightmares of Tessa Justin. I did not know what the future might hold for that young lady: but on the form of her first ten years, I could hardly believe she would lead a trouble-free life. The attitude of Sister Lucy to these nightmares had struck Sister Agnes as strange. Sister Agnes herself was the object of Tessa's childish adoration. Like Sister Boniface, she considered Tessa to be an exhibitionist —

'But Our Lord teaches us to be especially loving to such children, does He not? The little children in the Bible who crowded round Him, whom He suffered to come unto Him, were they not exhibitionists in their own way? Asking for His love?'

As usual, Sister Agnes was probably right.

But she did not think of Tessa as being a liar. Meanwhile the evidence of her own senses began to tell Sister Agnes that someone unlawful was prowling about the convent at night. The whisk of a black skirt round a corner where skirt there should be none. The sight of a nun, seen from the back, vanishing in the top corridor. The noise of someone apparently inhabiting the empty guest rooms. A bathroom strangely occupied and then empty. Above all, a sense of a mysterious presence in and around the chapel. She began to watch.

'Your novena then — that first night in the chapel? That was a cover-up, a pretence?'

'Certainly not, Miss Shore.' Sister Agnes sounded quite shocked. 'I would never pretend to make a novena. Our Lord would never forgive me. Besides, I had a great deal to pray about, didn't I?'

It was Sister Agnes's growing awareness that a member of the community was involved in the mystery which had led her to try and warn me off on the occasion of our interview. Sister Agnes was as ever discreet in her mode of expression, but she made me understand that the presence of Jemima Shore, Investigator, within Blessed Eleanor's had constituted yet another problem – to put it at its mildest. She murmured something about the standards of television not being entirely those of the convent. I quite understood the point she was trying to make.

As for Sister Lucy – so many little suspicious things, from her movements and unaccountable absences at night, to the fact that Tessa's running-away note had been clearly typed on the dispensary typewriter used by Sister Lucy to write up her medical notes.

'She was not with us very long,' said Sister Agnes, compressing her lips in a manner once more reminiscent of Mother Ancilla. 'And Sister Boniface was never satisfied about the nature of Sister Lucy's vocation. Sister Boniface may be old, but here at Blessed Eleanor's we pay a great deal of attention to the views of the older members of the community. There will be changes here of course when Mother Ancilla dies.' Again that matter-of-factness about the inevitability of death. 'But in all these changes I can assure you that the wishes of those who understand our traditions will be consulted. And respected. Changes must be in accordance with the will of God. And some of our older members are very close to Him now after a lifetime of prayer and devotion.'

In spite of the extraordinary circumstances of our conversation, I felt that I was listening to some kind of manifesto for the future. I remembered the occasion when Sister Agnes had sought gently to dissuade me from entering the infirmary. Sister Agnes might not be a senior member of the community, but she too had never been quite persuaded of the strength of Sister Lucy's vocation.

'But you're not going to let them go?' I groaned. 'Forgiveness of your enemies is all very well, but the man is dangerous, and a murderer. While Sister Lucy is insane and probably a murderess as well. She certainly intended to kill Sister Edward even if in the end her death was an accident.'

'There is no question of forgiveness, Miss Shore,' said Sister Agnes, opening her dark eyes wide. 'Forgiveness is for

Almighty God, who sees into every heart, not for us. I simply did the best I could at the time. Getting them both out of the convent precincts. Finding Mr Skarbek in the sacristy, I recognised him without difficulty—we watched the repeat of your programme last night with the Juniors—very instructive by the way, although I'm not sure I agree with all your conclusions. He had no idea of what I knew. I merely suggested that he should leave the convent instantly. As an unlawful intruder. Otherwise I threatened to summon the police. Finally I told him I would send our infirmarian down to him, Sister Lucy, as he was obviously sick, breaking in like that to a convent. And he'd better wait for her in the community car parked under the trees. And she would drive him back to the village. And get him some attention.'

'But, Sister Agnes, he was dressed up as a nun,' I cried.

'Exactly. That helped to convince him. I said: "You must be sick in your mind to do such a thing." I suggested it, and he didn't disagree. Besides only his—er—body was dressed in the habit. His head was clearly visible. I simply pointed to his own garments and said, "Those are your clothes I believe. Please resume them," and I left the sacristy.'

It was difficult to believe that Sister Agnes had been all that bad an actress.

'All the same we'll have to summon the police in the morning.'

'As to that, we must trust in God, Miss Shore,' said Sister Agnes, sounding weary for the first time. 'He will dispose of it all. We must trust Him.'

Another appalling thought struck me.

'But the will, Sister Agnes. Do you realise that Sister Miriam's second will leaves all the property to the Powers Project? Even if Skarbek is nailed, the property will still go to the Project. There is nothing wrong with the Project itself: the rest of them are perfectly honest people, if somewhat extreme in their views about society. It will all be quite legal. You will be turned out, dispossessed. The workers' commune up to your front door. Your work here will end just the same.'

'The second will of Sister Miriam isn't yet found, is it, Miss Shore? Until it is discovered, her original will leaving everything to the community still stands.'

'But it will be found. Believe me, it will be found.'

I hadn't the heart to tell her that I now knew exactly where to find it.

'Then it will be found. We must still put our faith in Almighty God, Miss Shore,' said Sister Agnes. 'What else can we do?'

18

Into the future

But in the event it was not necessary to summon the police. Very early the next day the police came of their own accord to the Convent of the Blessed Eleanor. They roused a sleepy Sister Damian, and asked to see the Reverend Mother. Since that was not possible, she being far too weak, it was finally to Sister Boniface, supported by Sister Elizabeth and myself, that they broke the news of the fatal car crash on Church Hill in the early hours of the morning.

A dark night, a sharp bend on a steep hill taken too fast: it was what Alexander Skarbek would have called, for once with proper accuracy, a natural – if unfortunate – accident.

There were two passengers, both killed instantly. The police were sorry to disturb the Sisters of Blessed Eleanor's so early in the day, but the car was registered in the name of the convent. Furthermore they had to break it to Sister Boniface that one of the two dead people was a nun. Had been a nun.

'It seems that the nun was actually driving,' said the senior policeman with a sympathetic clearing of the throat.

'People always say that nuns are such bad drivers,' commented Sister Elizabeth sadly. 'Trusting in God to protect them, instead of looking at the road. And it isn't true at all.

But Sister Lucy really was a bad driver. Then of course she hadn't been a nun very long.'

There were tears in Sister Elizabeth's eyes. After a moment she began to quote Wordsworth to herself.

'There is a comfort in the strength of love;
'T will make a thing endurable, which else
Would overset the brain, or break the heart ...'

It wasn't clear to me to which love she was alluding, the love of God, or the love of Sister Lucy for Alexander Skarbek.

When Sister Elizabeth had finished, Sister Boniface said robustly: 'Sister Lucy didn't trust in God enough.'

The policeman said: 'The driver certainly didn't look at the road.'

I thought of Sister Agnes. No doubt she would always believe that it was Almighty God who had thus conveniently disposed of Sister Lucy and Alexander Skarbek. But I did not want to think like that. To me, it was a natural accident—natural, and on reflection, fortunate. Fortunate, for everyone. Even the dead.

We were sitting in the Nuns' Parlour by the front door, the police and myself having been fortified by the coffee, delicious and hot, which even at this early hour Sister Clare had managed to produce.

I waited till the police had withdrawn and the nuns too had gone away to begin the endless sad process of untangling and sorting out all the mischiefs which had recently taken place in their unquiet convent.

Alone in the Nuns' Parlour, I too had a sad task to perform. Putting the brides of Christ out of my mind, I went over to the polished table on which lay the portfolio of wedding photographs of successfully paired-off old girls. The art of Lenare and Yevonde, Bassano and Vandyk, and the few more recent examples, had spilled out onto the table. I put my hand inside the portfolio and felt another thinner piece of paper amongst the pasteboard. I drew it out: it was an envelope.

On the envelope was written: 'This is the very last will and testament of Sister Miriam.' I recognised the handwriting – Rosa's own. Even in her anguish, it had really not changed much since we were at school together. Here among the brides, the brides not of Christ but of wealthy stockbrokers and poor Irish doctors and foreign princes and struggling Catholic lawyers and all other types of happy Catholic grooms, the will of Rosabelle Powerstock had lain safely hidden.

It was instinct which made me now seek out the chapel. Above all I had to be at peace. There at least would be repose and silence. There would be no more prying ghosts to disturb its ornate tranquillity.

Once in the chapel I sat down in the pew nearest to the statue of the Sacred Heart. The heart, my symbol. That pew in which I had first encountered Sister Agnes keeping her watch, and saying her novena at the same time. The candles, a little forest of them this morning, flickered. It was in their light, close by the shrine, that I read the last message from my friend:

'I, Rosabelle Powerstock, known as Sister Miriam of the Order of the Tower of Ivory, being in sound mind in spite of everything that has happened to me, do hereby revoke all other wills. In the confusion in which I find myself, I have prayed to God and His saints and to Our Blessed Lady to guide me.

'I wished to place my property in the hands of the poor, in accordance with the message of Our Saviour Lord Jesus Christ. Yet recently I have been aware that I have not yet found the right hands in which to place it. There are pressures all round me, within myself and without. I no longer know what is the right decision to make. It must therefore be for others, who have always been so much stronger than I, to decide.

'I therefore leave the lands surrounding the Convent of the Blessed Eleanor, in their entirety, to Jemima Shore. She will know what to do with them. Everything else I leave, as before, to the community of the Tower of Ivory, of which I die, as I have tried to live, a faithful member.'

It was signed: Rosabelle Powerstock, and in brackets: Miriam. A.M.D.G. The will was witnessed at the bottom of the paper by Blanche Nelligan and Imogen Smith.

I sat for a long time holding this piece of paper between my fingers. I thought of many things. Of the past: Rosa. A friendship from which I had taken so much, yet had abandoned. And forgotten. For Rosa a friendship which had marked her whole life; even seeing me on television in some shallow programme, calling for social reform from the security of my own detached position, had been enough to make her try and sell all that she had, and give it to the poor. A friendship which had in the end unwittingly brought about her death. A friendship founded on trust which had not failed even in her last hours when she was confident that her old friend would perform the labours which she no longer had the strength to carry out.

Of the future: the future of this convent robbed of its lands. But maybe the women within it would be released from their incarceration, find themselves playing a more valuable role in society ... Of my own future: establishing a great settlement for the poor perhaps, helped by Tom, supported by the W.N.G. As Rosa had wanted. As Tom would want.

I thought of the present: of Mother Ancilla, dying in her bare cell upstairs.

After a bit I stretched out my piece of paper towards the shrine of the Sacred Heart and lit the corner of the will from a candle. It flared up. I felt a momentary scorch on my fingers, and then I dropped it. I felt nothing else at all.

I rose up from my pew to find Sister Agnes standing at the side door watching me. She had made one of her noiseless entrances.

'You were right to put your trust in God, Sister Agnes,' I said. 'There will be no further changes at the convent of the Blessed Eleanor.'

'Oh we shall have changes, Miss Shore,' replied Sister

Agnes. 'But we shall decide on them together. I should tell you that Reverend Mother has just given me her dying voice as the new superior. My first action will be to have the choice confirmed by an election within the community. Even the lay nuns will be given votes. It will be an open contest.'

I believed her. But somehow I felt Sister Agnes would be elected all the same.

There was nothing more for me to do here now. I asked if I could see Mother Ancilla before I went back to London. She was very weak and cruelly white, but perfectly composed. Sister Boniface was looking after her, under the doctor's orders: even at her age Sister Boniface did not seem displeased to have come out of her retirement as infirmarian.

I clasped the hand which had so often taken mine in its warm grasp: it felt very cold. A crucifix above the bed was the sole decoration in the cell. The air here was chilly, not warm as the children's wing always was.

'Mother Ancilla,' I said. 'You knew, didn't you? You knew about the will.'

'Oh no, my child, I knew nothing. I only suspected. She loved you so much. She had such confidence in you. Your judgement. Jemima's so brilliant, she used to say. And she used to ask special permission to watch television on the nights you appeared. She admired you so much. As did we all, of course, dear Jemima. When no will was found, and she seemed so unhappy, so confused, I thought she might have done something like that.'

Mother Ancilla took a sip of water. I helped her.

'But of course I couldn't be sure. And I didn't know where the will was. If I had known, I should certainly have produced it. We nuns are a very law-abiding lot, you know.'

I let that pass. 'But that's why you sent for me? Tell me now.'

'Perhaps. If she had left you the property, then it was in my mind that you might get to know us all over again. And you would understand about our work. And see that it is worth preserving. And you did, my child, didn't you?' Sister Agnes had told her.

I shook my head.

'It wasn't for that. It's because you were good. And he was evil.'

Mother Ancilla smiled.

'How simple, Jemima. Good and bad. Good and evil. How do we know? Our Blessed Lord knows but we don't. We just have to be sure that we are doing the work that God wants us to do on this earth.'

There was a long silence. She raised herself a little on her pillows.

'Now it is my turn to ask you a question, Jemima. One day, do you think that you might ever—'

'No, Mother, never.' Very firmly. 'I'm sorry. Faith is a gift, they say. If so, I haven't been given it.'

'But you want to believe, I know it, I feel it.'

'No'—gently. After all she was a dying woman. Even so I had to speak the truth. Another silence. Then—

'My child, do you wish you believed?'

And then some ugly honesty took over, the honesty I could never defeat, part of me. Against my will, hating myself, for a moment even hating her, I said with absolute truth:

'Yes, Mother, I do wish I believed.'

Mother Ancilla smiled. A seraphic child's smile.

'Well then, it's simple, isn't it? Our Blessed Lord will see to it, won't He?'

I shook my head. It wasn't as simple as that. It was nothing. I just couldn't help telling the truth. It was nothing to do with anything.

'He'll see to it that you receive the gift of faith. Or I'll get after Him.' Mother Ancilla's voice was fading away.

After a bit a nun, Sister Damian I think, came and tapped me on the shoulder and said: 'You must go now, Miss Shore.'

I got up quietly and took a last look at Mother Ancilla before I left her—forever, as I knew it would be. She was still smiling, faintly, victoriously. She would sort it out with

Our Blessed Lord. She had promised to get me the gift of faith. I felt quite sorry for Him – if He existed.

I drove back to London and repossessed myself of my empty flat. I flipped through my mail, which Cherry had left in neat piles as befitted the perfect secretary. Included among it was an official letter from Megalith Television congratulating me on the success of my repeats, especially the Powers Estate programme ('Into the top ten ratings'). It was signed by Cy Fredericks. At the bottom he had scrawled: 'Well done. The Gem of my collection.' It was an old reference. The letter also suggested a whole new series under the general title Into the Future. I tossed it aside: unlike the past, the future did not strike me as being particularly urgent.

I left a message for Tom at the House of Commons to say that I was back in London and would he ring me? My lucky dress with its motif of hearts was hanging ready in the cupboard. I picked up the *Evening Standard* and began to read it. Sometimes when I'm low and waiting for a call I read the *Evening Standard* cover to cover as though for an examination. But on this occasion I threw the paper on the floor, after the Megalith letter. I decided to go for a walk.

It was a beautiful evening. And I wanted to be calm and free. It didn't worry me at all that I should be out when Tom called.

If you enjoyed this Jemima Shore mystery, you'll enjoy her next outing in THE CAVALIER CASE, which Bantam will publish in hardcover in February 1991.

The Portrait

Two things happened on the night of twelfth of July, both of them important to the Cavalier Case (as it was later known). An old man fell down some stairs in a large house in Taynfordshire and broke his neck. And in London, sitting at her desk at Megalith Television, Jemima Shore Investigator fell in love.

Since the object of Jemima's passion was a person in a portrait who had been dead for well over three hundred years and the old man who stumbled down the stairs to his death was seventy-seven years old, half-blind and fond of his late-night whisky, it could scarcely have been expected that this conjunction of events would lead in time to that thrilling mixture of sex, violence and the supernatural, snobbery, historical romance and even sport which went under the general name of the Cavalier Case. It is true that there was one obvious connection between the two events. The person in the portrait, Decimus Meredith, 1st Viscount Lackland, poet and Cavalier, mortally wounded in the Battle of Taynford in 1645, was the direct ancestor of the old man who died thus accidentally if not unexpectedly.

But Thomas Antony Decimus Meredith, 17th Viscount Lackland, had led a career in direct contrast to that of his famous forebear. Decent obscurity might be a way of summing it up, beyond the fact he still lived at Lackland Court, the poet's house. There had been a respectable war record which far from ending in a hero's death had merely formed the prelude to the long quiet life of a country landowner; no poetry in sight (except the works of his famous ancestor reverently enshrined in the library) and certainly none composed. No, surely no-one could have foreseen the chain of events which would link the passion of Jemima Shore to the death of old Tommy Lackland, bringing a chain of destruction in its wake.

Of course there was another way of looking at it. Since the career of the new Lord Lackland—previously known as Handsome Dan Meredith—had been marked by a certain romantic turbulence, it was hardly to be expected that his inheritance of his cousin's title would prove to be utterly peaceful. What with Handsome Dan's two wives, Babs and Charlotte . . . his numerous girlfriends, last but not least Alix . . . Then there was the Meredith family, Zena, the three little ones, poor Nell, and in quite a different sense, poor Marcus. But as Jemima Shore sat moodily in her Megalith office gazing yet again at the portrait of Decimus Lackland, Handsome Dan himself was quite unknown to her, beyond a name cursorily encountered in the newspapers in the past. There was after all no reason why their paths should have crossed. And without the fortuitous appearance of the Lackland portrait (combined with one of Cy Fredericks' notorious "seminals") they would presumably never have done so. Once again the world would have been the poorer—or at least less colourful for the lack of the Cavalier Case.

The portrait of Decimus Lackland was propped up opposite Jemima's desk. It was in fact a large oil painting: over five foot high. The background was mainly dark, although some kind of pillar could be discerned and a heavy swag of rich reddish material—taffeta perhaps—encompassing it, with a snatch of obscure country landscape beyond. The light fell mainly upon the face and the high pointed white lace collar, falling over the further darkness of the armour. In the poet's face, as in the picture, darkness was set against light: the pale oval contrasted with almond-shaped black eyes, the dark fringe and the flowing lovelocks of the Cavalier. To Jemima, the face itself seemed to rise above the armour and transcend it as though at once disdaining the arts of war, and ennobling them by its participation.

There was a further patch of light on the splayed white hand with its long—perhaps disproportionately long—fingers; it rested on the head of an enormous dog—a hound? a mastiff? Jemima was not good on dogs. A few words were sketched in spidery gold in the corner of the picture: although Jemima could hardly make them out herself, she had learned from the back of the portrait (which confidently proclaimed it on a faded typed label to be "by Sir Anthony Van Dyck") that the legend read: AMOR ET HONOR.

Love and honour: a good if enigmatic motto, perhaps all the more good because it was so enigmatic. Jemima sighed. Love . . . It had to be said that her private life at the present time was fairly lovely without being exactly what you would call honourable (having been exactly the reverse for nearly a year); it was also just slightly claustrophobic, hence perhaps this sudden passion for the romantically unattainable Decimus Lackland. For only recently Cass Brinsley had come back into her life, his marriage on-the-rebound-from-Jemima having broken up with the same startling suddenness as it had begun. Jemima herself still did not fully understand the reasons. All she knew was that Cass was back, and since she was too much of a lady—well, most of the time anyway—to express sentiments like "I told you so," the situation between them seemed outwardly remarkably unchanged.

That is to say, she still found Cass fantastically attractive and probably always would, fascinated by the formality of the lawyer's demeanour in public combined with something much less controlled in private. It was also true that their first sweet reconciliation when he actually spoke the words she had longed to hear: "I was mad . . . how could I ever forget you . . . never for one minute *did* I forget you . . .," had lasted sexually speaking all one evening, then all one night, then most of two days of a lost weekend. There was no doubt that reconciliation (its own silent revenge on the younger rival who had dared to marry her Cass when she, Jemima, had persistently declined to do so) was a sweet process when it involved sex.

All the same . . . The trouble was that after that, a long time after that, but a moment that would still inexorably arrive, Jemima was still Jemima, she who did not want to marry Cass or anyone else come to think of it, someone who pleased herself and in doing so liked to please others. As and when she chose. Freely and in freedom. In short, once again not settling-down material. Whereas Cass, she had an awful feeling, was so keen to settle down that he would run through several marriages in an attempt to do so. "I thought it was *women* who were supposed to long to get married," he had exclaimed with mock bitterness only last night.

Jemima gazed into the slanting dark eyes of Decimus Lackland and sighed. Love and Honour. Had he found love within marriage immediately? She knew that he had been married off to the famous Olivia of the "Swan" poems when he was a mere sixteen and she fourteen. Presumably love itself, the love celebrated in his poetry, had come later, and the marriage itself had been founded on the seventeenth-century concept of honour: worldly honour in the shape of money, since Olivia Lackland had been an orphan and the heiress to Lackland Court in her own right. Do I perhaps need an arranged marriage? pondered Jemima gloomily. After all who ever really married for love in any century? Cass, had he really married for sudden overwhelming love of the young and charming Flora Hereford (as Flora Hereford herself presumably believed)? Or had he married because Jemima Shore would not say yes to him—nor no, for that matter—and to marry Flora was the most hurtfully decisive thing he could do under the circumstances?

Another sigh. In her present mood, how much easier to fall in love with a portrait who demanded no commitment, than with a real live man, determined, in that dreadful phrase, to "settle down"! (Why *down,* for God's sake? The mere word gave the game away.) In her present mood, it was particularly easy to fall in love with the man who had written to a woman that poem every schoolchild learned, but was in fact far more explicitly sensual than one realised at the time; "I fain would be thy swan . . ."

The portrait had arrived two days before as a result of a cri-de-coeur from Jemima's friend from Cambridge days, the brilliant, engaging—and disorganised—Dr. Rupert Durham. Since Jemima, like all Rupert's friends, was accustomed since Cambridge to do far more onerous things for him than merely housing a portrait, she was delighted to be able to assist him so easily. It turned out that Rupert Durham had been bequeathed the portrait by the nonagenarian widow of a former President of his old college. (She had fallen a victim to his famous charm at a college dinner intended in theory to raise funds for the college, not a portrait for Rupert.)

As ever with Rupert Durham, questions of scholarship—art scholarship in this case—came first. In fact he had spent some time digressing on the National Portrait Gallery's own fine recently acquired Van Dyck portrait of the poet and what he called "the whole ridiculous early Lely red herring" before Jemima had actually realised what she had been asked to do. Which was to give Decimus Lackland house room, as it were, until Rupert managed to uncover just one portion of a wall either in his large book-filled rooms at Cambridge, or, even less likely, in his room off Ladbroke Grove. Here he had moved "temporarily," without unpacking anything except books, about five years ago after being thrown out for the third and final time by Jemima's friend Becky Robertson. ("The trouble with Rupert," Becky had told Jemima rather wearily on the telephone, "is that he may have a first-class mind, but his famous intellectual powers apparently do not extend to concentrating on one woman at a time. I mean, since when was absent-mindedness a plausible excuse for large-scale infidelity?")

As a cat-lover, Jemima did occasionally cat-sit for friends (one of these episodes—in a flat in Bloomsbury—had resulted in one of her more harrowing investigations a few years back★). She also occasionally allowed visiting cats who belonged to really good friends, although the air of injured betrayal with which her own cat, the proud and independent-minded Midnight, greeted these intrusions, was hard to bear; Jemima also suspected that in cat-terms he might be right— it *was* the ultimate betrayal to allow another cat on his territory. Altogether, housing a portrait would be much less trouble, reflected Jemima innocently, having no hint of the upheavals, beyond anything within the compass of the most devilish cat, which this elegant ikon would bring into her life.

Jemima's reverie was interrupted by an inordinately long blast on her buzzer. Even before she picked up the instrument, she knew that the caller must be Megalith's Chairman. She also knew that she had only a brief moment to answer before Cy Fredericks' busy fingers passed on in an increasing frenzy to other buttons . . .

"Jem, my gem," Cy was indeed saying in great agitation into her ear. "Where *are* you?" But before Jemima could answer, reasonable enough, "Right here in my office, just where do you expect?" she was cut off, and a noise of infuriated buzzing began to spread audibly through the other offices. With a last sigh—

★Related in *A Splash of Red*.

Decimus Lackland with his romantic looks must be temporarily put aside—Jemima performed the necessary ritual for acknowledging Cy's call by buzzing in her turn his secretary, the estimable Miss Lewis.

"What's it all about?" Jemima asked casually when she had established that she was sitting quietly in her office, and expected a second call from Cy in about ten minutes' time when he had explored all the other possibilities (including the messenger's room and the gentlemen's cloakroom). Miss Lewis and Jemima were old allies; both believed ardently, where Cy was concerned, in the principle that forewarned was forearmed.

"A ghost, I think. Cy wants you to interview a ghost," replied Miss Lewis with equal casualness. Being a loyal ally did not preclude her from occasional throwaway lines like this.

"Of course, what else?" murmured Jemima easily, wondering whether she would after all warn Miss Lewis that she had heard Cy inviting both Jane Manfred and Baby Diamondson to visit India with him in the autumn at a party the night before. The problem was not being not so much that both had accepted, but that Jane Manfred was married to Baby Diamondson's first husband, a fact Cy might have overlooked at the time but the ladies concerned would certainly not, throughout a three-week trip.

All the same, she was grateful that she had had at least some warning, when she found herself sitting in Cy's baroque office and listening to his excited disquisition on the general nature of ghosts.

"So you see, Jemima," he was saying, "it really would make a seminal programme." Experience had taught Jemima not only to beware the word "seminal" on Cy's lips, but also that Cy's notion of a "seminal programme" differed widely from the meaning generally attached to the word.

All the same: "Tell me more, Cy." That seemed the most circumspect thing to reply under the circumstances. Especially since Cy was certainly going to call her more in any case. Why this sudden interest in ghosts, she wondered? There had to be a lady—probably two ladies, knowing Cy—at the bottom of it all; as in a murder mystery, once she knew who, she might know why. And what to do about it. If some passing fancy was responsible, then she might by delaying—and if Miss Lewis was in a cooperative mood—sit the whole thing out, and avoid altogether the big series Cy was now busily outlining. But if someone serious was involved—Jane Manfred for example—then quite different tactics had to be employed, an altogether longer and subtler battle might have to be fought—a battle which would not necessarily be won by Jemima.

"Lady Manfred has seen a ghost." Under the circumstances these words, announced by Cy with much gravity as though Lady Manfred had left her husband—hardly likely owing to the totally delightful relationship both complaisant and complacent which existed between them—were to Jemima's ears doom-laden. Before Jemima had decided quite how to deal with this extremely threatening situation, Cy proceeded as though she had actually contradicted him. "No, you must understand, Jemima, this was a . . ." He looked round and ended triumphantly as though using the word for the first time: "A seminal experience."

There was nothing for it but to bide her time in patience. And as a matter of fact what Cy had to relate was not without a certain touching quality. For the ghost Lady Manfred had so surprisingly seen, was, it transpired, her *own* ghost; no, not her own ghost in that sense, how could she see her own ghost, queried Cy in slight irritation.

"Her *doppelgänger,* maybe?" References to Cy's own culture—he undoubtedly knew or had once known about the romantic theory of the *doppelgänger*—could sometimes waylay him for hours. On this occasion it was not to be.

"Her *own* ghost! The ghost she had bought, acquired, acquired with the house, the ghost of Taynford

Grange," explained Cy. "You see, my dear Jem, up till a short while ago, Jane Manfred, the most charming woman, I must really bring her into your life."—Jemima thought it tactless to mention the innumerable times Cy had already brought Lady Manfred into her life—"Up till now poor Jane has not *seen* the Taynford ghost, despite the absolutely enormous price Max paid for that house, and a house in the country too." Cy shuddered metaphorically. He was not fond of the country, to put it mildly, considering even Saturday dinner and Sunday breakfast in a stone-built Cotswold palace like Taynford Grange an exaggerated demonstration of his friendship.

"At first there was some thought that perhaps, change of ownership," Cy continued, "the original family, the—what were they called? The family had certainly been there since Charlemagne." He paused, wondering momentarily if he had the right country, right history, then proceeded, "yet Jane felt, indeed had complete confidence, that the ghost would soon *settle down*."

"And it didn't?" prompted Jemima. (That word again: she felt some sympathy for the ghost.)

"It did not. Then there was some thought that perhaps the builders, or more to the point the decorators, or more to the point still, the decorator, might have upset him. As Jane said—she's so amusing, Jem, you two share a sense of humour, as I hope you will soon discover—as Jane said, 'I know that Gawain is a brilliant decorator, there is John Steff, I suppose, if he wasn't so tied up at Oare, still Gawain is brilliant, incredibly creative, but I'm not sure I'd come back from the next world to see him.' Jane Manfred, as quoted by Cy, was referring to a famous decorator, known fondly to his friends as the Green Knight, and by those not privileged to enjoy his friendship as the Green Nightmare.

"It seems that Gawain plans to build a conservatory on the north side of the house, which needs excavation. And that might have unsettled our ghost. Very daring, said Jane, but he's currently interested in the northern challenge. Gawain of course, not the ghost. What challenge would that be, Jem?" enquired Cy, without clearly having any interest in the answer. He was back to the ghost and Lady Manfred.

"And now at last she's seen it!" Cy concluded happily. "And she feels accepted at last. And that, my dear Jemima, is how our series has been born. A series of ghosts and their owners, Jem, beginning with Lady Manfred. Taynford, such a beautiful house, she's promised, she'll see to it that Max agrees. Ghosts—and what they tell us about our time and ourselves; ghosts, who sees them, who doesn't, a new form of who's in, who's out, if you like, don't let *Taffeta* get hold of that one, don't breathe a word; ghosts, how they have influenced history, ghosts, how does history influence them . . . ," Cy rattled away.

"It could be seminal," he concluded. And this time Jemima knew she was finally lost. She had one last weapon on her side, or thought she had: that programme about social attitudes to birth control among the women of Afghanistan as influenced by the Russian occupation—which meant three months' research and filming away from everything, including Cy, Jane Manfred and sundry ghosts; but it also meant three months away from Cass. It was easy, in certain moods, to underplay the sweetness of their reconciliation; and hadn't it been that selfsame kind of programme about child-brides in Sri Lanka, her prolonged incommunicado absence, which had caused him to engage in his precipitate marriage in the first place?

So: "What kind of ghost, Cy?" asked Jemima.

"A romantic ghost," Cy pronounced with great benevolence. For Cy, too, knew that Jemima was lost; vague as he might be about many things such as the challenge of north-facing conservatories, Cy had not built up Megalith Television to its present eminence without being at once feline and ruthless when necessary. What Jemima did not know, for example, was that he had only this morning lured her arch-rival Serenity

Saville away from Titan TV, with the offer of just that programme about Afghanistan. And, Serenity, a girl with the face of a Madonna, known for some reason as "the S.S. trooper" to her colleagues, had accepted.

"You'll enjoy it all, my Jem," Cy, secure in this knowledge, was promising. "A romantic ghost: a Cavalier, a handsome soldier from the Civil War, long hair, soulful expression, Jane Manfred said. A bit like a violinist, except of course he was in armour. But she will tell you the full history of it all."

For a moment Jemima's heart had given an uncomfortable lurch. Armour, long hair, soulful expression . . . could it be, no, impossible. Besides, if Decimus Lackland's ghost walked anywhere, it walked presumably at Lackland Court . . . Wait a moment, *wasn't* there a ghost? Wasn't there something rather odd in one of Rupert Durham's books about the ghost of Decimus Lackland? A historical reference? That must be it.

The ghost of Decimus Lackland . . . her mind pursued this train of thought while she continued to smile at Cy with an angelic expression worthy of the S.S. trooper herself. Now *that* was a ghost worth investigating. Wait a moment . . .

"I'm sure I shall enjoy it all, Cy," Jemina said in her sweetest voice; in fact so sweet was it, that Cy shot a sudden look of suspicion. Docility in Jemima was rare, and in Cy's opinion, generally the prelude to some devious act. Even when their relationship had been a great deal more intimate than it was now—years back an episode never referred to but in fact the foundation of a warm relationship—docile was never a word which Cy would have applied to Jemima. Then the telephone rang on Cy's private line, and Miss Lewis buzzed him on the intercom at one and the same moment. They were both saved.

At almost exactly the same time as Jemima was vowing herself enchanted at the prospect of a whole series on the subject of "Ghosts and Ourselves"—the working title—the new Lord Lackland, a.k.a. Handsome Dan Meredith, was professing himself rather less enchanted with a conversation he was having, perforce, at Lackland Court.

The conversation was being held with his late cousin's elderly butler and Dan Lackland was sufficiently put out by it to be gazing out of the stone windows of the house, rudely turning his back on the old man. Yet even his worst enemies would concede that Handsome Dan's manners were normally immaculate to one and all, including women of course and servants, naturally.

"What on earth do you mean, Haygarth, his late Lordship was frightened?" There was silence, silence with a quality of obstinacy about it, Dan felt.

"Come on, man, out with it. Frightened of what?" The old butler was shortly to be retired under the will of the 17th Lord Lackland, and the 18th Lord had time to reflect that his retirement was perhaps not an unmitigated disaster.

"He was frightened, m'lord," repeated Haygarth stolidly.

"Frightened of death, d'you mean? Well, we're all frightened of that if we've any sense, death is a frightening business, and his late lordship, being nearly eighty, had more time to be frightened of it than most."

"His late lordship was not frightened of death, m'lord," said Haygarth; there was a distinct note of indignation in his voice, and Dan Meredith thought he declared extra flush in the butler's cheek. "Ask any of us who were at Dunkirk with him."

"Quite so, Haygarth, quite so," answered the new Lord Lackland hurriedly. Give Haygarth his head about the war and they'd be here all day; what with Charlotte, children and nanny arriving at Taynford station any minute, Babs threatening to drop Nell herself at exactly the same moment with all the possibilities for trouble *that* implied, especially if he had to offer her a drink. As for Zena—when had his sister Zena's presence ever made for peace? "Now, there's a good fellow, tell me exactly what the trouble was. Keep it brisk, if you don't mind. Her Ladyship doesn't like to be kept waiting, and if she did, that nanny doesn't." He laughed companionably before remembering that even in a short space of time, Haygarth and the nanny had managed to get at daggers drawn.

"His Lordship was frightened of the ghost," said Haygarth carefully. "The ghost that steps out of the portrait. He thought that the ghost had decided to kill him."

2

Toast to Decimus

"He—Handsome Dan as he used to be called—Lord
Lackland in other words, suggested meeting you at the
Plantaganet," said Cherry importantly. From Cherry's
tone Jemima could tell that her faithful P.A., one who
was not easily impressed, was impressed upon this
occasion. Since Jemima herself continued to look blank,
Cherry added, "The Plantaganet. The tennis club. In
Fulham, down by the river. You know, the one they
always write about in the Press." She sounded just
slightly reproachful, as though Jemima, her heroine,
had on this occasion let her down.

"Of course I've heard of the Planty! Actually I've
played there." Jemima hoped that her slightly base use
of the Yuppie nickname for the celebrated club would
regain Cherry's esteem. "That disastrous Megalith ver-
sus Titan tournament, wasn't that played at the Plantaganet?"

"Disastrous! But we won."

"We may have won but that was the fell occasion on
which Cy first met Serenity Saville," replied Jemima
grimly; she had just heard the news about the S.S.

trooper and her Afghanistan programme. It was true that Jemima had recently had her own triumph: all the same these reverses must be remembered and if possible revenged, otherwise Cy would get quite out of hand.

Her own triumph was quite considerable, for all that. For her devious and somewhat prolonged campaign had finally succeeded: the "Ghosts and Ourselves" series would now lead off with a programme about Decimus Lackland and *his* ghost, instead of one about Jane Manfred and *her* ghost, in other words the resident ghost of Taynford Grange. Various people had been of assistance in this campaign. Rupert Durham for example had proved a staunch ally once she had been promised that the programme would put an end to the "ridiculous Lely red herring" once and for all. The habitual chaos of his private life by means incapacitated him from a nice line in academic in-fighting, Jemima noticed, and his mild eyes beneath their large spectacles glinted at the thought of extinguishing once and for all the ludicrous theories of "that woman." What woman. Presumably some rival academic, not one of his rather numerous female acquaintances. (Rupert had addressed Jemima as Becky for most of lunch, with occasional excursions in the direction of Sylvia, Sue and Vicky.) For all his amatory vagueness, however, Rupert Durham was full of good practical advice as to how to lobby who on the whole subject.

What was more, he showed a marked disinclination to repossess his own portrait, when Jemima politely suggested it.

"Where London is concerned, I'm not exactly living in Ladbroke Grove at the moment. At least I don't think I am, am I?" Rupert ran his hand rather desperately through his curly hair, so that the springy brown halo divided itself into two horns. "And Cambridge is impossible." He did not say why. "So, Becky darling—"

"Jemima," said Jemima politely but firmly. She had extremely fond memories of a hectic summer romance with Rupert during her second year at Cambridge; at least he concentrated his mind wonderfully when making love, which no doubt explained his continuing success with the opposite sex (punting on the Cam was another matter). But that was another place, another time; she had no wish to revive the memories. And she had observed that Rupert Durham's technique, conscious or unconscious, was to accompany the wrong (but more intimate) Christian name with the kind of intimate approach one name justified but the other didn't.

"*Jemima!* Then there's another thing. My own television series—did I tell you about it? No? Nothing in your class, just a modest little thing. But one way or another—look, you wouldn't mind holding onto it just a little longer? Till I sort everything out."

"I shall be delighted," answered Jemima with perfect sincerity. If Rupert's chaotic personal life combined with a "modest" television series—which of course he had not previously mentioned—meant that she kept the portrait, she welcomed both.

"I know what we'll do to celebrate," said Rupert, with evident relief—even a picture had the potential power to tie him down—"We'll go to the N.P.G. after lunch" (they were at Orso's) "and compare my version with theirs. You'll find the differences interesting. No, wait, I have to meet someone. You go, Sylvia. Now, back to this old buzzard we need for the programme and how we nail him."

It was in this manner that Jemima found herself ten minutes later on an upper floor of the gallery, threading her way past portraits of voluptuous reclining beauties with visible swelling bosoms and lambent pearls at the neck and ear. Jemima thought of Pope on Lely. How did it go? She would have to ask Rupert. Something about "the sleepy eye that spoke the soul." Here were sleepy eyes in abundance. Indolence must have helped to pass the time wonderfully for these apparently passive, certainly privileged women. Olivia Lackland on the other hand even if passive had not been indolent: for she had had a devotion to learning which according to Clarendon had marked her out from the rest of her sex.

But wait! Jemima had gone too far, gone as far in fact as the Restoration. And there was the Merry Monarch himself, gazing at her, bold, black-eyed and cynical, in frank sexual appraisal from the end of the room (Jemima was sure that he bent the same gaze on every female who entered). Jemima retracted her steps and in a kind of antechamber dedicated to the "Arts and Sciences," found at last the real thing. All the same, Lackland in his armour seemed oddly placed among men in the voluminous dark robes of peace, a man in an open white shirt holding an admonitory skull . . . the ambivalence of his career as artist and war hero struck her anew. There was no dog in this picture, although the pose was otherwise very similar. With his right hand—with its disproportionately long fingers—the poet held a baton. His other hand was hidden. Even the legend beneath the portrait seemed to emphasise the dichotomy. "Decimus Meredith 1st Viscount Lackland 1612–1645. Poet and Cavalier," she read. Then Jemima stepped back to study the portrait at leisure, hoping to hold her own version in her mind's eye—and found herself for one moment ensconced in the arms of the only other adult visitor in the room, who had in fact been standing directly behind her.

Hastily apologies on both sides followed. In her embarrassment Jemima hardly took in the appearance of the fair-haired man at whom she had thus apparently flung herself. She had the impression certainly of someone tall and thin, as well as fair, that he was wearing some kind of dark suit, and illogically, she knew, or thought she knew, that he was English—that was because, like Cass, who was also English, the stranger smelt of Eau Sauvage shaving lotion (which was actually French).

The tall fair-haired stranger on the other hand recognised Jemima Shore immediately and followed his own apologies with a quick discreet smile which acknowledged that fact without presuming upon it. It was moreover the smile of a man used, for well over twenty years, to please by his smile; a man used furthermore to pleasing generally, not only women but crowds. Lastly, it was the smile of a man not unusued to recognition himself. As a matter of fact, if Handsome Dan Meredith had been wearing a white T-shirt, immaculate white shorts, white socks, white shoes and had been carrying a couple of tennis rackets, Jemima might indeed have recognised him in her turn. But the well-fitting and well-fitted dark blue suit gave her no clues. Besides, Jemima herself was soon utterly absorbed by the portrait before her, as she tried to figure out the differences between the real Van Dyck and "her" copy.

Jemima was oblivious therefore to the intense, level scrutiny which the stranger, confident of his anonymity, now proceeded to focus upon her as she studied the picture. Perhaps that was just as well. There was something just slightly calculating about Dan Lackland's expression. This was not the purely sexual appraisal of the Merry Monarch, forever lustful, forever held back from consummation by the confines of his heavy gold frame. Lust was certainly not absent from the gaze of the new Lord Lackland: yet it did not seem to be his sole emotion as he inspected Jemima Shore.

Lord Lackland silently left the gallery. Outside, in St. Martin's Lane, he turned left and marched rapidly in the direction of Wilton's Restaurant in Jermyn Street. To an outsider, he would have looked not so much calculating as abstracted. At Wilton's, the friendly—but not obsequious—greeting at the restaurant, which was the sign of its excellence, still did not remove the slight frown from his face.

"Her ladyship is already at the table, m'lord," murmured the head waiter in what was obviously just one variant of a familiar pattern in which lordships might already be at the table awaiting ladyships, graces awaiting other graces (both ducal and physical) and so forth and so on.

It was not until Dan Lackland actually reached his destined table in an alcove that he relaxed. And then the imposing woman sitting there, striking in a red Chanel suit which set off her glowing red-black hair and smooth olive skin, had to command him to do so.

"Darling boy, you smile when you see me," said his *vis-à-vis*—surely a few years older than Dan Lackland himself? "Don't forget." There was something not entirely maternal about the admonition.

"An odd coincidence," he said. "That's all." And he did give the lady opposite the kind of boyish, apologetic smile which she presumably had in mind. "You know I'm working on the Lackland Court problem. And I've had this approach . . ." He leant forward.

Back at the gallery, however, Jemima Shore was not smiling either. She too appeared abstracted. For some reason her thoughts had suddenly turned away from the portrait itself to the ghost of Decimus Lackland; the bizarre, even horrifying story she had recently been told.

Already her imagination was beginning to play upon the story. In spite of herself, she could not help fleshing it out in television terms, a drama, an investigation. In her mind's eye, Jemima saw Decimus in his lace-decked armour, bidding farewell to his wife. It was a farewell which had of course been anticipated in another celebrated poem: "I could not love thee dear so much"—no, that was Lovelace and Althea. "I could not love thy *kiss*—" And then, long before television, Victorian painters had loved to illustrate the scene: the handsome Cavalier bending from his tall black horse towards his fainting wife with her similarity downcast eyes and her neat little rosebud mouth.

Jemima had an idea that one painter—Frith perhaps? No, someone later, Millais?—had done two pictures of Decimus and Olivia entitled respectively *Their First Kiss* and *Their Last Kiss*. The first picture had shown a similarly modest highly Victorian-looking maiden seated on a rustic bench under a vast sheltering tree.

The handsome Cavalier had his lace matched on this occasion by plum-colored civilian velvet instead of armour, as he launched himself towards the shrinking Olivia, plumed hat in hand.

But were females really so innocently abashed at a mere kiss in the seventeenth century? Jemima reflected on this with the stirrings of indignation. Surely here subsequent Victorian attitudes were being imposed upon a more robust society. Olivia Lackland herself would survive to bring up that dewey-eyed infant in the second picture: Antony Decimus, her only child. A widow but not altogether helpless. Furthermore she would survive through the rest of the Civil War period as a woman alone: it was she who, following *Their Last Kiss,* would conduct the famous defence of Lackland Court which marked—according to the legend—the first appearance of Decimus' ghost. And she would survive in the harsh times of the Commonwealth—harsh for Royalists that is—and plead successfully for her son's estate from Oliver Cromwell.

The Petitioner, that was another Victorian picture, if not actually depicting Olivia Lackland, some other Royalist widow; more downcast eyes, graceful black garments (but lace-trimmed to reveal Cavalier status) and the grimly patriarchal figure of the Protector himself looming over her, bulbous nose, visible warts and all. According to Jemima's recollection, the gaze which the Protector was bending upon the lovely Petitioner before him, while not the frank appraisal of Charles II, was not quite without its hint of sexual element. As though even Olivier Cromwell was not averse to the spectacle of a beautiful—and vulnerable—female casting herself upon his mercy. A female who might be raised up, pardoned—or flung down at the whim of the dictator.

Was it in this sweetly self-abasing fashion that Olivia, widow of the "Malignant" Royalist Lord Lackland had pleaded for her son's confiscated property? Everything that Jemima had read about her heroic withdrawal from society following the Restoration. Not for her the louche high jinks of the Merry Monarch's Court. The same, alas, could not be said for her wastrel son, Antony Decimus, who had been the King's boon companion. But then heroes' sons were notoriously prone to dissipation. As the son of both a hero and a poet, what chance in life had the 2nd Viscount Lackland ever really had?

On the other hand, it was possible that Olivia Viscountess Lackland in her petitioning had simply used that secret weapon of apparent frailty always available to the woman in the man's world. Pride and dignity in a woman might be all very well in private but were hardly likely to sway the all-powerful Lord Protector to mercy in public. Nor could Jemima Shore herself, ostensibly living in a far more liberated world from the woman's point of view, really criticise such prudent self-abasement in Olivia Lackland. With her hand on her heart, could Jemima really swear that she had never exercised such "wiles" herself in the course of a highly successful professional career? What about that time she had dropped, well, a tear or two, in Cy's presence over that Sri Lankan child-brides budget? It had of course worked wonders. All in a good cause. The tears moreover had been quite genuine, even if they had been tears of rage, not weakness as Cy had imagined . . .

Jemima put this uncomfortable moment of self-criticism firmly aside and turned her thoughts back to the death of Decimus and the origins of the ghost story which obsessed her. She saw again the big black horse returning to Lackland Court on the evening of that dreadful day when, in the words of Clarendon, the sun itself setting had not been more red than the blood which stained the King's field. Over the crupper of the horse lay the body of his master. Lifeless—no, not quite.

There was time for Decimus to be laid down, for the frightful wounds to be tended by "clouts" or bandages of linen. There was time for Decimus to embrace his sorrowing and exhausted wife, still weak from the strain of bearing the much desired son and heir. Most of Jemima's knowledge derived from that memoir of the poet "lately dead" by an anonymous author, most probably the Lackland chaplain, entitled "Heaven's True Mourning" or "The Cruel Death of the Most Noble Viscount Lackland." According to this account, Decimus gave Olivia certain last commands concerning his son; he also gave her commands concerning his burial.

Just before ten o'clock Decimus died. The slow blooming of the Lackland chapel bell marked the event. That was significant because everyone in the village and around would have known that the lord was dead.

No doubt Decimus' last commands concerning the boy were carried out by the admirable Olivia. The instructions for his burial, on the other hand, in the family vault in the chapel, had definitely not been carried out.

That was because some time in the night, under cover of darkness, while the desolated Lackland servants slept and no watch was kept on the corpse—No, Jemima stopped. That was not quite right.

It was Olivia Lackland who had collapsed and been carried away. But there had been a watch kept and she should have remembered that because she found the thought of this particular character so poignant. There had been one person in the room lit only by black candles, Alice, the old nurse, who had in fact been Decimus' own wetnurse. The poet had been the fifteenth child and the tenth son of Sir Marcus Meredith and his City-heiress wife—hence the commemorative Latin name Decimus. He had also been the only boy to survive; Alice must have done well by him. Decimus! You could not imagine such a name being bestowed on a baby today, at any rate not being a tenth child. Admittedly the Merediths had ended up with a mere four children—out of fifteen—since two of their five girls had also died in infancy.

So Dame Alice knelt alone by the great bed draped in its black velvet hangings; plenty of those available in the early seventeenth century when Death was never further away than the threshold of the room. According to "Heaven's True Mourning," Decimus had been laid in the bed in which his own mother had recently died, as his life slowly bled away. That "pious and revered daughter of a City-merchant who brought honour as well as fortune" to the family name, in the words of the memorial, had preceded her single surviving son by only a few weeks. "She led the way, he followed trustingly as when he was a child."

At some time, then, in the night, when the black candles had burnt low, in that "dead of night when men most easily give up their souls to God," robbers had come silently and secretly to Lackland Court. They had found their way without difficulty through the Great Chamber: with the King's cause so heavily defeated that day, and the lord dying, they had not thought to put guards.

Perhaps Alice slept on her watch, wearied by the long day of horror and its tragic climax. For when she awoke the body was gone. The heavy black coverlet was torn aside, and the corpse was vanished. The old woman had some story of men-at-arms, knights, black knights, visions of the devil, but surely these were merely unhappy visions as she slept. The body of Decimus Lord Lackland had never been found.

It had in fact never been seen again since that night, not his bones, not his skeleton, no trace. The coffin alone had been placed in the family vault: sadly and symbolically empty. The tablet above it had in sonorous and long-winded Latin recorded the capture of the body "and yet his soul they could not take"—*sed animam non raptare posse*. And even that tablet had not been destined to rest very long in place. The chapel, which was much older than the house itself, had been very badly damaged by mortars during the siege of Lackland Court three years later. In a reverse of the usual pious story of miraculous preservation it was the chapel which had burnt and the house which had emerged virtually unscathed. (The Parliamentarian excuse for pounding the house of God was the fact that ammunition and troops were stored there, something hotly denied by the Royalists.) In the eighteenth century the chapel had been allowed to become a suitably ivy-clad folly; the tablet, Jemima believed, had been removed to Taynford Cathedral.

Returning to the abduction of the body, who could have done such a thing? The Roundheads—the Parliamentarian army, as Jemima must learn to call them—were naturally blamed as they were blamed for every desecration. Was it their need to extinguish the legend as well as the life of the Cavalier hero which had led to such a gross deed against the dead? Contemporary sources were either unhelpful or contradictory on the subject, according to Rupert, and Jemima, having checked them for herself, agreed.

Clarendon, for example, in his long eulogy of the character of the poet and his wife, elected not to mention the disappearance of his corpse. "Heaven's True Mourning," while suggesting that the deed was an act of vengeance on the part of the Parliamentarians, on a par with the impiety of those who would five years later kill King Charles the First, had nevertheless not named those personally responsible. Wicked John Aubrey on the other hand, ever one to promote a colourful tale, suggested that Lord Lackland had had a mistress who lived close by—the notorious Lady Isabella Clare—and that she had sent her own men to steal the body and give it secret burial.

As Rupert Durham crushingly said: "Well, he would, wouldn't he? You know Aubrey—" Jemima was just beginning to know Aubrey. "He would have written for the *Daily Exclusive* if he'd been alive today. There's absolutely no proof that Isabella Clare was Decimus' mistress, and as for writing the Swan poem to a woman like that, the mind boggles. We've only got Aubrey's word for the whole thing, and *he* wanted to have a dig at Decimus, I believe. Didn't like the poetic halo around his head. He came up with the same kind of story, if less dramatic, about Decimus' rival, Falkland." And so the matter rested. Until the ghost-who-could-not-rest, the ghost of Decimus, returned to Lackland Court during the 1648 siege and guided the widowed Olivia to victory.

According to tradition Decimus stepped out of the portrait to do so.

"Yes, the portrait," said the present (and 18th) Lord Lackland to Jemima Shore. "As the story goes, he steps out of the big portrait at the head of the stairs. The Van Dyck. The finest version, or so *we* believe. What's more, we all think it's the original, and not the one at the N.P.G., even if Oliver Millar doesn't agree. Something ridiculous about the hands, the hand. I believe you know that picture," added Dan Lackland carelessly. Jemima nodded. She had not, however, recognised him from their previous odd little encounter, believing him to be familiar to her merely from his famous past as a tennis star.

They were sitting in the coolly elegant surroundings of the Plantaganet Club. Enormous windows opened on the river. Even the factory chimneys on the bank opposite had the air of being composed for the sake of the perfect modernist view. The fact that through another vast plate glass window before their eyes a tennis game was being played made such talk of a seventeenth-century ghost seem for a moment peculiarly bizarre.

Counting the seventeenth century, there were in fact, thought Jemima, three levels of reality. For the surroundings of the Plantaganet bar, a high-ceilinged glass and mirrored area with huge purple bougainvilleas in white tubs (where on earth were they grown?), small tables adorned with pale pink button roses, and a barman in a bright pink jacket, bespoke the leisured luxury of another age; some ocean liner of the thirties, perhaps. The players, on the other hand, whether on the visible "Royal Court" behind the glass, or passing through the bar area on their way to other courts or back to the changing room, indicated both by their dress and their complexion, a rougher or at least a sweatier way of life. And the pictures were all enormously blown-up photographs of tennis stars past and present—including, she noticed, Handsome Dan himself instantly recognisable by his thatch of blond hair, in younger days.

The exact nature of Dan Lackland's involvement with the Plantaganet was not quite clear to her. But he introduced Jemima to various members with some style as though he was in fact a form of host. These included various young or youngish women—her uncertainty about their age was due to the fact that tennis gear, with women as well as men, proved a remarkable disguise. The essentially schoolgirlish nature of such clothes could prove delusive: whether very short pale pink pleated skirts revealing brown thighs—did all members of the Planty have to have an all-the-year-round tan by law?—or bright pink track suits concealing unsightly middle-aged spread. One way or another, it was impossible to guess the age of most of the women she met.

Take the energetic girl—or woman—introduced to Jemima as Alix Carstairs, who appeared to run the Club: how old was she? Alix Carstairs sported a thick pigtail of auburn hair beneath her bright pink bandeau and her face, devoid of make-up, was prettily freckled; she might have been any age between twenty-two and forty-two. As she gazed at Jemima, she had the bold bright eyes of some kind of bird; not necessarily a friendly bird, although her demeanour was extremely polite. On learning that Jemima liked to play tennis, Alix Carstairs urged her to come and play a trial game on spec: "To see if you like us."

But the sub-text was, thought Jemima, "And to see if we like you; which I, Alix, may not necessarily do." Charlotte Lackland, on the other hand, Dan Lackland's wife—his second wife, according to the reference books—was extremely friendly and as a result Jemima warmed to her. Charlotte's slight figure—she couldn't have been much more than five foot—coupled with her long straight fair hair tied by a ribbon in a ponytail, and her round blue eyes, made her age once again difficult to guess. Didn't she have—according to the reference books again—three children? But she was gazing at her husband with those round blue eyes as though she was a child herself.

It came as a further surprise to Jemima therefore to discover that sweet little Charlotte, improbably mother of three, also ran a well-known patisserie called eponymously Charlotte's Cakes (whose proverbially charming girl assistants were generally nicknamed, doubtless incorrectly, Charlotte's Tarts). She had been taking part in some form of tournament:

"We were slaughtered," she groaned. "It's true, darling. I'm going to take my serve right back to Costa next week and see if anything can be done about it, otherwise—"

But Dan Lackland hardly seemed to hear her, and soon Charlotte wandered off.

For a moment, Jemima tracked her progress amid the flower-decorated tables; most of the members either kissed or were kissed by her. Then Jemima's attention was caught by a man at the bar. He was gulping down what looked like iced water (but was perhaps a vodka tonic) and dressed, despite his considerable bulk, in a track suit—bright pink like the barman's coat—which was emblazoned with the crossed capital P's of the Plantaganet: to Jemima, with her present bent towards history, they had the look of two crossed swords with large hilts.

She looked again. The wringing wet and curly hair, and a face not much less rubicund than the track suit, the unfamiliar gear, had prevented her from immediately recognising—yes, it was . . . The new Home Secretary. Stuart Gibson. So that was indeed iced water, since he was a self-proclaimed teetotaller as well as health freak. Jemima glanced round and saw the one man conspicuous not so much by his neat dark suit but by the fact that he was ostentatiously doing nothing. That must be the Home Secretary's detective. And who was, or rather who *had* been, the Home Secretary's opponent? Medium height, stocky build, distinctly hunched: in his conventional white shorts and zipped-up blue jacket, he looked to be in his forties.

"That's my cousin Marcus." Lord Lackland had evidently read her thoughts. "Gibson's P.P.S. Playing tennis against the boss goes with the job."

"If he's as good as you are—" began Jemima politely to make up for her wandering attention. Then she perceived that in some way the subject of his cousin was inimicable to Handsome Dan; his expression had clouded: piqued vanity perhaps because a pretty woman had looked at another man? "He's not likely to be as good as me since he had polio as a boy," Lord Lackland replied quite shortly. "But he's pretty good all the same, gets around the court at the most amazing speed. Stout fellow, Marcus." Jemima felt abashed. She hastened to return to the third—or rather the first—reality of the seventeenth century.

"So Decimus—the ghost—does step out of the portrait! Just as it says in 'Heaven's True Mournings.' The memorial." Jemima hoped that this proof that she had done her homework would start the soothing process. Now for the question, the crucial question which had brought her so eagerly to the Plantaganet Club, the question on which the future of this particular episode in the "Ghosts and Ourselves" series might well depend.

Jemima sipped her Planty Punch (which was actually a non-alcoholic mixture of fruit juices, beloved of the Yuppies who used the Club for its healthful pink froth).

"By the way, have *you* seen the ghost, Lord Lackland?" she asked casually, following the question with a smile, as though the answer to it hardly mattered. But her precise tone, even the sheer sweetness of her slightly cat-like smile, might have been recognized by those she had interviewed on television in that famous hard-hitting programme about women's treatment in the Trade Union movement—"Sisters or Brothers?"

"Call me Dan, for God's sake! I've hardly got used to this Lord Lackland bit. I keep looking round nervously for poor old Cousin Tommy when I hear the name!"

"Dan then! *Much* nicer. And I'm of course Jemima." She smiled again, looking more cat-like than ever. "I just wondered if you'd ever seen the ghost yourself."

Handsome Dan drank from a glass that looked as if it contained whiskey.

"Ah, Jemima—what a pretty name that is, by the way. Do you know, I had an ancestress called Jemima, said to have been the daughter of James II, hence the name. It was originally a form of James. But you knew that." Jemima didn't. "I hope to God she wasn't," he went on. "His daughter, I mean. *Not* one's favourite monarch to put it mildly. Where was I? The ghost. Ah. Jemima, I see you don't yet know everything about the Decimus Ghost. Which is what we generally call him. Or it. But somehow *him* seems right."

"There must be a great deal I don't know. So— enlighten me."

"Children can see the Decimus Ghost quite safely. And many have. Down the centuries. If you believe the stories. He likes children. Because he came back the first time to save his little son. Nell—that's my funny little daughter by my first marriage, not so little now of course, fifteen? I'm hopeless about my children's ages— Nell saw him when she was quite small. And she continues to see him. If she's to be believed."

"Have you yourself seen him often? That's really what I'm getting at."

"Only children can see the Decimus Ghost in safety. If anyone else sees the Decimus Ghost, that's an omen."

"An omen?" Jemima was genuinely startled. This really was news to her.

"An omen of death. His death. Or her death. Or possibly the death of a member of the family. So—" Handsome Dan paused and drank again. "In answer to your question, Jemima, no, I haven't seen the Decimus Ghost and I very much hope I never do." He drained his glass. It seemed like a kind of toast—to Decimus per- haps, *in absentia*.

ANTONIA FRASER'S
JEMIMA SHORE

Jemima Shore didn't plan on living a life steeped in detection and mystery. But at the age of fifteen, while staying at a Catholic boarding school, she found herself plunged into a bizarre situation involving a suspicious miracle and a flamboyant, manipulative Italian princess.

Now Britain's most popular newswoman, Jemima lives day in and day out with mysteries and danger from every walk of life. That first story, "Jemima Shore's First Case" and all her adventures are now available from Bantam Crime Line Books:

Enjoy any of Antonia Fraser's Jemima Shore mysteries, available wherever Bantam Crime Line Books are sold or use this page for ordering:

At Annie Laurance's Death on Demand bookstore, murder is often more than just a reading experience and the mysteries are just leaping off the shelves.

CAROLYN HART

Carolyn Hart's Annie and Max are two of mystery readers' best loved characters and in these award-winning books you'll join them on their adventures of mystery, danger and several volumes of murder most foul.